Praise for *The Keys to Gramercy Park*

"What a story! Lush with historical detail, *The Keys to Gramercy Park* exposes the shadowed flaws in human nature, while shining hope on the glories of embracing new beginnings. This artful balance of light and dark is presented in thoughtful prose that remains with you long after you reach 'The End.'"

–Rachel Scott McDaniel, award-winning author
of *In Spotlight and Shadow*

"In *The Keys to Gramercy Park,* author Candice Sue Patterson takes the reader on a journey of light and dark, love and mystery. The story twists and turns through the lives of people living more than a hundred and fifty years apart yet linked by a common thread—the discovery of counterfeit money. A cast of characters spanning the spectrum of the human condition will entertain, enthrall, and engross the reader to the end."

–Pegg Thomas, award-winning author of *Sarah's Choice*

"Candice Sue Patterson masterfully weaves a 19th century net of collusion that reaps 21st century consequences in this intriguing time-split novel. Rousing ambition converges with deadly covetousness, breaking gentle and hard hearts. While Mrs. Patterson's work is introspective, ultimately readers are invited to look beyond themselves to the Creator and Lover of their souls."

–Jericha Kingston, author of *Waiting for Lily Bloom*
and *Borne by Love*

The Keys to Gramercy Park ©2023 by Candice Sue Patterson

Print ISBN 978-1-63609-533-2
Adobe Digital Edition (.epub) 978-1-63609-534-9

All scripture quotations, unless otherwise noted, are taken from the King James Version of the Bible.

This book is a work of fiction. Names, characters, places, and incidents are either products of the author's imagination or used fictitiously. Any similarity to actual people, organizations, and/or events is purely coincidental.

Cover Image: Nikaa / Trevillion Images

Published by Barbour Publishing, Inc., 1810 Barbour Drive, Uhrichsville, Ohio 44683, www.barbourbooks.com

See the series lineup and get bonus content at DoorsToThePastSeries.com

Our mission is to inspire the world with the life-changing message of the Bible.

ecpa Member of the
Evangelical Christian
Publishers Association

Printed in the United States of America.

Doors to the Past

The KEYS *to*
GRAMERCY
PARK

CANDICE SUE
PATTERSON

BARBOUR
PUBLISHING

DEDICATION

To Mrs. Green, my high school drama teacher. When I walked into your class for the first time, I wondered why I was there. You did too. As I grew more comfortable with the odd methods you used for teaching us how to get into character, I understood why I was there. You did too. Little did I know your teachings on characterization would be something I'd use years later when writing novels. Your class was always a blast. Thanks for the memories.

CHAPTER ONE

EDWARD

Manhattan, May 1862

$\mathcal{E}$dward Davidson had an odd fascination with pretending he was everyone but himself. The butcher. The baker. The candlestick maker. Any of the young boys grappling in the alleyway between Palmer's Dry Goods and the sewing machine factory.

The pop of flesh striking flesh brought him satisfaction. Shouldn't but did.

He stepped a few feet into the shaded alley for a better view of the performance. He'd been around their age, if he estimated correctly, when his beatings had started. Not the ones from his father. Those had started much earlier. The scraps he'd found himself in with the neighborhood boys had started at ten, though his brother, Franklin, had done his best to stop them before they began. Sometimes Franklin was successful. Most times not.

When not, Edward would pretend he was Franklin, the Robin Hood of New York City, risking his life for truth and justice.

The smaller of the two boys in the alley stepped into a crater filled with muck, lost his balance, and collapsed onto the filthy ground. The larger one rolled the kid onto his back and straddled him, pinning both arms to the ground. Both fists jabbed without mercy. Disappointment filled Edward. He never could save himself, but he was hoping this kid could.

"That's enough!" Edward's voice echoed off the brick buildings. He strode forward, dodging the filth, spine erect, his steps calculated to hide his limp.

Punches continued flying, teeth bared. Hate of this caliber was hard to control.

"I said 'enough.'" Edward grabbed the larger child and yanked him off the smaller. The child writhed on the ground, holding his face. "Are you trying to kill him?"

Chest heaving, the bigger kid blinked. The haze of anger cleared, and clarity dawned. His skin was dirty, and he smelled as if he'd been wallowing in a hog pen. He pushed away from Edward and pointed at the injured boy. "That'll teach you to steal from me again."

The smaller boy moaned.

The attacker stepped away and assessed Edward's suit. Snot dripped from the boy's nose. He swiped it away with the back of his wrist. "You look like a man who could spare alms for the poor."

Edward had to keep from slapping the kid. "I won't turn you over to the authorities for your misbehavior. That's alms enough."

Snarling, the kid spit on Edward's polished shoe and ran from the alley before Edward could teach him respect. He uncurled his fists and flexed his fingers. The smaller child, still rolling on the ground, turned his face away and spit blood. It was a good thing Edward came upon the scuffle, or this one would have been left for dead.

"What'd you steal from him?" Edward knelt on his good leg and helped the kid to a sitting position.

"It was mine. He stole it from *me*." Blood garbled his voice, his lips already swelling double in size. "I wanted it back."

Blood trickled from both nostrils. Bruises began darkening both eyes, one almost swollen shut. Edward placed his silk handkerchief in the kid's dirty hand. Uncertain why, he believed the boy. The child had a humbleness about him that the other did not.

"What was it?" Edward studied the gash on the kid's right eyebrow. He'd be fine without stitches, but it would leave a scar.

Edward was familiar with scars.

"A ruby brooch." The kid coughed and spat more blood. His little hand reached inside his pocket and came out empty. He punched the ground. "It was all I had left of my mother."

A single tear burst from the corner of the swollen eye and disappeared into the handkerchief. The loss transported Edward to the day he'd parted with his mother's precious heirloom. Merely a ribbon, it was gold to Edward, for the ribbon had secured his mother's braid when she'd rocked him to sleep. She would tickle his nose with the ends of her hair, and he'd laugh. Then she'd sing a lullaby, and her soothing voice would float him to a world of rest and peace while his fingers kept hold of that ribbon.

After her death, he'd stolen it from her bureau before his father emptied the house of her belongings. Edward carried the ribbon in his pocket wherever he went. Then one day he'd made the mistake of using it as a bookmark at school and it had vanished into the clutches of a monster.

"You okay, mister?" The child put a hand on Edward's arm, yanking him back to the present.

"I ask the same of you."

The kid shrugged.

"Let's get you on your feet." Edward struggled to a stand then helped the kid up. "You think you can get home?"

"I can still see a little. It's not far."

"Look, kid, never let them win. No matter what you must do, don't let them win."

"This being spoken by a winner or a loser?"

Smart kid. "Both."

The boy held up the handkerchief to give it back, but Edward waved it away. "Keep it. Here."

Edward fished in his pocket then dropped a few coins into the kid's hand. "Get home quickly before you lose those too. Should feed you for at least a week."

The boy patted Edward's arm. "Thanks, mister. For everything."

He took off out of the alley as fast as his small legs and injuries would allow. Hopefully, the little scamp would be all right. Edward limped between the tall buildings, straightening his suit coat.

Back onto the street, sunlight hit his eyes, making him squint. Carriages filled the streets, the smell of horseflesh and droppings strong. A couple sidled past arm in arm. The fringe on her parasol swayed in tune with their steps. Edward nodded to the man and stepped into the crush of bodies.

A twinge ran up his leg. He'd done everything he could to hide his deformity—purchased a specialized brace, wrapped it in cloth to both muffle the sound of the creaky joints and cushion it against his skin, thought about each step before taking it. Even then it gave him away.

And when it did, he was that young boy in the alleyway.

A troop of soldiers dressed in blue, muskets cradled in their palms and resting against their shoulders, marched along Fifth Avenue. Edward scanned the troop, looking for his brother but not finding him, and turned down Mercer Street. The once-lovely homes from his youth had become bordellos. Advertisements hung in the windows, detailing the euphoric experience to be found inside. Though tempting, Edward had come home for one purpose only, and it dwelt in a row house on Wooster Street.

The neighborhood landscape had changed little in the seven years he'd been gone. He didn't recognize any of the faces, but that was to be expected in a place like New York City. He stepped up to the deteriorating gate that separated the street from his childhood home. The window frames needed a fresh coat of paint and the ivy needed to be removed, but it was still the same prison. Edward smoothed his new suit coat, checked his timepiece, and walked to the door.

After knocking, he didn't wait for a reply. He cared not what the warden thought of his audacity. The house smelled stale, and the temperature was stifling. His father sat in the parlor, staring out the large window. The small table beside him held a glass of amber liquid.

Edward cleared his throat. "Hello, Father."

The man didn't turn from the window. "Ah, the prodigal son returns. Back from the pig shed?"

Edward swallowed the insult. "Quite the opposite. My silver mine in Utah is doing exceptionally well."

That got his father's attention. He twisted and looked at Edward. Then his lips curved in disapproval. The way he'd always looked at his crippled son. "Silver, huh?"

"The gold was nearly gone when I reached California. I invested elsewhere, and it served me well."

"I see that," Father mumbled.

Edward removed his new suit coat and draped it on the back of a dusty chair. "I brought you something."

He reached into his pocket and removed a glinting pocket watch with an intricate carving of a knight's shield with elk antlers jutting from each side. A bee, wings outstretched, lay in the center of the shield. The glass face was clear as crystal, and it ticked the sound of masterful workmanship.

Father took the offering, and Edward waited for the man's satisfaction.

"How do I congratulate one son for building an empire while his brother risks his life in war?"

Edward's spirit deflated. Leg growing weak, he perched on the edge of the chair. "They wouldn't have me. You know that."

"Yes, that foot of yours has been the bane of your existence from the start." Father fingered the pocket watch. "A real man would have defied them and enlisted anyway."

Anger warmed the back of Edward's neck. "I was in Utah Territory when the war started. It took months for word to reach us. By then, my mine was already established and making money. You'd have me leave it all to join a war they'd refuse to let me fight when we'll soon win anyway?"

"Get your head out of the sand, boy. Have you not read the papers? The battle at Shiloh nearly took us out. Over thirteen thousand men, gone. Perhaps your brother among them. While you're sitting in a fancy suit counting your coins."

Edward's jaw twitched. His mind's eye took him to the alleyway, his father atop him throwing punches. Then he thought of Mr. Richard Olney, the pious man from Virginia who'd fallen prey to Edward's scheme. Edward lifted his chin and tilted his head the way Olney had during their transactions, arrogance leaching from every pore.

"I had hoped this visit would go differently, but I now see that no matter what I do, I will never gain your approval."

Father's cheeks turned purple. "You've never tried, always sniffling and sneering. Why can't you be like your brother?"

Edward stood, towering over the frail old man. He was strong enough now to dole out his own beatings. "Franklin and I may be mirror reflections, but we are different people. You've always failed to understand that."

"Take it." Father shrank against his chair, thrusting the timepiece at Edward. "You want to do something noble? Sell it and give the money to the Union army."

He'd sell it all right, but not a shaving would go to the government.

Edward slipped the watch back into his pocket, hung his coat over his arm, and turned to leave. "I feel sorry for you."

"Sorry for me? You're the one who's crippled."

Edward halted, realizing his emotions had caused him to forget about straightening his steps. He pivoted to see his father, determined this would be the last time. "Your soul is crippled. That's far worse than a foot."

Father attempted to rise from his chair, no doubt to lay his hands on Edward for such disrespect, but Edward was gone before the man could fully stand. The sound of breaking glass hit his ears as he stepped through the gate and onto Wooster Street.

Edward walked for what seemed like hours, burying years of pain his father had caused and contemplating what to do next. He'd exhausted his resources in the Utah Territory. Going back would get him arrested. Or killed. Especially now that Mr. Olney had had time to realize that the booming silver mine Edward sold him didn't exist.

He smiled. Olney was much like his father, only wealthier. Well, less wealthy now that Edward had swindled him out of fifty thousand dollars. Tonight he'd treat himself to a luxurious stay in the Fifth Avenue Hotel.

Manhattan was a beautiful city in the areas owned by John Jacob Astor. The streets were cleaner here, the air fresher. What would it be like to be one of the richest men in the world? Edward would love to know.

He cut through Union Square Park to the newly built Gramercy Square. Trees lined the streets, offering blessed shade to the countless brownstones filling the community. A wrought-iron gate fenced in a lovely garden where only the inhabitants of the square who owned keys could recreate. A sanctuary amid buildings and industry and immigrants.

Mansions towered over the garden beyond the gate. Mansions full of crystal and fine china and pianofortes. Maids and butlers and plush beds. Mansions that entertained the most respected families in the country.

Gramercy Park.

The name itself commanded respect.

He closed his eyes and imagined himself stepping from one of those homes each morning, status and money buoying his steps. He would have such a life someday.

Somehow.

He focused on the property that was swampland the year of his birth.

In Edward's twenty-six years of life—if one could call it that—Samuel Ruggles had drained, filled, and built a beautiful community that housed the most affluent members of society. If a man could transform a swamp into the most opulent real estate in the city, then Edward could step from his brother's shadow and become a man worthy of such envy.

CHAPTER TWO

Andrea

Manhattan, Present Day

*A*ndrea Andrews believed gates surrounded Gramercy Park for one of two reasons: to protect the historic garden or to imprison dark secrets. Being an investigative journalist with a minor in history, she liked the secrets angle best. Since she wasn't one of the privileged few who held a key to the locks, however, she'd never get to find out.

Her fingertips skimmed along each wrought-iron bar as she trailed down the sidewalk enjoying the last vestiges of summer, trees bursting with green and the colorful pop of flowers adorning the brownstones along the square. If only she could spend this glorious afternoon outdoors and not waiting tables.

Gant & Company treated their employees well, and she loved serving its eclectic patrons—everyone had a story, and she enjoyed listening to their life experiences—but the city itself had stories to tell, and she desperately needed to hear one. The position for writer-at-large was opening at her day job with *Smithsonian* magazine, and if she was going to prove to her boss she deserved the promotion, she needed to stumble across one of those tales.

Beyond the bars, the plush garden flared with color, the oxidized bronze statue of Edwin Booth in the center acting as guardian. The Empire State Building made a stunning backdrop with the trees of Gramercy Park framing the entire image like a painting.

An oasis in a concrete jungle.

Some of the most powerful families in the country had lived behind the gates along this square. Still did. Too many power holders throughout history gained their positions by trampling over others in some form, so it conflicted with her fascination with the men who built America.

"Daydreaming again?"

The familiar voice across the street pulled Andrea back to reality. Hands on her hips, Caylee waited for a response.

"Guilty." Andrea waited for a car to pass then crossed the street.

"That statue's not going to talk to you. You know that, right?" Caylee moved them out of the path of an oncoming bicycle. Her platinum-blond bob swayed with the action.

"Joy-kill." Andrea adjusted her cross-body bag higher onto her shoulder. "Cute haircut."

"Thanks. Practicality is not the killer of joy."

"Negativity is." Andrea smiled.

"Girl, you wear me out. So does working the evening shift." Caylee linked her arm in Andrea's and tugged her along.

"I agree. If the tips weren't so good, I'd quit."

As in Andrea's case, the gig was supplemental income to Caylee's actual job. The twenty-four-year-old was working hard to secure a role on Broadway in a Shakespearean drama turned musical.

Caylee rolled her eyes. "At least you get tips."

Andrea bumped her friend's shoulder with her own. "You make more per hour. It balances out."

"Irrelevant."

"And you don't have to deal with customer complaints."

"You were serving Elliot Monhagen!" Caylee threw her hands up with dramatic flair. She would never let Andrea live that down.

"I didn't recognize him. How was I supposed to know about his perfume sensitivity and disdain for hot peppers?"

"How can you live in this century and not recognize *People* magazine's sexiest man alive?"

"Keeping up with who's married to each Kardashian and knowing a social media star's allergies will not alter my life experience."

"Not true. If you'd have been on point, he might have left you a four-figure tip like he's been known to do. If you'd keep up on current events instead of living in the past, you would know these things."

"Ugh, and you say I'm exhausting."

Caylee laughed and ascended the stone steps into the old brownstone converted into Gant & Company. The posh restaurant was famous for small amounts of artistically placed food sold for an enormous price. Andrea followed, and the aroma of marinated hanger steak in a red wine bordelaise filled her senses. Her stomach growled. The granola bar she'd brought to eat on break would have to suffice until her shift ended.

She parted ways with Caylee at the hostess stand and went to the break room. After stashing her belongings in a locker, she finger-combed her hair into a messy bun atop her head and secured it with an elastic band. She washed her hands, checked her appearance in the mirror, and silently gave herself the daily pep talk confirming her life choices. Pasting on a smile, she entered the dining room.

Five hours later, her feet and back ached, but her tip jar was full. She rolled her neck and stretched her shoulders while she waited for the chef to finish dripping sauce around the plate of braised lamb. "Order up," he yelled, as if Andrea weren't standing right in front of him. She arranged the entrées on a serving tray and delivered them to table 4.

New customers awaited her at table 6. The two men were deep in conversation when she interrupted, but they acknowledged her with friendly smiles. Both appeared to be around her age, maybe slightly older in their early thirties, good looking, and well dressed. "Good evening. I'm your server, Andrea. If you know what you'd like to drink, I'll get those for you while you take a few minutes to look over the menu."

All professionalism left the building when the man with black hair grinned. Her pulse jolted when he looked at her. Thick eyebrows offset stormy-blue eyes that confessed he was used to this reaction from women. Her heart did a weird fluttery thing that made her inwardly groan. Something about him seemed familiar, but she couldn't place it, and Caylee's earlier comment about her lack of knowledge on celebrities and current events made Andrea fear she was missing something important.

Before retrieving their drinks, she detoured to the hostess station to ask Caylee to sneak a peek, but Rory had taken her place.

"Is Caylee on break?" Andrea asked him.

"She went home." Rory leaned in and whispered, "Not feeling well."

Code for she took off early to go home and study her lines.

"Can I help you with something?" Rory glanced behind her at a group entering the front door and started gathering menus.

"I'm good. Thanks." Andrea would have to go on being oblivious. Ignorance was bliss, right?

She retrieved an extra set of silverware for table 2, delivered an appetizer to table 10, and then brought two iced teas to the handsome men at table 4 who seemed to be locked in some kind of debate. The ginger-haired man moved his coaster to his left, indicating she was to put his drink there, and continued with his argument.

"There's no way to fix it. New York City is the most populated in the U.S. The heavy traffic and brutal winters cause poor road conditions, and there's nothing you can do about that. All reconstruction does is clog traffic and make it worse. Let this be some other guy's problem."

The black-haired man shook his head and leaned back in his chair. He thanked Andrea for the drink then asked, "How long have you lived here?"

The question caught her off guard. She was usually the one asking questions. Customers loved to talk about themselves. "Six years. Why?"

His intense study of her face made a flush of delicious heat crawl across her skin.

He scratched his cheek, the black stubble on his face almost grown in. "I've lived here my entire life. Well, except for my years at university. David seems to think there's no way to fix the issues that plague the New York City Department of Transportation. I contest, however, and I'd love to know your thoughts."

Andrea blinked. "I just came to take your order."

The ginger-haired man, David, chuckled. Stormy Eyes curled his lips into a smile. "I'll have the mole chicken. And your thoughts as a tax-paying citizen on how to improve our roads."

She wrote his order. "Are you responsible for New York's road infrastructure?"

"It's merely a passion of mine."

"He's—" David shot forward, his mouth grimacing. He growled. "I'll have the sea bass."

"Good choice." Andrea wrote it down, slipped the order pad into her apron pocket, and turned to Stormy Eyes. "Germany, Russia, Japan. All have cities comparable to ours in traffic and weather, and they manage their roads through tolls and taxation of foreign travelers."

Stormy Eyes crossed his arms, amused. "World traveler?"

"History geek. In college I wrote an essay on the history of highway engineering."

He tipped his head. Probably curious why someone with a college degree was waiting tables. "I'm intrigued. Tell me more."

His gaze flirted with her. Not the first time she'd earned that reaction. Though flirting back was tempting, she didn't flirt with customers. Especially ones who used terms like *university*. That indicated Harvard or Yale or some such prestigious institution, which immediately put him out of her league. "I'll put in these orders and check on you soon."

She did so; then she waited on a few more tables, packed a to-go bag, and helped with a minor crisis in the kitchen, all while trying to escape the memory of that man's amazing eyes. If they were truly windows to the soul, his told Andrea he was a good, caring guy who took life seriously but still liked to have fun.

Or he could be a serial killer.

In this city, one could never be certain based on first impressions.

Beau
Manhattan, Present Day

Beau Davidson-Quincy's interests had just turned from road repair to coaxing his waitress into a date.

"You're crazy." David dipped a forkful of bass into his puree and moaned his approval. "She's not going to date you. She doesn't even know who you are."

It was clear by the absence of dollar signs in her eyes.

"That's what makes her appealing." Beau sipped his tea to quell the heat of the ancho and hot honey. "I'm tired of being dated for my assets."

"First-world problem." David wiped his mouth with a napkin. "And there's something to be said for assets. First thing I noticed on Courtney when I asked her out."

"Funny. You're also a pig who just closed on a three-million-dollar home on Fifth Avenue. Enlighten me on your knowledge of first-world problems."

David shrugged. "I'm a married man now. Got a kid on the way. I needed a home my family could grow in."

"With a bowling alley in the basement?"

"Kids love to bowl. I think."

Beau laughed. "Man, you are way over your head with fatherhood."

"I'm drowning." David pushed his plate away, only scraps remaining. "Courtney bought me a book I'm supposed to read. Something about expecting expectations or something. I don't know. Every time I pick it up, I start sweating. Her belly grows every day, and I'm running out of time."

"Sounds like you need to get home, then." Beau pushed up from the table and placed a few bills next to his plate. "I've got it this time. You enjoy that book. I'm going to find our server and see if she'll go out with me."

David stood. "Good luck. My bet is still on her saying no."

"Thanks for the confidence."

"Ditto."

They shook hands and pulled close enough for back slaps. Beau grabbed his jacket draped over his chair and curled it over his arm. Candles flickered on tables around them, though most of the seats were empty now. "Quit stressing. You're gonna make a great dad."

"Here's hoping. Take care, brother."

David left. Beau pretended to head for the bathrooms but arced right when he spotted Andrea at a small podium with a computer.

"Ma'am?"

She pivoted. "Did I forget to bring you something? I'm sorry."

"No, you did a fine job." For all his confident bragging, his nerves kicked in. "It's not customary for me to do this—in fact, I've never asked this of a server before—but I was wondering if you'd like to go out sometime."

This was bad. He sounded fifteen and inexperienced with women. He was neither.

Eyebrows arched over hazel eyes. "Out, as in a date?"

"Yes." He should've kept their conversation to road conditions.

"I...um...I've never been asked out by a patron before, so it's not customary for me to agree."

Beau leaned an elbow on the wooden stand and noted the blond strands that had escaped the sexy mass on her head. Smooth, lightly tanned skin made her teeth gleam. He concentrated on the small mole in the hollow of her neck where her collarbones joined. "Is that a no?"

"Yes. I mean, yes that it's a no." Her hands searched the area around the keyboard then dug in her apron pocket.

"Your pen is in your shirt pocket."

"Of course it is." She retrieved it, a lovely pink staining her cheeks. "I knew that."

He glanced around the dining room. Many of the tables had cleared, the overall hum in the restaurant quieter. "You seem flustered," he said in a low tone. "Is it because of me, or my offer? If I make you uncomfortable, I'll apologize and leave."

Her mouth opened and closed a few times. Man, she was beautiful. "No, you don't make me uncomfortable. I just...well, I have a cautious nature, and you're a stranger."

"Beau." He stuck out his hand.

She looked around then smiled. "Andrea. I guess you already knew that, though."

Her skin was every bit as soft as he'd imagined. "Well, Andrea, now that we're not strangers anymore, would you like to go out sometime?"

"And do what, discuss the city's roads and traffic jams?"

"We'll discuss whatever you like."

An Asian man in a suit and tie walked by, frowning.

"That's my manager." She clicked her pen a few times then caught herself and tucked it away. "It was nice to meet you, Beau. I'm sure you would show me a wonderful time, but I'm going to decline until we know each other better."

Logically, since he was a patron who wouldn't get to know her at all, it was her way of turning him down. Rejection wasn't something he was familiar with.

Perseverance was.

"Here." He took the receipt from his wallet, asked to borrow her pen, and wrote his number on the back. He'd normally hand out a business card, but he didn't want to scare her away or tip her off to who he was just yet.

"No pressure, but you're welcome to call me. We'll get to know each other."

She took the paper and tucked it in her apron.

"Have a good night, Andrea. Be safe going home."

He walked to the exit. Now to wait and see if she called.

CHAPTER THREE

ANDREA

Manhattan, Present Day

*A*ndrea waited for a cab beneath the industrial-style lights blazing outside of Gant & Company. She normally split cab fare with Caylee since they lived one block apart, but the drama queen had bailed on her tonight, leaving Andrea on her own. Rory joined her, waiting for a cab that would take him in the opposite direction. Sanjay skipped the extra expense during fair weather and walked the eight blocks to his apartment. He was also six four and built like a bodyguard, which decreased his chances of an attack by half. This part of Manhattan wasn't as rough as other sections of the city, but one could never be too careful.

Especially a female.

Rory tucked his hands into his pockets and inhaled a loud breath. "I love the city at night."

"It has its appeal."

Lights against the backdrop of night, movement that never ceased, the distant noise of cars and sirens and horns. Where many lulled themselves to sleep with the gentle sounds of nature, energy rocked the inhabitants of New York City into slumber.

Sure, she loved the open sky of her childhood home where she could gaze at the stars, listen to the crickets' serenade, and wake to the smell of whatever her mom was cooking downstairs. But this life she'd made on her own, and the independence that brought, was healing.

Though she should at least visit her parents soon.

A cab approached, and Rory stuck out his arm. The car parked curbside. "You take this one, love."

"You sure?"

"I'm nothing if not a gentleman." His English accent grew thicker when using such phrases, and it always made her smile.

"You are that." She patted his cheek. "Thank you."

Rory opened the door, and she climbed inside. "Greenwich Village, please. The Winderfield."

The driver glanced in his rearview mirror then pulled back onto the street. Halfway down the block, Andrea saw a familiar face turn to the entrance gate of Gramercy Park. "Can you stop for a moment, please?"

The driver eased to the side of the road, eyes wide. "Everything okay? Paper bags are in the seat if you're sick."

"I'm okay. I just…" She turned to look out the back windshield.

Bathed in light from the old-fashioned lampposts, Beau—Mr. Stormy Eyes—entered through the gate. Metal clanked as he closed it behind him. A few seconds later, he disappeared into the garden.

"I'm not sick." She smiled to reassure the driver. His eyes narrowed in the rearview mirror in disbelief. "I thought I saw someone I knew. I'm ready now."

Dark eyes assessed her a moment more before the driver pulled away and continued to her apartment complex. Andrea's spirit sank. She shouldn't have been entertaining the idea of accepting a date with a stranger anyway, but now she definitely couldn't. The only people who had access to Gramercy Park were the millionaires, celebrities, or artists who lived there. She didn't fit into any of those categories.

Now his use of the word *university* made sense.

Why would a man who held a key to the kingdom want to date her, anyway? Clearly, her social standing was beneath him. Had he thought her easy? Vulnerable? Ignorant? She certainly didn't fit into any of those categories either.

She fingered the receipt in her pocket where he'd written his phone number. Whatever his intentions, she'd never know because the first thing she'd do when she arrived home was throw it away. Her priorities were a full night's sleep, an afternoon at the New York Public Library digging through research books, and an all-nighter tomorrow, writing the first draft of her article on waterborne diseases and how the commission of municipal plumbing saved thousands of lives in the slums of New York City.

It wasn't the breakout story she was counting on to gain her that promotion, but the unique angle she planned to take should at least make it stand out.

The cabbie flicked his turn signal and drifted to the curb in front of her building. She thanked him, passed over three dollars and seventy-five cents, and stepped onto the sidewalk. Her keys rattled against the small can of bear spray attached to her key ring. She punched in the five-digit code to open the main door and sailed past the old wooden post boxes that held the tenants' mail. John Jacob Astor originally built the Winderfield as a hotel in 1872. In its day, those boxes were behind the registration desk and held any correspondence for the guests along with the keys to each room. The history behind the Winderfield had drawn Andrea here in the first place and justified why she paid more than Caylee did for her newer apartment one block south.

Yawning, Andrea climbed the stairs to the second floor and unlocked her door. She kicked off her shoes, walked to the kitchen trash can, guided only by the glow of the night-light, and dropped the wadded-up receipt inside.

Now to feed Sammy Davis Jr. his dinner.

She turned on lights as she went back to the living room.

The large blue betta fish knew the routine. His fins worked faster as he watched her open the plastic bottle and raise her hand to drop the flakes. Her mom had teased her for naming the fish after the bluesy jazz singer, but the betta had what looked like a tiny mustache and he was blue, so it fit. She'd wanted a cat, but no pets were allowed. Not ones with legs, anyway.

After a quick meal of ramen noodles and a leftover biscuit, Andrea double-checked the door locks, turned out the lights, and went to her room. Walking from memory seemed like a good idea until her toe smacked something hard.

She yelped. Biting back what else tried to escape, she felt along the wall for the light switch. Where was it? Her hand grasped at nothing but plaster. She'd heard a crack. Hopefully, it hadn't come from her toe. Ah, there was the light.

Toe throbbing, she inspected the nail and discovered she'd broken off a chunk. Blood pooled around the cuticle. A cherry on the top of this perfect night. As she limped to the bathroom for a bandage, she noticed the corner of the baseboard had broken off.

One problem at a time. First, her toe.

She cleaned it up and applied a bandage, debating whether to leave the baseboard issue for the morning. Tomorrow needed to be dedicated to research, but she should at least assess the damage tonight and see if she needed to stop and buy anything for repairs on the way home.

The ends where the baseboard had popped loose were splintered, making it hard to repair. Original to the building, it was thick and ornate and would be impossible to replace with a modern-day decoy. She hung her head. Fantastic.

A flash of green caught her attention, and she got on her knees to inspect. Using the flashlight on her phone, she probed the damage.

The plaster held a perfect notch behind where the corner baseboard once was. Was that fabric? Maneuvering her fingers in the small space, she tugged out an old cloth pouch. Her pulse raced with excitement over finding a secret stash in the wall. Nancy Drew come to life!

The thin cord that cinched the bag broke when she untied it. She finished prying it open as carefully as she could manage and dumped the contents on the rug.

A roll of bills emerged, along with a handful of coins and a tattered slip of paper. Antique money, much larger in size compared to modern currency. Three one-hundred-dollar bills, two fives, seven tens, a fifty, and four twenties. Some of the bills were black and white with red emblems, some were green, and others were pink. None of the coins were consistent in size, and many were chipped. The paper read *16GPS*, the scrawl barely visible with the age of time.

The artistry on the bills was amazing. They varied from pictures of past presidents to Greek women to ships. The five-dollar bills held actual signatures on the bottom in place of serial numbers.

Strange.

Who had put that pouch of bills in the wall and why?

How old were they?

Why had they been forgotten?

She ran her thumb along her lower lip, thinking. There was a story here. Perhaps the one she needed to secure her promotion. She didn't have any of the answers to her questions tonight, but the investigation would begin at daybreak.

CHAPTER FOUR

FRANKLIN

Manhattan, July 1863

*F*ranklin Davidson wasn't sure which was worse—the maddening pain in his leg where his foot used to be attached or the metallic dust that coated his tongue from the train's brakes. Three days' travel from the Georgia mountains to home made worse by the dirtiest locomotive in existence. He should be grateful the Union army hadn't broken the rail line, but it was hard to be grateful without part of his leg.

The only good thing to come from the South was his new bride disembarking by his side. Without her gentle nursing and encouragement, he would have given up in that field hospital. Begged the angel of death to take him home.

Now to measure how a man was supposed to carve out a living with only one good leg.

Guilt pricked him. His brother, Edward, had done so his entire life, though his quality of life was questionable. Franklin had done everything he could to help his brother. Massaging his foot and leg when the pain became unbearable, protecting him from the ridicule outside—and inside—their home. Somehow his efforts always fell short. He'd never understand the bitter hatred their father had for his crippled son and why Franklin had escaped it.

Would Franklin now receive the same condemnation when he returned home?

Home. If one could call it that.

Franklin hadn't seen his brother in eight years, and he missed him.

After so long apart, he'd find it difficult to recognize the man if he saw him on the street, except for the fact they were mirror images of each other. Father had written to Franklin once, telling him Edward had struck silver in Utah. Good for him. After all his brother had endured, he deserved happiness. A life of ease. Hopefully, the passing of time had taught Edward how to manage money, as balance had never been one of his talents.

Descending the train onto the platform apparently wasn't one of Franklin's. Pain made him clench his molars to keep from yelling. He still hadn't gotten used to the wooden prosthetic. Margaret gripped his arm, holding him erect as best she could against her petite frame. The very one that had curled against his every night for the past week, offering comfort in ways her nursing at the field hospital had not. Those midnight hours were the only ones since he'd lost his foot when he felt like a whole man.

A porter watched them before timing his approach.

Franklin patted Margaret's arm to assure her he was steady. "Please have our trunks sent to the nearest carriage."

"Will do, sir." The porter gave a slight bow. His gaze fixed on the bulge of Franklin's boot a moment before straightening.

Now he knew how Edward felt his entire life. As less than everything. It was even the same foot as Edward's too. But where Franklin's was gone completely, along with half of his shin, Edward's foot was merely twisted inward. Both handicaps made the simplest of tasks difficult and invited scrutiny. For years Franklin had tried to ease the burden of his brother's tribulation, but now he carried the same affliction.

They moved through the station like salmon swimming upstream. As if the July heat wasn't stifling enough, the friction of moving bodies made it feel like hell. Oddly enough, that was where they'd be living. The pleasant neighborhood surrounding his childhood home between Houston and Canal Street was now considered part of Hell's Hundred Acres. He loathed moving his respectable bride to a district full of brothels, but he had no choice. Not until he found someone who'd hire a lame man at a decent enough wage. He prayed it wouldn't take him twenty years to save for a house of their own.

"Oh my." Margaret gaped at the mass of bodies moving outside the train station. Buildings towering stories high blocked any view of natural landscape. The open fields and lush forests where he'd camped with his troop had too often made him feel vulnerable and exposed. Thousands of bodies speaking various languages, traffic noise, and chaos were all Franklin had ever known.

"Pittsburgh is large, but nothing like this." Margaret's lips parted in surprise. "How does one know where to go?"

He patted her hand. "Just pretend the buildings are trees and the people are forest creatures scurrying around, and it makes navigation less daunting."

Mouth drawn to the side, brows furrowed, she looked around them. He attempted to see it through her perspective. Bodies everywhere. The stench of sweat and horses, mud, and refuse. His mind went fuzzy, and his heartbeat galloped. His ears awaited the boom of cannon fire. Perspiration dotted his upper lip as the screams echoing through the hills of Chickamauga reverberated in his ears.

Gentle strokes on his arm brought his breathing to a steady pace. Margaret. New York City. Home.

He recognized their trunks being loaded into the rear of a carriage and led Margaret that direction. This couldn't lick him. He had a wife to care for. While war still raged, the infantry had discharged him honorably. Time to discover some semblance of living.

Margaret grabbed a fistful of skirt and took his offered hand, rising into the carriage with a twirl of blue fabric before sitting. So graceful. Her dress fanned around her like a bell, nearly taking up the entire seat.

Heat climbed into his neck and face as he fumbled to get in beside her. What took a normal man seconds took him minutes, and he wanted to shake his fist in anger. Once he was seated, Margaret took his hand as if nothing was amiss and asked him questions about the businesses as they passed.

His shoulders relaxed with every street that fell behind them. They'd soon travel by the mansions along Fifth Avenue before continuing south to his father's home. Margaret pointed out the glass factory with a sign in the window advertising HELP WANTED, WOMEN WELCOME. With so many men away at war, especially now that a federal draft law had been enacted, women filled the roles of men in the household. Though immodest, one must do what was necessary for survival.

"Perhaps they'd hire me." The uncertainty in her voice cut him to his core.

"You needn't work. I'll find a position soon. Before you know it, you'll have your pick of any home you want."

"What about that one?" She pointed at a massive brownstone with servants milling about and winked.

He chuckled at her teasing, but his insides were bleeding. He'd likely never be able to provide her with nice things. Would his love and devotion be enough to sustain hers?

The carriage rolled along, jostling them as it avoided craters in the road and people crossing the street. As they neared Five Points, the clopping of horses' hooves changed to shouts and frantic cries. Something in the air was different. The atmosphere had shifted into something very dark. The hairs on Franklin's neck and arms rose. His pulse picked up pace.

The driver rounded, cheeks paled. "Sir, there's an angry mob coming. Get to safety. Quickly."

Angry men spilled from the alleyways like a tidal wave flooding the street. Margaret released a tiny scream. Franklin gripped the side of the carriage and jumped. His injured leg gave way, and he smacked the ground. Groaning through the pain, he stood and reached for Margaret. She'd already scrambled down. Hands clasped, they ran.

Why was this happening? What was going on?

His breaths came harder with every jolt of misery that shot through his leg. If they could get inside a building, they might have a chance, but he was slowing her down. "Margaret, go."

He pointed to the nearest tenement.

"I'm not leaving you," she cried.

"I'll be right there. Go!" He pushed her forward.

"No." She turned to grab his arm, and her mouth fell open.

Without slowing momentum, he looked back to see what horror lay behind them. The mob had reached the carriage. Hands held the horses steady as others yanked the driver from his seat. The rioters went through their trunks, strewing clothes and belongings into the street.

They reached the tenement as more of the mob poured around the carriage to continue down the avenue. Franklin banged his fist on the locked door. "Help us! Please!"

Margaret joined his crusade, screaming for help.

The door opened just wide enough for one terrified eye to be seen through the crack. "Please let us in," Franklin pleaded.

Before the person could react, Franklin barged his way in, dragging Margaret behind him. The door slammed, and he helped the woman bar the latch. He was back on the battlefield, cornered and terrified.

"What's going on?" Margaret asked as she helped the woman cover the windows.

"The Irish—angry over draft—think they not should fight war not theirs. Can't pay." The woman's broken English was further interrupted by her panted breaths.

"Pay?" Margaret assessed him with questioning eyes. Franklin stepped away from the door to help reinforce the windows.

"The lottery." A black man jogged down the narrow stairs, his clothes tattered and stained. "Privileged white men who can afford to pay the government three hundred dollars don't have to go. Neither do any blacks. That leaves the poor and immigrants to fight for our freedom. Freedom they think we don't deserve."

Franklin looked down at his worn uniform. "I'm not one of those men."

"Then grab a pot, 'cause we've got to fight." The giant of a man led them to the kitchen and began collecting every vessel.

When Franklin had all he could carry, Margaret held out her arms. As banging started on the barred door, they followed the man up the stairs to the rooms on the top floor where several other people stood clustered by the open windows, ducking under clotheslines. Two women pushed ironing boards against the wall to allow for extra space.

"They're caught in the alley," someone in the room yelled. "Let's get 'em."

They poured pots of hot starch out the windows onto the rioters below. Cries of misery blended with victory shouts as vessel after vessel was emptied. Huddled against a wall in the hallway, Margaret covered her ears with her palms. Her eyes pinched shut, tears leaked from their corners and down her cheeks.

Franklin pulled her against his chest, tucking her under his chin. His hand rubbed the back of her head where her pristine coif used to be. The air was thick with the acrid scent of lye soap and sweaty bodies. He'd thought New York City to be one of the safest places to bring his wife. Maybe he should have attempted to find Edward in Utah Territory and start a life with her there. Franklin would be slower than other men, but limping around in a cold, dark hole, mining the mountain's reserves was better than being trampled and killed in the streets.

The battle raged for what seemed like hours before the rioters moved farther into the city. Evening was falling, and with no driver or carriage, it would put them walking to his father's house in the black of night through the brothels filled with drunken and lascivious men. His leg hadn't hurt this badly since the cannonball had crushed his foot into the earth. He'd be no match for rowdy men wanting to have their way with his lovely bride.

The proprietors who ran and worked the laundry service of Hart's Alley were kind enough to let them sleep in the corner of the first floor overnight. As the sun rose the next morning, the streets were eerily quiet. Those who did venture out did so with the utmost caution. Yesterday's carriage lay in pieces, the horses gone. Franklin prayed the driver had survived. Their trunks and belongings were beyond salvaging, so they made their way toward Hell's Hundred Acres.

He kept Margaret close to his side as they walked along the houses and businesses, keeping a keen eye and ear for trouble. With every step, Franklin wanted to scream in agony. The strips of fabric cushioning his prosthetic had come undone, and the wood was rubbing blisters on his still-healing nub.

By the time they reached his father's dilapidated home, Franklin could hardly walk. Margaret's nose and cheeks were sunburnt, and they were both in desperate need of water.

As he opened the door to step inside, anguish rose, threatening to drown him. Not only was he ashamed to face his father in this condition, but he couldn't even carry his sweet bride across the threshold.

CHAPTER FIVE

BEAU

Manhattan, Present Day

𝓑eau had one hour before the meeting with his campaign committee, and it was his only chance to eat until Marcy served their dinner party at seven. The sweet cook would've gladly made him lunch, but with all the preparations she was already juggling, he didn't want to burden her. Meat and Greet was only a block away, and they made a mean Italian sub he could eat on his way back home.

After locking the door, Beau sped down the stone steps and through the low-profile wrought-iron gate surrounding his home. He checked for traffic then dashed across the street ahead of the oncoming city bus. Cutting through the garden would be faster than walking around the square, so he slipped his key inside the lock. A warm breeze stirred the trees and made the gate's hinges groan in protest. The walking paths were still damp from yesterday's rain but had given them a much-needed break from the heat wave.

Careful of the other residents, he jogged through the garden. There weren't any visitors these days except the residents who held a key now that the adjoining Gramercy Park Hotel had permanently closed. Limited and supervised access had been granted along with the price of their room. The pandemic had put a massive crunch on many of the surrounding businesses, but none so much as the hotel. Its loss, however, would further put a strain on the local operations that had survived, as people who could afford nine hundred dollars a night for a hotel room wouldn't be frequenting those establishments.

Commerce was another topic he planned to tackle if elected governor.

He also needed to have Wilson leave a slot in his schedule open for him to use his home gym. While Wilson Kennedy was a master at raising funds, marketing, and polling, he was not so great at remembering Beau had a life outside of his ambitions.

Beau exited the park and lifted his smart watch to dictate a text to Wilson when he saw a pretty waitress on a park bench, laptop balanced on her knees. Three days had come and gone, and he hadn't heard from her. He should respect her silence and move on. He had a meeting to get to anyway.

However, he always welcomed a challenge.

He crossed the street. Whatever was on her computer had her engrossed, because she didn't seem to notice his approach. He took the space on the other end of the bench, startling her. "Sorry. Wasn't trying to scare you."

He'd forgotten her mention of a cautious nature.

Her lips parted and stilled. He forced himself to concentrate on anything but.

"Beau."

"Andrea."

"You're…" She ran a hand down the leg of her dark jeans. Her white shirt matched her white sneakers, but her nails and bracelet were pink. "You're probably wondering why I haven't called."

"Disappointed, but your reasons are your own. I respect that." He rested his elbows on his knees.

"Truth is, I threw your number away."

Her statement hit him like the impact of sprinting into a brick wall. He tried to recall a time when he was flat-out rejected by a woman— or anyone in his life—and couldn't recall one. He was a Davidson-Quincy. That name carried weight. And influence.

More weight than he cared to carry on his shoulders at times.

She closed her laptop, put one ankle over her knee, and crossed her arms. Not angry. Defensive. "You look as if I just slapped you."

"You kind of did." He gave her a sheepish grin.

"I wasn't trying to hurt your pride. I just believe in being honest, even if it's blunt."

That made her even more desirable.

"You must be a writer."

Her tongue traced a path over her teeth. "What brought you to that conclusion?"

"Writers are blunt." He smiled when her mouth fell open. "Plus, your laptop and press pass gave you away."

He pointed at the badge clipped to her canvas bag.

"Ah." She rolled her eyes but smiled back. "And you must be someone with a trust fund."

Beau grabbed his chest, as if shot. "They always go after the trust fund."

She laughed.

"What gave me away?"

"When I left work the other night, I saw you go into the park." She pointed across the street.

"Ah. And that makes me…?"

"Way out of my league." She opened her bag and slipped her laptop inside.

"Au contraire." He leaned against the back of the park bench, stretching an arm toward her.

"Au contraire?"

"Don't writers like fancy phrases?"

"You're being stereotypical."

"So are you."

Andrea opened her mouth once again then closed it. "Touché."

"See, you do like fancy words."

"And you do have a trust fund."

"Opposites attract, you know." He nodded a greeting to a woman walking her terrier.

"I'm a simple woman who likes simple living. Money and status mean nothing to me."

He'd heard that a million times. Though coming from Andrea, it sounded genuine. "So, you have me completely figured out based on what facts?"

The statement hung in the air like a thick fog. He was curious to know if she'd discovered his identity.

"That you own a key to Gramercy Park." Crossing her legs, she turned toward him, hooking her arm over the back of the bench. Her words said she wasn't interested in him, but her body language proved otherwise. "I know nothing about you, and I mean no offense. Truly. But everyone around here knows that to gain a key, you have to own one of the historic mansions on the square and that none of those are sold for less than four million."

"You act as if the keys hold some kind of magic."

"Don't they? If I was paying seven thousand a year for keys to support the garden's upkeep, I'd expect some magic."

She'd surprised him yet again. "You've done your research."

"I'm an investigative journalist. Research is my life."

Not just any writer, then. He already struggled to escape the clutches of the media and journalists determined to ruin his campaign without the added headache of trying to date one. If only she were a sci-fi novelist.

"What else do you know, oh well-researched one?"

Her scowl was far from intimidating. "I know they change the locks every year for added security. I know that if a trespasser gets inside, they won't be able to get out, because the key must be used for both entry and exit. That's how they prosecute anyone who sneaks inside."

She continued ticking her knowledge off using her fingers. "I know the entire block used to be swampland, that there used to be a fountain where Edwin Booth's statue stands, and that number 22 Gramercy Park Square was the inspiration for E. B. White's *Stuart Little*. I also know that number 4 used to be the mayor's home, and that when the lamps were lit, it meant he was home. And that one of the few times Gramercy Park has been open to the public was during the Civil War when the Irish rioted in the streets in protest of the draft, and armed guards camped in the garden to protect the property owners."

All of it was public knowledge plastered on the internet. Not much investigating to it. The bigger question, did she know who he was?

"Well done, Ms. Andrea Investigative Journalist. Are you writing an article on Gramercy Park and its current inhabitants?"

"No. My passion is the past. I investigate history for *Smithsonian* magazine."

"Impressive." And a relief she wasn't a reporter who'd want to investigate him. Not that he had anything to hide. He was as pure as winter's first snow. "I'm surprised you live in New York, since the Smithsonian Institution is based in D.C."

"I love D.C. But my niche is the Gilded Age through World War I. Many of the kings in those eras either lived in New York City year-round or were frequent visitors. No matter what you're investigating, you always go back to the source. I work in the Manhattan office."

"Expert advice." He stretched out his legs, going for casual, even though she was speaking of some of his ancestors. "Would you like to go out sometime?"

She shook her head and gave him a shy smile. "I'm flattered. Really. We're just different enough that it wouldn't work out, and I need to concentrate on earning a promotion right now."

"All right. I'll settle for a casual friendship."

A line he'd never had to use before.

His watch buzzed with a notification. Thirty minutes until his meeting. He gestured to her bag. "Anything I can help with?"

"That depends. Do you know anything about old money?"

"Do you mean old money versus new money, the way the social elite used to refer to money passed down through generations?"

"No. Old money as in historical currency circulated prior to the 1920s. Long story short, I found a pouch hidden in the wall of my apartment the other day, and I'm trying to track its significance."

"Hidden treasure? Intriguing. What makes you think the bills are older than the twenties?"

"Currency changed drastically around that time, and these bills resemble nothing from the twenties to present day. Plus, my apartment building used to be the Winderfield Hotel—a once-prestigious establishment in Greenwich Village that was converted to tenements in the thirties. My conclusion is whoever hid them was a guest of the hotel."

"I know the place." Twenty-five minutes until his meeting. "That's an interesting conversation piece. Hidden in the wall for safekeeping, or hidden for nefarious purposes?"

"I plan to find out."

He enjoyed seeing her passion break through her guarded exterior. "I know a guy."

"Of course you do." She bumped her wrist with his in a playful gesture. He liked the contact way too much.

"Grant Caudalie. He owns a relic shop near Bryant Park. I'd be happy to escort you there, and we could try to discover the story behind your hidden money."

"Hmm. Would that be a date?"

"Of course not. Consider it fulfilling a duty to history."

She laughed and stood. "Nice try."

He stood as well, noting that the top of her head barely reached his chin. "In order for me to text you the address to Grant's shop, I'll have to have your number."

Her lips twisted in a cute I'm-trying-not-to-enjoy-this-banter-even-though-I-am way. She slung her bag over her shoulder. "You're very charming, Beau. And incredibly handsome. As much as I want to say yes, my answer is still no."

"What woman can resist 'very charming' and 'incredibly handsome'?"

"This one." She squeezed his forearm to soften the blow and walked backward a few steps, holding his gaze. Then she turned and walked the twenty feet into Gant & Company.

Man, he hated losing.

CHAPTER SIX

ANDREA

Manhattan, Present Day

*D*ust, smoke, and a hint of mothballs assaulted Andrea's nose as she stepped into Recycled Relics on Forty-Sixth Street by Times Square. An assortment of oddities dangled from the ceiling—a unicycle, tin circus toys, scary theater masks, and sharp torture devices she hoped were antique farming tools. The glass counter sat at the back of the main room where an employee stood behind the register, occupied with cleaning an object in his hand.

She glanced at the sign that read SMILE, YOU'RE BEING WATCHED with a picture of a security camera beneath it. An additional measure to the iron bars over the windows.

"Welcome. Can I help you find something?" The man looked up from the metal item in his palm. A knife.

"I'm here to see Grant Caudalie. I was told by a..." *Customer? Acquaintance? Guy who keeps asking me out?* "By a *friend* that Mr. Caudalie was the one to see if I wanted to discover the value of something I recently found."

He set the knife aside and poked his glasses higher on his nose. Light glinted off the shiny blade that tapered to a thick handle engraved with skulls. "I'm Grant. You must be Andrea."

Her hand paused halfway to her bag, unsure how he knew her name. Now the place was really giving her the creeps.

"Beau called and said to expect you."

The mention of Beau made the unease drain from her muscles. If

Beau trusted this guy, she would too. Her traitorous brain brought up his image, making her blood warm. He was kind and charming, and she wanted so badly to accept a date, but the last thing she needed right now was complication. She knew all too well, rich and powerful men were complications.

"Did Beau explain what I'd be bringing?"

"No, he said that was your story to tell. Which has me completely captivated." The gleam of a mad scientist lit Grant's face.

She pulled the cloth pouch from her bag and began emptying the contents, easing out the bills and the strip of paper so as not to inflict damage. The coins pinged on the glass counter. Grant spread everything out with the gentle care of someone used to handling antiquated items. He turned on an LED rating lamp, slipped on a pair of jeweler's glasses, and began inspecting each bill.

As she waited, she perused the gaudy antique jewelry and presidential buttons in the case. A black-and-white button from 1920 with the busts of Cox and Roosevelt caught her attention. The rare item was worth thousands. Ah, and he knew that, according to the price tag hanging below.

Slim, open-faced curio cabinets bracketed the counter. She took stock of what he offered, growing more curious of her treasure with every "hmm" and "huh" he uttered. A blue glass medicine bottle sat on display with other old medical items. One of the first Red Cross patches that would've once been worn on a uniform, a small case of doctor tools, a measuring device, and—was that a bone saw?

She returned her attention back to the glass bottle. Most from that era were plain and in rough condition. This one was pristine and held an emblem in the bottom corner. A shield with antlers protruding from the sides and a honeybee, wings outstretched, on the shield.

"Beautiful, isn't it? Blue glass was trending in the 1870s. A West Point doctor had the theory that the blue color of the sky had a connection to the success of living organisms. He thought that land near the equator was so fertile because the sky was a vivid blue. Therefore, the North and South Poles were desolate because of a lack of blue sky. He started growing all kinds of fruits under blue glass. Even convinced other physicians to place premature babies under it. He wrote a book claiming all kinds of positive phenomena came from using blue glass, and it swept the world by storm."

Andrea filed the information away, determined to bring it out later and research it for herself as a potential future article. "The emblem looks like some kind of family crest. Is that specific bottle from the West Point doctor?"

"Dr. Pleasonton, and not that I'm aware of. It's a bottle that once contained opium. From what we know about the drug now, it's likely the blue color was to help mask what it really contained inside versus thinking it would help aid in health. You interested in purchasing? I'll give you a good deal."

"Uh, no. But thanks for sharing the story behind it. Fascinating."

"Isn't it?" There was that mad scientist look again. It was rare she stumbled upon another human as passionate about history as she was.

"Can I ask where you found these?" Grant took off the glasses and laid them aside.

"Long story short, in the wall of my apartment."

"Wow, these are in great condition." He scratched his chin. "Would you consider selling? I'll offer you two hundred dollars cash."

The register dinged then popped open.

Too easy. If he wanted them after so short an inspection, they must be valuable. And for him to make a profit, he'd have to buy them from her below value. "Thanks for the offer, but no. Beau mentioned you'd be able to help me understand what I have here. If not, then I apologize for taking up your time."

Grant nodded. "Well played. Normally, I wouldn't be so forthright with information on an item that isn't in my possession, but since I owe Beau a favor, I'll tell you that the bills are definitely post–Civil War. Maybe even closer to the end of the century. I can also tell you they're counterfeit. See here, and here?"

He pointed to the lettering on the far left and then the right side of the ten-dollar bill. "The shading isn't flowing the right direction. And here." He tapped the twenties. "Each bill of this denomination has the same serial number."

Andrea leaned an elbow on the counter. "I didn't realize money that old had serial numbers."

"They didn't refer to them as serial numbers back then, but each bill was stamped with a number and signed in iron gall ink. Problem was that prior to the Civil War, most of the money in circulation didn't come from the federal government. A network of private banks circulated it. They each had their own design of bills, easy to counterfeit because it took so long for anyone to realize they were fake."

"So, bills with matching serial numbers spent at different times in different places would hardly get noticed."

"Exactly. Only a merchant or bank employee who knew what to look for would recognize it. Sometimes the type of paper used in counterfeiting rings could tip an expert to a fake."

"What about the coins? Are they counterfeit as well?"

"Most likely. They could be made of a cheaper metal merely dipped in silver and gold. I'd have to run a chemical test to be sure."

Andrea chewed on the information. "Since they're in the same pouch as the counterfeit bills, it stands to reason they'd be fake as well. Any idea what that code is on the slip of paper?"

Grant took his time stacking the bills and rolling them to fit easily into the pouch. "No idea. My guess is it only had significance to the owner of all this. My offer still stands. It's rare to find counterfeit bills dating that far back so well preserved."

"I'll consider it. I'm a journalist for *Smithsonian* magazine, and I need to hang on to them for now."

"*Smithsonian?*" His features lifted in surprise. "Isn't that incredible that someone of your profession would find counterfeit bills in the wall of her apartment? It's almost as if someone left them there for you to find."

CHAPTER SEVEN

EDWARD

Philadelphia, March 1864

*E*dward stepped into the vestibule of the Kingsley Hotel, twirling the gold-tipped cane he'd just won during a rousing game of poker. The bird-faced clerk at the desk scowled at his appearance. Edward tucked the cane to his side and matched steps with a loudly dressed woman about his height, with a dress matching in circumference. Her green hat held more fringe than the portieres at Madame Bragg's.

"Mr. Dickerson. A word, please, sir." The clerk lowered his chin, eyes glaring over his pointed beak.

The woman, confused over which one of them the clerk was speaking to, pivoted to see behind her and nearly took out Edward's eye with a tassel. She stepped out of the way, smiling, allowing the vicious fowl to pin him in place.

Wearing the placating expression of Mr. Key, the man Edward had bested at poker, Edward sidled up to the desk. "What can I do for you, Mr...."

"Hartford." The skinny man's thin white mustache twitched. Mr. Hartford slipped on his monocle, his giant nose more than qualified to hold the eyepiece in place.

Edward remembered the man's name, of course, his brain never failing to forget those who thought themselves better than he, but asking the man each time they conversed gave Edward an air of authority over the man, as if the clerk was no more significant in Edward's life than a pigeon begging crumbs on the street. He'd learned that tactic from the real Mr. Dickerson, a wealthy saloon owner he'd worked for in San Francisco before leaving for Utah Territory.

Mr. Hartford leaned over the desk and lowered his voice. "What you can do for me is settle your bill, sir. You've accumulated some extravagant charges, and in order to continue accommodating your expensive whims, we must have partial payment in good faith. I'm sure you can understand that."

Edward didn't consider meals from other establishments delivered to his room and extra room keys left at the desk for his rotation of high-class courtesans from the Palace "whims," but the old codger had obviously forgotten what it was like to be young and virile.

"Of course, Mr. Hartford. My apologies. Allow me to return to my room, and I will be back to settle up the entire bill, posthaste."

"Very well." Hartford removed his monocle, dismissing him. "I'll see you in a moment."

His dark eyes followed Edward from the room.

Edward snickered. He'd be back, but the bill would fall entirely on the owner of this establishment. The Kingsley wasn't the nicest he'd stayed in, of course. There were much finer hotels in the West. Ones that didn't scoff at a man enjoying female company. But the effects of morals, and of war, were more pronounced in the East. A truth he failed to find comfortable. Especially since the latest draft announced last month. Fewer and fewer men were about the city, making Edward's presence—and penchant for luxury—harder to camouflage.

He made his way to the second floor and to room 27. Light flickered from the wall sconces, casting shadows in the dim space. Just last evening, he'd made the acquaintance of Mr. Cornelius Vanderbilt in this very hall. The bewhiskered commodore was shorter and frailer than Edward expected for a man who owned a fleet of ships.

After unlocking his door, Edward left it ajar and stepped inside the room to illuminate a lamp. A pang of disappointment stole through him. He wasn't yet ready to leave Philadelphia, but he'd exhausted his resources here as well. What must it be like to have a stable home, a stable life? He'd never had as much and likely never would.

He thought of his brother and kicked the door closed. Last he'd heard, Franklin had come home from war, injured but married. A hero at Chickamauga. Franklin's noble heart was bound to charm a woman. But

Edward didn't have to like it.

The blasted war had caused a separation between them never experienced. Edward's first time away from the shadow of Franklin's wings had been both exhilarating and terrifying. Empowering. He'd planned on striking it rich and he and Franklin having all the adventures they'd dreamed about as boys. Now that Franklin had a wife, those dreams were as fleeting as steam from a boiling kettle of water.

But Edward was no longer simply the crippled brother of Franklin Davidson, but whoever Edward chose to be.

Tonight he would play the role of vagrant.

He changed out of his tailored suit and into tattered pants and a dingy shirt. With meticulous care, he maneuvered his whisker device over his head and behind his ears. A little coal dust to soften the edges and make him appear unbathed, and no one could tell the wiry hair was not his own.

His meager belongings fit into a bag, and what would not fit, he left behind. Attachment was for the weak. And weak was one thing Edward would never be again.

He doused his lantern, opened the door, and peered down the hall. Silent for the late hour. Keeping his steps light, he hurried to the servants' entrance. The maze of steps leading to each floor were narrow. A series of dumbwaiters lined the passage. The echo of voices and kitchen noises rose from below. This wasn't the first time he'd escaped through the servants' quarters in this hotel, but it was the first time he'd done so with luggage.

He weaved in and out of spaces and up and down flights of stairs to avoid being seen. Though it took longer to escape the building than he'd planned, the chilly night air invigorated him as he walked in the shadows to the west end of town.

The *clip-clop* of horses' hooves and *clink* of fine china gave way to the boisterous sounds of the taverns and brothels and slapping water against the dock. Clouds of his breath mixed with the scent of briny salt water in the air. Darkness shrouded the boats moored away from land. Following the instructions given by Captain Kent, Edward reached the east end of the dock and found the promised rowboat.

Guided by the light of the moon, he rowed half a nautical mile southeast to the *Galleon*. The ship loomed above him, its lowered sails rippling in the breeze. He shivered. It was much colder on the water than it was on land.

Edward ran his hand over the crust of barnacles corroding the exterior of the ship. He whistled the tune of the osprey twice, paused for five seconds, and did so once more. A rope ladder rolled over the side of the ship.

Edward had never considered himself a pirate, but he rather enjoyed playing the part.

Climbing the cursed contraption with his clubbed foot and a heavy carpetbag was nearly impossible, but he finally made it to the top and heaved the bag into the boat with a *thunk*. He swung one leg over, then the other, breaths heaving.

Boots against wood thumped a steady rhythm toward him. Captain Kent weaved through the crew, held up a lantern, and smiled, revealing two missing teeth, the rest rotting or broken. Unease rippled down Edward's spine. Nothing for it. To build his kingdom, he must start by fraternizing with the unsavory. When the prodigal son returned home next time, he'd be as wealthy as a king and so respected among his peers, his father would have no choice but to bow in submission.

Resolve straightened Edward's spine, making him stand tall. "You have the cargo?"

"Aye. You, the money?"

Edward bent and opened the bag.

Captain Kent cackled, its evil undertone reverberating off the water. "Then we have a deal."

The captain invited him inside to dine. The meal wasn't anything more than a hearty stew, but it warmed Edward's bones. As did the rum.

With dinner cleared, the captain offered him a cigar. "I think it best to stay out of other men's affairs, but the cat's curiosity has me on this one. Why does a man in the East have need of so much poppy?"

Smoke curled around Edward's face as he contemplated his answer. "I visited the dens in the West. Witnessed able-bodied men of all classes return night after night, unable to suppress the need for pleasure."

Those moments made the easiest swindles. Out of their mind with the drug, men had practically handed Edward their fortunes. Richard Olney surely had. "The poppy takes hold of a man and becomes his lord. Willing slaves they are for more. That makes the one who possesses it dominant. When the craving becomes a desperate need to survive, they'll part with everything to have it."

"And you'll be the one to hand them what they want." Captain Kent took a long drag on his cigar. "Why not the untamed West? Why here?"

Going back west would guarantee his hanging. Despite the rum making his brain fuzzy at the edges, he wasn't about to confess his past to the captain. Sure, the West made more sense. After all, poppy had been introduced to the country when the Chinese brought it with them during the gold rush. His plan might add more risk in the East, but he wouldn't be competing with so many chemists.

Edward fought back a yawn. " 'Under the pressure of the cares and sorrows of our mortal condition, men have at all times called in some physical aid to their moral consolations.'"

The captain frowned.

"Edmund Burke, philosopher. I read about him in a library once." Edward put out his cigar. "This war has shattered the best of humanity and exposed the worst. The men who aren't dying are being sent home wounded and miserable. Given morphine—when available—to cope with pain and the reality of their changed existence, they need this 'physical aid.'"

Captain Kent rested his head on the back of his chair and closed his eyes. "Aye. We're all in need of something to prop us up as we transition from infant to aged."

After the captain fell into a steady slumber, Edward shuffled below deck to inspect the crates. The flame from the lantern flickered as he hung it on a wall hook. The wooden lid moaned as he pried it off one crate. Nestled among the straw were dozens of small glass bottles. He opened one and sniffed. His first delivery of many.

While some fought for freedom and others trusted in the foundation of politics, Edward was relying on the one thing that would ensure the security of his future.

Opium.

CHAPTER EIGHT

FRANKLIN

Manhattan, June 1865

*I*n one of the country's darkest hours, Franklin stood in the constable's office, straining against the pain of handcuffs biting into his wrists. He'd committed no crime that would justify arrest, but the officers had refused to listen to his pleas. Whatever the mistake, he had to clarify the situation and return home to Margaret, newly with child. These past weeks in Pittsburgh hunting for work had cost him more than he'd bargained for.

The constable looked up from his paper, the wax in his blond mustache giving his smirk a sardonic twist. "You're a hard man to catch, Mr. Dickerson. What do you have to say for yourself?"

Franklin shifted his weight evenly on his feet. Not an effortless task in leg irons and a wooden limb. "As I've told your officers several times, my name is Franklin Davidson. I live south of Houston Street on the corner of Mercer and Wooster. I clean the floors and presses for the *Houston Tribune.* You may check with my family or my employer to verify my identity."

"So you say, *Franklin Davidson.* Or is it James Palermo? Or Moses Grande?" The constable's brown eyes grew dark as he stared a hole through Franklin.

"I do say. What all of you have failed to tell me is what crimes I'm accused of committing."

"There's quite a list. Can you spare an hour? Oh, of course you can. Now that we've caught you, you have all the time in the world."

Franklin wasn't a violent man, especially toward others placed in authority, but he considered punching the officer beside him for his snicker. Too bad his hands were bound. The constable rubbed one side of his mustache between his fingers as he read his notes aloud.

"Unlawful entry, robbery, forgery, selling of property that doesn't exist, assault and battery, an accumulation of unpaid debts to several businesses, spending of counterfeit money, forcing yourself upon a woman—no matter how low in class she may be—and our latest tip that you're a conspirator against our great president with the late John Wilkes Booth."

Indignation rose like floodwaters. Franklin stepped forward, finger pointed at the constable. "Hogwash! I sacrificed my life for this country and held nothing but the utmost respect for our dear president. Check with Captain Landon of the Fifth New York Infantry. We fought side by side every day. He'll verify who I am."

Franklin forced a calm he didn't feel and relayed the story of how he lost his foot to a cannonball while saving two of his comrades as he inched them and himself to safety. He hated recalling that awful day, and certainly didn't want to be arrogant about his actions, but felt he had no choice. "Upon returning home, President Lincoln himself issued me a Congressional Medal of Honor."

The constable's arrogance slipped. He looked at his papers. "You're either telling the truth or you're a good liar. Why aren't you wearing your new clothes from Tilden's Haberdashery, Mr. Dickerson? Upon insisting the clerk meet you after hours to pick up your order of tailored suits, you then beat the man unconscious and left Fifth Avenue without settling your bill. Did you decide the role of vagabond suited better for the role you were playing today?"

Franklin wanted to laugh at the absurdity. As if he'd ever be able to afford so much as a button from a store on Fifth Avenue. He lived in a poverty-ridden neighborhood in a crumbling house his precious wife did her best to make a home. While he was grateful for his job, it didn't bring in enough to afford anything other than necessities to survive, and that list didn't include clothing of any kind. Margaret had patched their clothing so often the last few years it was looking like quilts.

"I've never been to Tilden's Haberdashery. You have the wrong man."

"Officer Briggs, check the Fifth New York Infantry's registry for a Franklin Davidson. Then retrieve Mr. Silas Hutcheson from Tilden's Haberdashery. We'll see what he has to say about our Mr. Dickerson.

"Officer Reynolds, lock him up and then bring someone from the *Houston Tribune* that can verify his identity."

Hours passed as Franklin sat in the cold, stinky cell. His stomach rumbled and his nerves frayed with every thought of Margaret. His father had taken a tumble right after he'd left for Pittsburgh to find work, and he could hardly get out of bed. Franklin didn't want the hours of tending the man and the stress of Franklin's absence to affect their growing child.

What if they kept him here? Would they send word to his wife while he awaited trial? How long would a trial take? Once declared innocent, would they compensate him for all the wasted time?

Sweat drenched every inch of him. Noise from the other inmates quieted as evening fell. Officers made their rounds. One relayed to another that President Andrew Johnson was forming a special department to seize and stop the spreading of counterfeit money. Able-bodied men with military or law enforcement experience were encouraged to apply. Franklin tucked the information away to chew on later and floated in and out of sleep on the stained bed.

The clang of metal jarred his attention. Still shackled, Franklin was led down the corridor and to a room where the constable waited with a man he'd never seen before. Mr. Silas Hutcheson, Franklin guessed by the bruises and stitches. The man's eyes widened when he saw Franklin. "This is the man."

Franklin fought back a growl. "I've been in Pittsburgh the last fortnight attempting to secure a position with the Pittsburgh Steam Engine Company." Franklin's good nature stretched as taut as a piano wire. "An advertisement in the *Times* declared they hire veterans of war, and the pay is considerably more than I make at the *Tribune*. I'm an honest citizen who just wants to put this war behind him and support his family."

Mr. Hutcheson shook his head but remained silent.

The constable yawned. "Is there a contact at the steam company who can authenticate your visit?"

"I interviewed with Mr. Colin Contigo. We met on three different occasions."

"And did Mr. Contigo offer you a position?" the constable asked.

"He did not." The backs of Franklin's eyelids rubbed like sandpaper when he blinked. "Veterans overrun the city. There were no current positions open that would accommodate my type of injury."

Mr. Hutcheson snarled. "That story is almost as good as the one you fabricated for why you couldn't pick up your order during normal business hours."

Franklin ran a hand down his weary face. "I'm sorry for your predicament, Mr. Hutcheson, but the man who attacked you wasn't me."

The man opened his mouth to speak, but the door opened and Lysander Millet, Franklin's manager at the *Tribune*, came inside. His beady eyes went from Franklin to the constable and back to Franklin, confusion evident. Mr. Millet spoke. "This is my employee, Franklin Davidson."

The constable frowned. Millet verified his identity again, stating that Franklin was a hard worker despite missing half of his leg. "We hired him on September 3, 1863. I remember because that's my son's birthday. I've never known this man to use any other name and don't know how he'd commit crimes in Philadelphia, Pittsburgh, Boston, and San Francisco, as you've stated, while recuperating for months in a field hospital and then remaining faithful to the *Tribune* every single day. A body wouldn't have time in the brief hours of night and still be able to attend work looking rested and proving useful."

The constable scratched his cheek. "Glowing praise. Franklin Davidson was listed on the Fifth New York Infantry's registry. We sent a telegram to Captain Harold Landon, and he too verified your character."

Rapping his fingers on the desk, the constable held up a wanted poster with Franklin's face on it. Then another. And another. "What I can't figure out is how your face ended up on posters from various cities if you did not commit these crimes. The woman you attacked even described your limp."

Foreboding snaked around Franklin's legs and slithered up to his neck, nearly choking him. Why hadn't he considered this before? He hadn't even known his brother was back in New York. Franklin hung his head, heart sick. "I think I can explain."

"Please do so." The constable rubbed his eyes.

"I have an identical twin brother. His name is Edward. He's known for getting into trouble."

"I'd call this more than trouble." The constable leaned back in his chair.

Hutcheson balled his fists. "Agreed."

"Silence." The constable's patience was clearly growing as taut as Franklin's. "Officer Briggs verified your leg as a wooden prosthetic. If the man in this poster is your twin brother, how do you explain his limp? I've yet to meet identical twins who share war injuries."

Exhaustion settled over Franklin all at once, and he dropped into a nearby chair. "He was born with a clubbed foot. He still has both of his feet, but one curves in, causing the limp."

Hutcheson's mouth fell open.

"Is there any record proving your births?" the constable asked.

"Beekman Hospital should have records. We were born at home, but the midwife filed the certificates there. I also have a record at home."

"Take a closer look, Mr. Hutcheson. Are there any noticeable differences between this man and Mr. Dickerson?"

Franklin stood so the man could examine him, but Mr. Hutcheson shrank against the wall. The officer on duty prodded the clerk forward and stayed beside him for protection. As if there was any harm Franklin could do while shackled.

The little man studied him with accusatory eyes. When he got to the right side of Franklin's face, his shoulders wilted. "The man who attacked me had a deformed ear. This man doesn't." He blew out a breath. "I can also verify the man who attacked me wore a metal brace for a clubfoot. I saw it when measuring his inseam, though I pretended not to."

Franklin lifted his pant leg to expose the wooden limb.

The constable stood. "You're certain the man who attacked you had a deformed ear?"

Mr. Hutcheson frowned. "I make it a point to know all of my customers' idiosyncrasies."

"Why didn't you mention it when you filed the description?"

"I didn't think about it until now," the clerk snapped. "I was quite indisposed. But yes, I'm certain of the ear."

"Does your twin have a deformed ear?" The constable pushed his chair beneath the desk.

"He does," Franklin answered.

He left out the detail that his brother was born with two normal ears but in a fit of rage one night after their mother had died, their father boxed the side of Edward's head with a glass vase so hard it busted into shards and cut his ear in a dozen different places.

"Very well. I'll send an officer to the hospital first thing in the morning. If there's record of a twin named Edward, I'll let you go." The constable headed toward the door.

Millet held up a finger. "May I go now, sir? Morning comes early."

The constable nodded. "You may go. Thank you for coming in."

Millet's amber eyes radiated sympathy. "I'm terribly sorry for your predicament, Franklin. But if you're not able to report to work in the next two days, I'll have to hire another man. You've already been gone two weeks, and we're desperate for help."

"I understand." Franklin's gut churned. "Constable, my wife was expecting me home this morning. She's with child and I don't want her worrying. Can you send word to her I'm all right?"

"See to it, Officer. I'm going home to get some sleep."

Exhausted, Franklin ignored the comment. What privilege to sleep in one's own bed. Especially when innocent.

Millet and Hutcheson left. Before the constable stepped out, he turned to Franklin. "Do you have contact with your brother? Any idea where he is?"

"No, sir. I haven't seen or heard from him in almost nine years." Franklin ran a hand down his face. "After today, I don't know that I care to ever again."

CHAPTER NINE

BEAU

Manhattan, Present Day

*B*eau smoothed his tie against his shirt as he stepped into the breakfast room. All except his dad's puff of white hair was hidden behind an open copy of the *New York Times*. A feast of hard-boiled eggs, pastries, bacon, pancakes, and sliced fruit lined the antique sideboard. Beau poured a mug of dark roast and filled a plate.

The newspaper rattled. "Can you believe this guy?"

Beau took the chair next to his dad. "Who and what?"

"Timothy Greene. He's proposing that we fill the nursing shortage with artificial intelligence. Madness! Robots giving humans medications. That's fine and dandy until one of them administers the wrong one, too much, or the power goes out."

"Odd choice of topic to bring out during a campaign." Beau sipped his coffee. "No mistake, the shortage of nurses is a concern, but one easily avoided had administration made wiser choices from the start. Tim should devise a way to encourage nurses to return, not to replace them with robots."

Dad handed him the paper. "He's not really running for the people anyway. Plus, he has an ulterior motive. Those robots would be made from recycled materials and the power source eco-friendly. A power source made overseas by a company he's invested in. His slogan 'Go Green with Greene' is ludicrous."

Beau wasn't surprised. The man had heavily invested in green energy since the early nineties.

"I don't see him getting far with AI. Especially considering how many years it would take to get an idea of that caliber from prototype to production."

Marcy's blueberry pancakes were phenomenal this morning.

"When is your interview?" Dad asked.

Beau swallowed his bite of egg. "Wednesday at ten. I have a PR engagement this afternoon at the children's hospital then a meeting with NYDOT at two."

"Full day. Governor Demcon is a good man. You'll have big shoes to fill."

Dad folded the paper and ran a finger along the edge of his teacup. The same gesture he'd performed at breakfast for years when awaiting Beau's response to a statement. A silent message to read between the lines, tread carefully, and provide the correct answer. Not that his dad had a temper. Quite the opposite. But one didn't want to disappoint Theodore Davidson-Quincy.

"Yes, sir. We the people." Seconds ticked on the grandfather clock as Beau worked on the last of the pancake.

Frown lines creased the weathered skin around his dad's mouth. "I'm surprised Wilson approved of that slogan."

"Why, sir?"

"It's antiquated. Today's voters want someone who's looking toward the future, not the past."

"Yes, but to make wise decisions for the future, one must consider the past. Something our forefathers did right was not consider themselves above the people. My slogan will show voters I include myself among them. Not just working for them but *with* them."

"And you assume to gain constituents through a pronoun?"

It had certainly worked for other politicians.

"I'm not naive, sir. When I say I'll be working with them, I mean literally. I plan to roll up my sleeves and work alongside the voters to find solutions to the problems. Gain perspective from all angles before attempting to pass a decision in their best interest. And I won't just go to them, but I will bring them to me. Show them we're in this together."

The pursing of Dad's lips said he had his doubts. "Could work. Nothing politicians haven't promised voters before, though. You'll have to prove yourself."

"Yes, sir." Beau went for the carafe and poured a second cup of coffee. It was going to be another long day with a full schedule, and apathetic faith in Beau's abilities just made it longer.

"You're so like your mother." Dad's voice was almost wistful.

Was the man showing a rare moment of emotion, or was it the side effect of his new heart medication? Beau waited as his father processed his thoughts.

"Headstrong yet gentle. Always thinking of others." Dad swallowed and glanced away. "If she were still with us, she'd pat your cheek and tell you to do your best. That win or lose, she was proud of you."

With slow, shaky movements, Dad stood and pushed the newspaper in front of Beau, the hard edge returning to his jaw. "Since she's not, I'll tell you to study your rival, take big risks, and don't be afraid to play dirty. The Davidson-Quincy empire wasn't founded on platitudes and servanthood. I'd still like to see you take over the family business, but if you're determined to do this, do it right."

A cavern of grief opened in Beau's chest at the memory of his sweet mother and the distance that had widened between him and his father ever since he announced he had different ambitions. Twenty years had yet to erase the pain of losing her. How did he repair the loss of someone standing right before him?

Malcolm entered the room dressed in his usual black suit. "The car is ready for you, sir."

"Perfect timing." Dad tugged on the gray blazer folded over his chair. "I hope you can join us for dinner. I'm entertaining a new client. Elias Woodrow from the Woodrow Corporation."

Beau was always the dutiful son. "Big business?"

"They're out of Nova Scotia. We're negotiating a sale for a block of town houses on Fifth. As a bonus, they'll get a great deal on a block of historic apartments in Greenwich Village."

Beau pushed back his plate, uneasy. "Which one?"

"The Winderfield. See you at seven."

Andrea's apartment complex. A large corporation would likely demolish the place and build something grand or evict the current tenants and remodel it into a business that would grow a healthy profit. Either way, Andrea was going to lose her home.

Beau ran a hand down his face. Dating her just got a lot more complicated.

Franklin
Washington, D.C., September 1865

Patriotic bunting swathed the city. While citizens rushed to conduct their business and commerce thrived, the movement was genteel compared to New York City. Franklin walked with Margaret tucked close to his side. Before long, her growing belly would swell so large she'd be forced into confinement, and Franklin wanted to get her settled into their new home before then.

Clean, modest homes with small gardens and trellises spilling over with flowers lined Delaware Street. Despite the devastating absence of Mr. Lincoln and the turbulence still sweeping through the country, this city gave one a sense of security, of hope that the nation would rebuild one day and thrive again. He thanked God multiple times a day for his position at the newly formed Secret Service. Not only would his pay provide amply for their needs, but it got them out of Hell's Hundred Acres. Away from his temperamental father. Away from debauchery and crime. Including the trail his brother had left behind.

Though the constable had released Franklin the morning after his arrest, the event still haunted Franklin's peace. For years he'd prayed that Edward would find purpose and self-worth in the West. Instead, Edward had found his sin nature in those hills and apprenticed under Satan himself, if the list of his crimes was any indication.

However, without the mistake in identities, Franklin may not have heard ahead of time about the department President Lincoln had commissioned, leaving them to drown in New York City. The information had allowed him early entry to an interview. Once again, Franklin's life was falling into place while Edward's fell to pieces.

His chest filled with a melancholy he hadn't known since the day they'd lowered their sweet mother into the earth. Franklin had protected Edward as best he could his entire life, but he could no longer help his brother. Edward had crossed a line Franklin couldn't. For the first time, they'd essentially become enemies, one on each side of the law.

His stomach roiled the way it did of late when he thought of Edward. A hand rubbed up and down his arm. "How much longer are you going to keep me in suspense?" Margaret beamed. "I'm near to bursting."

He chuckled, steering them around a ratty mutt that had lain in their path and rolled over for a belly rub. His new prosthetic fit much better than his old, easing his mobility and comfort. "Patience, my dear."

"I've been patient for two and a half years."

He halted their steps and turned Margaret to face him. He cupped her cheek. "As patient as a saint, and I love you for it. I'm finally able to make good on the promises I've made you. Starting with a safe and happy home."

Guiding her by the shoulders, he spun her to face the small stone two-story house. The railing leading up to the front door needed to be replaced, and the windows needed a good scrubbing, but it was theirs. Her intake of breath was the confirmation he needed. He smiled, watching her hands fold over her heart.

"It's the prettiest little house I've ever seen." She threw her arms around him. He swayed, and they both laughed. The swell of her belly pressed into his.

He kissed her temple. "You might not think that when you see the inside. We'll have some work to do."

"I've never been afraid of work."

No, she was quite the little soldier.

She pulled away. "Will your father be all right by himself? I wish he'd have come with us."

Franklin looped her arm around his and led her to the front door. Franklin was glad Father hadn't accompanied them after the last tirade. "He was too stubborn to leave, so he'll have to manage on his own. I refuse to raise children in that cesspool."

Or around the man himself, truth be told. His father had taken an instant shine to Margaret, and the man's age and infirmities had mellowed his ire, but it still struck like lightning at times, and Franklin didn't want his family in the path when it did.

He'd seen firsthand how the man could treat children he didn't deem worthy. Franklin wouldn't dare subject his family to such abuse. He'd failed to shelter Edward from the rage and wouldn't make that mistake twice. As often as he'd be away hunting counterfeiters, Franklin needed reassurance of his family's safety.

Margaret rested her head on his shoulder as they walked up the crumbling brick path to the front door. Franklin rummaged through his pocket, pulled out a key, and slipped it into the lock. After thrusting open the door, he swept his wife into his arms and grinned at her squeal. The mound of her stomach reminded him of a ripe watermelon waiting to be picked. Her weight and yards of faded and patched fabric made it difficult to guide them over the narrow threshold. The first thing he planned to do was buy her new dresses and undergarments. She deserved no less.

For the first time in his life, he was free from his chains. Free from the tyranny of his father, free from the temptation surrounding his former home, free from the horrors of war, and free from the responsibility of his twin. Come what may, he was his own man now, working for the government to rebuild a tattered nation. Working to rebuild his tattered life.

He prayed that, whatever it took, Edward would find his way to the light and one day to his own carefree existence.

CHAPTER TEN

ANDREA

Manhattan, Present Day

*M*idnight was really too late to start a lengthy documentary, but Andrea was still caffeinated from working the evening shift, and she could sleep in tomorrow. The notch of plaster exposed in the wall kitty-corner from her place on the loveseat taunted her, and she was dying to discover the story behind the counterfeit bills.

So was her boss. When he'd reminded her of Pat's retirement party and the open position, she'd made the mistake of revealing the sensational story she was working on. *Smithsonian* had published articles about counterfeit money before, and he reminded her that the angle from which she wrote it had better be different.

No pressure at all.

She was fine. Everything was fine.

Her fuzzy blanket offered a measure of comfort as she cocooned herself within and turned on the TV. A local news station played in the background while she scrolled through the app menu for the History Channel, which she paid to stream. The name Beau Davidson-Quincy yanked her attention to the sliver of screen not covered with icons. A young brunette reporter walked what appeared to be a hospital hallway, her back to the camera, chatting with a man whose voice sounded a lot like Andrea's Beau.

Well, not *her* Beau but...

She collapsed the app menu. The camera switched angles, and the image hit her like a sucker punch.

It was her Beau.

Shock had her so spellbound she didn't hear what the reporter said to make him flash his perfect white teeth. "I'm honored to work with hospital administration and the Bick Corporation to remodel the playground. We all agree that fresh air and sunlight are just as vital to these children's recovery as their therapy and medications."

As he talked about the addition of therapy dogs, a ribbon scrolled along the bottom of the screen, bearing a headline that read GUBERNATORIAL CANDIDATE DONATES THOUSANDS TO ST. JOHN'S CHILDREN'S HOSPITAL.

She stared at the screen, unmoving. Beau was running for governor?

The camera switched angles again, and the reporter asked questions about Beau's candidacy. Andrea listened to his perfect response in stunned horror. He was Beau Davidson-Quincy of Davidson-Quincy Investment Group, one of the most successful investment corporations on the Eastern Seaboard.

Her head dropped into her hands, mortification strangling. She'd turned down a date with one of the richest bachelors in New York. She not only felt incredibly stupid for not recognizing him but for treating his offer so flippantly.

She was probably the first woman ever to turn him down!

Oh, why had she done that?

Because, to her knowledge, he'd been a stranger. Because a relationship wasn't her priority right now. Because his residency in Gramercy made it clear they were too different to even bother with dating. Now the bottomless chasm between them widened even further. She hated being in the spotlight, and she definitely wasn't political-figure girlfriend material.

She'd learned that lesson before.

Disappointment bloomed in her chest. She liked Beau. A lot. His wit, his kindness, his charm. Why he was interested in her, she'd never understand. They were as suited for one another as an iceberg in the desert.

She muted the TV and sighed.

Girl, shake it off.

It wasn't the first time she'd embarrassed herself in front of a guy, and it likely wouldn't be her last. Avoiding him wouldn't be too hard since their social circles were as far apart as one galaxy to the next. She needed to forget about Beau and focus on her abilities and finding the answers to the counterfeit money hidden in her wall for the last century.

The room went dark as she closed her eyes. Breathe in. Breathe out. She envisioned herself climbing a mountain. One day, when she reached the top, victory would taste as sweet as spring water. She was strong, independent, and smart. She had this.

Her eyes opened to Beau's beautiful face playing on the television screen.

Nope, didn't work.

She flung a pillow at the TV, missing by two feet. The movement startled Sammy Davis Jr., and he dashed behind his plastic plant, stirring the water. He was the only male she needed in her life right now.

The app menu pulled up in the same place she'd left off. She clicked on the History Channel app and then on the *A Run for Your Money* documentary she'd recorded about the Secret Service and their quest to seize counterfeit bills after the Civil War.

Had someone hidden them in the wall to elude the Secret Service? Why had they been stashed away and then forgotten? What was the significance of *16GPS* written on the paper? They didn't have GPS back then.

Those questions and a dozen more raced through her mind two hours later while she tried unsuccessfully to sleep.

CHAPTER ELEVEN

EDWARD

Manhattan, February 1866

*T*he fierce winter wind stung the tender skin on Edward's face. Though yellow and green around his eyes from a good beating, he'd healed considerably since they'd left him for dead. He bent his head as he walked along the side of the frozen street. Licking dry lips, he ran his tongue over the scab where the skin had split with the force of a fist. He'd been lucky not to lose any teeth.

Smoke rolled from the rooftops of the brothels. He imagined the warmth to be had inside, the food his hungry stomach longed for, the diversion from his miserable existence. But he was penniless. Everything he owned he now carried on his being. Those thugs had taken every-thing—his latest winnings from a poker game, his bag of counterfeit bills, his only set of engraving plates, and his best suit and shoes.

Without those plates, he had no way of printing counterfeit bills to pay his creditors. All the progress he'd made in the opium trade would be for naught. Unless he could plead for more time. Then he could engrave new plates and stay in the booming market. Addiction equaled profit. Soldiers home from war craved the liquid injected into them to relieve the horrific facets of the battlefield.

Opium's calming properties made it the perfect substance to slip into female health tonics and syrups for fussy and teething babies. Men and women alike imbibed for recreational purposes, increasingly popular among the middle and upper classes as a fun little escape from their problematic lives.

Fools, all of them.

But those same fools could make him a very rich man.

As long as his father would part with Edward's half of the inheritance, meager as it was. Then he could give his creditors enough to bide him time to engrave another plate. If not, Edward would put the man in his place and take whatever of value he could carry off.

The roof sagged on the old place. Any more snow and it might cave in completely. Then the man could live in an environment as cold as his heart. Edward's shiver was more pronounced, as much from trudging through ankle-deep snow in boots with holes in the soles as the anticipation of facing the tyrant. If his body wasn't sick with fever now, it surely would be later.

If not for the curl of black smoke escaping the chimney, Edward would think the place abandoned. The snowy path to the front door remained untouched. No light filtered through the windows. The fence on the west end of the house listed sideways like a drunken man attempting to walk a straight line. Apparently, his brother and wife didn't live here any longer, or the property would be in better condition.

Could it be the favored son who could do no wrong had a falling out with the dictator? Wouldn't that be a twist?

Preamble never honored in this house, Edward pushed open the front door without knocking. The lock caught, but a harder shove made it fail. The door leaned just enough that the lock no longer fit into the mortise plate. The air smelled of woodsmoke and urine. A half-frozen cockroach crawled across the floor. Edward squashed it with his boot. He'd stayed in worse hovels, but the sight of his once-pristine home in disrepair took him by surprise.

He closed the door as best he could. Cold air seeped around the frame. He inched through the chilly hallway, grateful the temperature warmed as he neared the parlor. A skeleton sat facing the fireplace, a few wisps of white hair sticking up on end. His father fastened gaunt eyes on him, hope shimmering in their depths before his lips folded in disappointment. "Oh, it's you."

Hatred still reigned supreme. Despite the man's haggard appearance, there was nothing wrong with his memory.

"It's me. Your favorite son."

"Pshaw."

Edward approached the dying embers and tossed a few more logs inside. Stoked the flames. The heat emanating from the wood seeped into his bones, bringing a comfort he hadn't felt since his last stay at the Kingsley Hotel.

"Where's Franklin and his blushing bride? Enjoying a night at the opera? Or perhaps attending Mrs. Astor's Valentine's Day ball?"

"I see time hasn't tamed your tongue any." Spittle dribbled down his father's chin as he spoke.

"Nor has it yours. It appears we're destined to carry our disdain into death." Though this man was a lot closer to its door than Edward.

A wet, crackly cough rumbled through his father's chest. His cheeks went from pale to red to purple, then back to pale. He cleared his throat. "What do you want? You look less bountiful than the last time you came, flashing your fancy watch and golden cuff links. Your mine run dry, or did you gamble it away?" He leaned forward, squinting. "Is that a cut on your lip? Boy howdy, someone worked you over good."

"Disappointed it wasn't you this time?" Edward was no longer afraid of the ghost of a man that sat before him.

"You always were mean as the devil."

"You made me that way."

"I made you strong."

"You broke me to pieces!" Edward lowered his raised fist. The calming breath only made him cringe. It smelled like a hog pen in here. "I came to collect everything you owe me."

"I owe you nothing."

He owed Edward everything. Kindness. Respect. Love.

Things he wasn't foolish enough to believe he'd ever see. So, he'd come to stake a claim on material possessions. If there was anything left worth having. "I want my half of the inheritance now. I'm not waiting until you're dead."

"Inheritance?" Laughter turned into another round of coughs that nearly shook the crumbling house from its foundation. "Look around you, boy. Does it look like I have the means to leave any kind of inheritance?"

"I know about the government bonds Mama had as a dowry. I want half. Along with half of her jewelry."

"I don't know how you found out about those bonds, but it doesn't matter. I've already given them to Franklin. A down payment for the humble house he purchased for Margaret. In Washington, D.C., of all places. Did you know of his new position at the Department of the Treasury as a Secret Service agent? He travels the country, sniffing out and apprehending criminals like you."

Rage bubbled from the well of Edward's soul. His limbs shook, and it took all his control not to tear the man's face off. When Mother had died, his father had rid the house of anything that had belonged to her except her jewelry and those bonds. Half were to go to him. Like everything good, it had all gone to Franklin.

Snatching the lantern on the table beside his father, he stomped into the main bedroom, leaving the old man in darkness. He yanked out bureau doors, ripped clothing, upended the bed, smashed the bowl and pitcher, all the while stuffing any trinket he thought may have value into his pockets. Then he did the same with the bedroom he and Franklin had shared as children. Then the kitchen. Through the blood rushing in his ears, he registered his father's voice crescendo to a yell before a choking hack took over.

He wished the man a slow death, vomiting up one chunk of lung at a time.

By the time Edward had destroyed every room of the home, his father had gotten to his feet. A twisted, bony finger pointed at Edward. "You will pay for this."

"I've already paid for it a hundred times over with every lashing you gave me growing up." Edward flew at the man to give him the beating he'd always dreamed of issuing but stopped when a dark stain wet the man's trousers. The liquid made a line down the fabric of his pants all the way to the ankle.

Edward's gaze flicked to the chair, layered in stains. The wood floor beneath the chair held the same evidence. The source of the ungodly stench. Instead of remorse or pity, laughter shook his body. He threw his head back and laughed. What a glorious ending to this sordid tale.

Chin quivering, his father lowered his hand and blinked.

"Don't fear me, Father. This will be the last time I will come to see you. I want to remember you just as you are—old, weak, and helpless as a baby—for the rest of my life."

Edward turned to leave.

"Where are you going?" His father's voice sounded much like a child's.

"To pay a visit to my dear brother, of course. It's been far too long." More spittle ran from the man's mouth. "What do you plan to do?" Edward spun on his heel and walked to the door. "Whatever I want."

"Don't you hurt him. Or his sweet wife! They have a—"

The slamming door silenced his father's words. The wind howled between the buildings and the air bit his skin, but Edward didn't feel a thing. He was invincible. The trinkets in his pockets should bring enough for a hot meal and a ticket to Washington, D.C.

The next day, Edward disembarked at Union Station empty-handed and disheveled, ready to greet his brother and new sister-in-law. Franklin would straighten this out. He'd take care of Edward. He always had. He wouldn't leave Edward destitute. Their bond was too great.

First, he needed to discover where they lived. The stationmaster told him where he could find the Department of the Treasury, so he'd start there. The long, cold walk wasn't as harsh as the one the previous evening to his father's house. If one could define it as that anymore. Between the stench and the company, it was more like purgatory.

At least the temperature was warmer here and the wind had calmed its fury. Edward's had calmed too. Happy to see his brother after ten years, he quickened his steps. Not all of Edward's past need come to light. Some methods of survival were too unconventional for Franklin's approval. Perhaps he'd invite Edward to stay. This was one city he'd avoided due to all the security, but maybe that was the more genius plot. Many wouldn't be fool enough to commit crimes in the very place where a horde of forces held headquarters. They'd be sniffing other cities, leaving Edward to his vices.

A man in an overcoat atop striped trousers walked down the steps of the Treasury, wearing a petite version of a top hat. Ears the same red as his moustache, he frowned at Edward.

"Franklin? I thought you'd gone home to your wife. Is she well?"

Edward blinked. Explaining situations to strangers was something Edward never did, so he slipped into the role, inflecting his voice just like

Franklin's. "Uh, quite well. Thank you for asking."

The man's expression lifted then fell. "My lands, what happened to your face?"

"Nothing to worry about. I took a spill rushing home earlier." Edward lifted his scarf higher on his neck and chin and pointed to the icy patches on the road.

"Sorry to hear it but glad you're all right. Did you leave something inside?" The man studied him, his forehead bunching. "Harris has already locked up for the day."

"Nothing urgent that won't keep until tomorrow."

"We're set to leave on the seven o'clock train. There won't be time to fetch it tomorrow." The man gripped his elbow. "You seem out of sorts. Did you hit your head in the fall?"

Unease and an uncomfortable jab from the man's thumb pressing into a nasty bruise settled over Edward. A train with this man to where?

"I took quite a tumble. I'll be fine, I assure you. Only a little muddled."

"Your eye. It's already starting to bruise. Go home, my friend. Rest up with that pretty wife of yours. It may be months before you see her again."

Months? Franklin didn't work behind a desk, then. "Good advice. I'll do that. I'll take the next carriage to my home on…"

Edward feigned confusion.

"On Delaware Street. Number 216." The man's eyes fell to Edward's shoes and bounced up again. "I believe I should escort you to the nearest doctor."

Edward moved away from the man's extended hand. "No, no. I'm fine." He threw out his hands. "I was jesting." His laugh sounded hollow. "See you in the morning, my friend."

Before the man could respond, Edward took off at a brisk pace across the street, dodging piles of snow and ice. He went one block before stopping the first person he found and asking for directions to Delaware Street. Twenty minutes later, the carriage let him out on the corner, and he walked the narrow lane toward house number 216.

The clomping of horse hooves sounded behind him from an approaching carriage. He lowered his hat over his eyes and kept his head down until it passed. A few houses away, the carriage pulled to a stop, and a man stepped out.

Franklin.

Edward's feet hastened that direction then halted when Franklin assisted a woman with a large belly out of the carriage. The sight trampled him like a racehorse. He dashed behind the nearest hedgerow and peered around the lamppost. He squinted into the distance for a clearer view.

Franklin steadied the pretty woman on her feet then patted her shoulder. She gazed up at him the way Mama used to look at Father before she died, and Edward's heart turned to stone. The woman, Margaret, his father had called her, cradled her bulging stomach beneath mounds of brown fabric. A red ribbon secured the end of her chestnut braid. It swung across her shoulders as she waddled to the front door, Franklin guiding her by the elbow.

Breath left Edward. He couldn't move. Couldn't speak. A sharp pain ripped through a tender place in his chest. Moisture filled his vision. She was beautiful. And she wore a ribbon at the end of her braid, just like Mama.

Swallowing, he absorbed the tender way Franklin cradled his hand in the small of her back while he unlocked their front door.

Franklin had always been gentle with Edward whenever a kid in the community had decided Edward needed to be taught a lesson. He would bandage Edward's wounds and speak in gentle tones. Distract him with a joke or crazy tale. Sometimes he read to Edward late into the night to ease the viciousness of the day. From the terrors sleep would bring.

Now Franklin would do those things for Margaret.

A cavern opened in his chest. Edward had always longed for a proper family. With Franklin's wife and soon-delivered child, Edward would finally have it. Such good fortune might tempt him to change his ways.

"Franklin." Edward stepped from behind the snow-dusted hedge.

Franklin spun, and his jovial mood stiffened. He whispered something in Margaret's ear and stalked toward Edward. The pretty woman went inside the house and closed the door.

"Brother." Edward held out his hand.

Franklin stared at it.

Edward's arm went limp against his side. "It's me."

Sure, it had been ten years, but Edward couldn't possibly be unrecognizable if the man at the Department of the Treasury had mistaken him for Franklin.

"I can see that." Franklin examined Edward's face. "It seems the actions you've doled out have returned to haunt you."

Edward took a step backward. "You've talked to Father."

"Occasionally, but that has no bearing on my comment. Does the name Silas Hutcheson sound familiar? Or perhaps Tilden's Haberdashery?"

Edward's stomach soured. "What do you know of it?"

"I know that you're a wanted man in several regions for a list of crimes longer than my legs. I know because, only six months ago, the authorities arrested me for those crimes."

"I don't understand." The vapor of Edward's breath clouded the image of his brother's disdain.

"Honestly, I don't either. What I do understand is that you've shown up at my door, beaten and desperate, needing my aid once again. This time you will not receive it, brother. I have a wife and child to support and protect, and your choices will not weigh us down. Good day to you."

Franklin spun and marched to the door.

Shock melded with anger. "I came for my half of those war bonds. Mama would want me to have my share." Edward held his head high, hands fisted, ready for a fight if necessary.

"Why, so you can squander them away? I guarantee Mama wouldn't want that." Franklin's hand curled around the doorknob.

"Don't deny me, brother."

Remorse radiated from Franklin's lined and weary eyes. "You deny yourself with every nip of bitterness you allow to feast upon your soul." He ran a hand down his face. "I will always love my brother, but until you repent and turn from your wicked ways, we are henceforth strangers."

The door slammed on Edward.

He swallowed, stunned. Franklin didn't need him anymore. Didn't want him anymore. Breathing became difficult. He leaned over and gripped his knees.

Franklin had it all—the family, the respect of society, the inheritance.

Edward had nothing. No one. He would wander and beg until he found solid ground again, while Franklin lived in this quaint little house with a beautiful wife and a child who'd be born perfect because Franklin was perfect.

Edward was completely alone.

With every intake of cold air as his feet dragged him away, his mind cleared. His heart hardened. How dare Franklin turn on him like their father? Like everyone else? How dare he?

Let him have it all. For now. One day, when Franklin least suspected it, Edward would swoop in and take what was rightfully his.

CHAPTER TWELVE

ANDREA

Manhattan, Present Day

*1*6 Gramercy Park South was home to the Players, a members-only organization dedicated to the arts. It was also the legacy of Edwin Booth, brother of John Wilkes Booth, Abraham Lincoln's assassin. Andrea studied the brownstone standing stalwart and regal like a queen awaiting her coronation crown.

"Why are we here again?" Caylee whined like a teenager who didn't want to go to school.

Andrea led her to a patch of sidewalk out of the way of foot traffic. " '16GPS' was written on a piece of paper I found inside the pouch of money. The code made little sense, since they didn't have GPS devices back then. Then yesterday when I was mapping directions to a store on my phone, it hit me. I googled '16GPS near me,' and it brought up this address. It might turn out to be a dead end, but we're pursuing it anyway."

Caylee threw her head back and pointed. Giant hoop earrings bumped against her outstretched neck. "Why do those lamps have spikes?"

"To discourage people from jumping off the loggia."

"The what-tia?" Caylee's head whipped to Andrea, sending her newly dyed blue hair to swaying.

"The open-sided extension of the house. See that balcony above the lanterns? There's only a handful of original gas lamps in the city, and those are two of them."

"Ugh. I hate old things." Caylee picked at her chipped yellow fingernail polish.

"I know, but we agreed that if I was going to let you teach me twenty-first-century pop culture, then you were going to let me take you back in time."

"Fine." Caylee frowned. "But I refuse to wear a corset."

"And I refuse to dye my hair blue."

"Hag."

"Millennial."

They burst out laughing. Bantering was something they'd done well from the first day they'd met. Andrea linked their arms and dragged Caylee up the stone steps. "You can learn so much from me."

"Likewise. For starters, how to accept a date when a hot billionaire asks you out."

"I never should've told you."

"You did because you know you're helpless without me."

"Likewise. I brought you along because I thought you'd appreciate the dedication to performing arts. Edwin Booth is honored as one of the best actors of all time. They say he played a stellar Hamlet."

"Shakespeare is depressing. Too many people die."

"Agreed, but it made William a legend."

Caylee stopped her before she could open the door. "Wait. If this place really lives up to its hype, you can't just walk in there and start asking questions. You'll have to play the part."

"The part?"

Chin to chest, Caylee groaned. "The part of an Elizabethan noblewoman seeking answers. Just follow my lead."

"Hold it." Andrea grabbed her elbow. "Before you lead us any further onto this crazy train, you need to know that the setting is the Gilded Age, not the Elizabethan period."

Siren-red lips frowned. "What's the difference?"

"Two hundred and fifty years."

"Nerd."

"Dunce."

Caylee tugged on the handle. "Your first lesson in modern living—nobody uses the word *dunce* anymore."

The door swung wide into a large vestibule with polished hardwood floors and plush, ornate rugs. A large marble fireplace made for a breath-taking centerpiece with a leather couch and two armchairs surrounding a Chippendale table. The crystal chandelier sparkled tiny prisms of light around the space.

It reeked of money and decades of tobacco, and held enough intriguing history within the walls to make Andrea salivate. She wanted to walk every inch of the building unhurried and unaccompanied. Except she wasn't a member.

A heavyset man with a stern scowl approached. Andrea expected to be thrown out within seconds. "May I help you ladies?"

Andrea opened her mouth to answer, but Caylee beat her to it. "Yes, dah-ling."

Would anyone notice if Andrea crawled under the Chippendale table and disappeared?

The man grimaced as if he'd tasted something rotten.

With a flick of her wrist, Caylee brushed hair that didn't exist off her shoulder and continued with her flapper-girl accent. "My friend here found some antique money hidden in the wall of her apartment, and the trail led us to this fine establishment. We thought maybe an intelligent man such as yourself could offer some insight into our little mystery."

His scowl slid from Caylee to Andrea. "That true?"

She was going to throttle Caylee. "Yes, sir. I don't know if the money is connected to the Players whatsoever, but this address was on a piece of paper inside the pouch with the money, so I thought it wouldn't hurt to inquire."

The tightness in his jaw relaxed. "What kind of bills?"

Andrea reached inside her purse and unearthed one ten she'd slipped inside a protective sleeve. The man studied each side. "Interesting. I've never seen anything like it."

Caylee threw her hand onto her hip and fingered her Mardi Gras beads as if they were pearls. "Probably because they're counterfeit."

"And you presume they originated here?" His ruddy cheeks turned purple. "As I don't recognize you as members, I must ask you to leave this establishment immediately."

"Oh, we didn't mean that. I—" Andrea went silent at his raised palm.

"Enough. Leave now, or I will call security."

Caylee opened her mouth to argue, but Andrea dragged her by the arm to the exit. At the door, she broke from Andrea's hold, turned to the man, and said, "Applesauce. The dame's in a jam, and you threaten to call the buttons. Come on, Andy. We're tooting the wrong ringer."

Andrea flew out the door and down the steps, not caring that she'd left her friend behind. Should she laugh at Caylee's harmless—outlandish—behavior, or move very far away? It was a good thing there were millions of people in this city and facing that man wasn't likely to occur a second time.

Feet slapped the sidewalk beside her. "Can you believe that sap?"

"Break character anytime. We've left the *joint*."

Caylee had the decency to look regretful. "Sorry. Once I get going, it's hard to stop."

"I noticed." The muscles in her legs burned from the brisk pace.

"That was fun. Next time—"

"Next time I'll go alone and call you afterward."

"But that was my best ad-lib performance yet."

"Once again, wrong era." Andrea slowed, her breaths coming fast. "The Roaring Twenties were *after* the Gilded Age."

"Well, I tried."

"A for effort."

Caylee huffed. "I wonder what people in the *Gilded Age* would've thought of his rudeness."

"Or your blue hair."

"The shade is called lapis lazuli. Named after a metamorphic rock."

"Perfectly named, since you just melted my chance at getting some answers."

They stopped at the street corner and waited for the pedestrian light to give them the right-of-way. The false lashes framing Caylee's eyes waved as she blinked above pouty lips. "I said I was sorry."

"Ugh. I know you mean well. All is forgiven."

They walked across the street and around the square until they reached Gant & Company, then parted ways so Caylee could start her shift. Andrea hailed a cab, disappointed over the wasted trip. Maybe she'd let a few days pass and then try again by herself. In the meantime, she had a junior article to write on the Star Wars X-Wing Starfighter recently donated to the Smithsonian's National Air and Space Museum. Between that and the edits she needed to finish on the waterborne diseases article, she shouldn't have time to be depressed over the day's events.

Three hours later, she stood from the sedentary position at her desk, legs aching, and did several reps of squats and knee-highs. Her arms were poised in the air for jumping jacks when her cell rang. An unfamiliar number. The area code was local, and her spam detector didn't flash across her screen. Let them leave a message, or answer?

On the fourth ring, she answered the call.

"Miss Andi Andrews. Author of 'The Untold Stories of the *Titanic*.' Great article, by the way." The masculine voice rolled over her like warm water in a shower.

Beau had taken time from his busy campaigning schedule to look her up. His flattery bolstered her ego.

"Mr. Beau Davidson-Quincy, development mogul and potentially my next governor. How on earth did you get my number?"

Stupid question. The man could ask to eat cheese on the moon, and someone would grant his request.

"I stopped by Gant & Company to see if you were working today, and I had the most interesting conversation with the hostess."

"Blue hair?"

"She's the one. I didn't even ask for your number. She just gave it to me. Once I had it, though, I thought, why not?"

"Yeah, why not?" She didn't mean to sound sarcastic. It just seemed that Caylee was determined to upend Andrea's life one way or another that day.

A beat of silence. "You seem unhappy about this. I apologize. I should've waited for you to give me your number."

"No, you're fine. I…I've had a long day, and I'm frustrated about things not related to your call."

She meant it. She enjoyed talking to Beau. Knowing his identity now made it awkward, though.

"I don't mean to brag, but I am a very good listener."

A smile tugged at her mouth despite wanting to be annoyed. She hit the SAVE button on her laptop and then closed the monitor. "I hit a roadblock today with my counterfeit money investigation."

"How so?"

"I finally figured out the code on the paper was an address—16 Gramercy Park South."

"Ah. The Players."

"Wow. If you know that by memory, you must be familiar with the place."

"Confession—membership is a rite of passage in my family when we turn twenty-one. Well, for the men anyway."

Of course it was. Membership only cost a piddly twenty-eight hundred dollars a year.

She was glad Beau hadn't been enjoying the benefits of his membership during Caylee's embarrassing performance.

"You got quiet," he said. "What are you thinking?"

"About how different we are."

"I hope you'll give me an opportunity to show you we're not all that different."

He was too smooth for her own good. She knew this. It was a fact. And yet she couldn't resist his magnetism.

Something that sounded like a bag of potato chips rattled in the background. "Why don't you tell me about this roadblock."

"It's kind of a long story. Are you sure you have time?"

"I'm all yours."

A delicious heat pooled in her belly. She was going to melt into the floor, and poor Sammy Davis Jr. would swim around for days without food before someone noticed she was missing.

Flopping onto the loveseat, she hugged her fuzzy blanket to her chest and told him about her visit to the Players. He listened, he engaged, and by the time she was done, he was laughing.

"Alfred is all bark and no bite."

"I didn't know that."

"Tensions are high there right now. There's been some scandal with pilfered funds, and with the roller-coaster economy, it's been struggling for years."

"I wasn't insinuating that the club was responsible for the counterfeiting, but Caylee made such a mess of things, I didn't have time to explain."

"This Caylee is...quite the lady."

"Gotta love her." Even if Andrea wanted to shake her most of the time.

"How about I join you next time? You can come as my guest, and together we'll work on getting some answers."

Her foot ticked against the coffee table. "That sounds dangerously like a date."

"Doesn't have to be dangerous. Unless you want it to be."

She wasn't sure how to respond to that.

"It's a joke. In all seriousness, though, come as my guest. We'll ask questions, we'll eat, we'll talk. No pressure on anything past that."

She would love the chance to investigate further. To see the place where so many historical icons spent their leisure time. And the chance to know Beau better, if she was honest.

"You're overthinking this, aren't you?"

"I'm the queen of overthinking."

"I'm not trying to bribe you, but this may be your only opportunity to see Mark Twain's pool cue."

She giggled. "His pool cue?"

"I'm not joking. It's on display. But if that alone doesn't entice you, what about a behind-the-scenes tour of Edwin Booth's living quarters?"

"You don't have that much clout."

"Ah, but I do."

She clutched the blanket tighter. "Not fair. You're taking full advantage of my affinity for history."

"That's what Caylee said you'd say. She also told me not to take no for an answer."

That girl.

Before she chickened out, she blurted, "Fine."

"Is that a yes?"

"It's a yes. Don't make me regret this."

"I won't. I promise."

CHAPTER THIRTEEN

Washington, D.C., September 1866

*C*ora was the most beautiful baby he'd ever seen. Fair complexion like her mother's, rosebud lips pressed into a pout beneath a button nose. Eyes closed in slumber, her tiny eyelashes fanned the tops of rosy cheeks. Perfection swathed in a tiny bundle of pink fabric. How Margaret could care so little for the child was beyond him.

At first, he'd blamed himself. Infiltrating a counterfeiting ring took weeks, sometimes months, and his absence was taking a toll on them both. But the pay was great, and he was good at identifying the dealers and earning the trust of the informants. This work was vital to rebuilding a better nation, and for the first time since he'd lost his foot, he had a purpose. He felt whole.

Except his wife felt empty.

Cora whimpered. He reached into the cradle and scooped the baby into his arms. Rubbing circles on her back quieted her spirit, and she soon slept again.

"You are good with her." Franklin turned to see Mrs. White smiling at them from the hallway. An angel of mercy in the form of a neighbor, she'd helped Margaret during the delivery and in the days that followed.

"She's..." Emotion welled in his throat, and he swallowed it down. Then his nose registered a baby-like stench. "She's soiled."

Mrs. White laughed, expanding her wrinkles to greater heights. "I'll handle that. You go check on Margaret."

"Teach me how to change her."

The woman's thin gray eyebrows arched to her hairline. "You want me to teach you how to change a soiled diaper? Never in my seventy-nine years have I heard a man make that request. Especially with a willing and able-bodied female in the room."

His ears couldn't believe it either.

He gave the woman a wan smile. "We rely on you far too much as it is, Mrs. White. I need to learn so that when I'm home I can help."

"And that is why our sweet Margaret is blessed to have you. Truly, caring for Margaret is a privilege. After losing our daughter in '42, it took me many years to open my heart again. Margaret has become like my flesh and blood now."

Holding Cora steady, he patted the woman's willowy arm. "We echo that sentiment."

She explained how to change a diaper then guided him as he tried the process on his own. The result was far below satisfaction but should hold. Mrs. White encouraged him to show Margaret later, hopeful the gesture would bring her a bit of joy. Perhaps he could coax her to take a walk with him as he pushed Cora in her new carriage. Summer was waning, and autumn was Margaret's favorite time of year.

His steps were silent on the thick rug that led to their bedroom. Dust motes danced in the scant rays that barged their way through the closed draperies. Margaret lay beneath the covers, pale and bleary-eyed. She stared into nothingness. Her chest barely moved with breath. With each passing day, she was slipping further away. If God didn't intervene soon, Franklin would lose her altogether.

He padded to the bed, holding a sleeping Cora, and occupied the side of the mattress. "Mrs. White taught me how to change a diaper. I thought you might want to tease me for it."

Margaret blinked but otherwise gave no sign she knew he was there.

"I only impaled my finger twice."

A sigh.

"Only a little blood."

In times past, she'd have jabbed him in the ribs and ridiculed his crooked pins. Now he couldn't get her to look at him. "She's grown so much since I saw her last."

Silent moments passed.

Tamping down his frustration took a valiant effort. "Look at her,

Margaret." His command was gentle. "Look at our beautiful daughter and feel something. Look at me and feel *something*."

As if her head was too heavy for her shoulders, she turned her neck to face him. A lone tear slid down her cheek. "I do. Feel something." She swallowed. "I love her with all my being. But I can't bear the thought of leaving this bed to care for her. The sadness…is too great."

She had a safe home, a husband who adored her, and a beautiful child. Why such sadness?

Her gaze retreated to the window, expression once again shuttered. It didn't escape Franklin that she'd made no mention of loving him. Could it be that he'd already lost her?

Dr. Fullerton had diagnosed her with female madness, a condition that afflicted new mothers at times. The emotions of the condition could range from hysteria and violence to sadness and suicide. Margaret's version was the latter. What the doctor couldn't explain was why this madness afflicted women at all. Shouldn't motherhood elicit only feelings of love and joy? Did this mean the madness had been suppressed this whole time?

The doctor's regimen of daily fresh air, at least a half hour of social stimulation, and a tonic that smelled comparable to the diaper he'd just changed only worked if the patient took part.

Franklin rested his hand atop hers. "Take a walk with us? The Isengoles have purchased the most ridiculous little statues for their porch you just have to see."

Her head shook in the barest of rejections.

"Summer will be gone before we know it. Why don't we sit on the bench beside your roses? Mr. Moniker has been tending them for you. They've filled the entire yard with their heady scent. The anticipation of autumn is in the air."

He smiled at the memory of her choosing those roses specifically for their "heady scent."

"I just can't, Franklin," she whispered.

Unable to bear her melancholy any longer, he took a sleeping Cora back to her cradle, nestled her inside, and found Mrs. White in the kitchen. "Will she ever get better?"

Mrs. White's downcast gaze told Franklin of her doubts.

"I feel so powerless." He rubbed the moisture from his eyes.

"You are."

He buried his face in his hands, counted to five, and then jammed his fists into his pockets. "If I knew what to do, I'd do it."

Mrs. White set a cup of tea on the table for him. "Pray."

She settled in the chair beside him. "We're going to need reinforcements."

"What do you mean?" He sipped the bitter tea, skipping the cream and sugar.

"The Secret Service takes up much of your time. While I'm happy to help you both, Gerard is ailing. You need a cook and maid and a nanny."

"A nanny?" He wanted Margaret to raise their child, teach their child, love their child. Not a stranger who did so for payment.

"What other choice do you have?"

Her elderly face was weary from fatigue. He couldn't keep expecting her to aid in Margaret's and Cora's care. And he couldn't support his family without this job. Mrs. White was correct. He had no choice.

With the scant amount of assets that were sold upon his father's death, Franklin would take his half of the inheritance and hire help. The other half would go to Edward if he ever stopped being a scalawag.

In the meantime, he'd pray his wife would find her way back to the living.

CHAPTER FOURTEEN

BEAU

Manhattan, Present Day

Beau hoped to discover more on this date with Andrea than answers to her mystery money. Like where she grew up, if Andi was just a pen name or if she'd let Beau call her by it, what made her tick, and if the electricity between them equaled compatibility. She drew him unlike any woman in years. Bad timing in the middle of a gubernatorial race, but his mom had always told him that love often struck at unexpected moments. It was too soon to call it love, but he sure wanted to find out. If he won the office, he'd need a good, sweet woman to keep him grounded.

Thunderheads darkened the sky, casting ominous shadows on the buildings as they raced north. His version of a first date included picking her up at her apartment, treating her to a nice dinner, and walking along the waterfront at Battery Park. Instead, she'd insisted on meeting him at the Players and paying for her own dinner. The strings he'd pulled to make sure this night was unforgettable for her would hopefully quell any apprehension about future dates. For now, he waited on the sidewalk away from the crush of bodies hurrying to beat the weather and hoped the rain held off until they were inside.

A cab parked against the curb, and Andrea stepped out. Blond hair fell in waves around her shoulders. Despite the congested sidewalk, her gaze locked on his, and his pulse kicked up pace knowing that smile was just for him.

"Is this okay?" She held out her arms, one hand clutching a small purse with no strap. "I wasn't sure about the dress code."

Now that she'd given him permission to observe, he took advantage. A thin strip of leather wrapped around her slender neck twice before blending into a knot above the neckline of her floral shirt, the long ends dangling. A tailored blazer dressed up a perfect pair of tight jeans she'd paired with black heels. "Andi, you are stunning."

"Stunning? I like the sound of that." Her mouth twisted flirtatiously. "So much so, that I'll let you get away with calling me Andi. Something I rarely allow outside of work."

She took his offered arm and, to his pleasure, clung tighter than he thought she would. "You look great yourself, Mr. Governor."

He winked and led them up the stairs. The lobby was empty for a Friday, but it was early enough yet that the dinner crowd hadn't arrived. Smoke curled above the heads of two men sitting in the wingback chairs by the fireplace. Instead of flames in the hearth, an arrangement of candles in various sizes glowed.

"Mr. Quincy. Good to see you." Alfred stepped from a side office, hand extended. "Who is your lovely guest?"

"Andrea Andrews. I believe you met the other day."

Alfred raised a brow at Andi, and she reminded him about the counterfeit bills. The man frowned. "We have an appointment with Oliver," Beau said.

The frown morphed to a sheepish grin. "Of course. My apologies for the previous misunderstanding, Miss Andrews."

"Forgiven." It was clear by Alfred's uplifted posture her smile won him over.

"Oliver's office is on the second floor at the end of the hall." Alfred bent in a slight bow.

Beau pulled her close to his side so they could maneuver the stairs together. Andi leaned into him and whispered, "Are you treated like royalty everywhere?"

Man, she smelled good. He couldn't quite place the enticing, airy scent, but it made him hungry for more. "It comes with the name. Don't think too much of it. I didn't earn it on my own."

"Au contraire, Mr. Donator-to-children's-hospitals-and-public-education."

"I'm only trying to leave the world in better shape than I found it."

She paused in the middle of the staircase, bringing him to a halt.

"Words like that make you hard to resist."

"Then stop trying."

A breathy laugh escaped her lips and they continued up the stairs, passing the portraits of Jimmy Fallon, Angela Lansbury, John Barrymore, and Nikola Tesla, all either members or former members of the club.

Illuminated sconces reflected off the deep red walls. The air smelled of history and decades of tobacco and perfume. Theater memorabilia decorated every corner and table. Andi's head swiveled from one side of the room to the other, taking it all in with the excitement of a child on Christmas morning.

She released his arm and ran her fingers over a small plaque on a table pushed against the opposite wall. "Samuel Clemens used this table?"

Beau tucked his hands into his pockets. "Rumor has it, he penned the first words to *A Connecticut Yankee in King Arthur's Court* here."

Her fingertips skimmed over the polished wood with reverence. "Mark Twain has always been one of my favorite authors."

"I'm partial to H. G. Wells, but I've yet to find any of his relics here."

She studied him. "*The Time Machine?*"

"Classic."

"Hmm…I had you pegged for a nonfiction man. Practical books of substance."

"You shouldn't judge a book by its cover."

"We know this, and yet we do."

He took her hand. "I'd like—"

"Mr. Quincy, good to see you." Oliver, the director, appeared in his office doorway. "Please, come in."

Tucking away his confession for later, Beau put a hand in the curve of Andi's back, and they stepped into the office. The room was a mix of retro and modern with leather furniture, antique collectibles, and contemporary decor with bold colors. It reminded Beau a bit of his dad's office. The designer had walked them through samples for days.

Oliver gestured for them to sit. "We appreciate your most recent and substantial donation to our organization, Mr. Quincy." He sat behind his large desk and folded his hands. "How can I help you regarding your discovery?"

Andi removed the money from her purse and passed the bills across the desk. A corner of his mouth ticked when he saw she'd put them in protective sleeves. This told him she took meticulous care of whatever was in her possession. A fine quality he'd like to explore further.

She offered more details about the stash than Beau had been privy to, allowing him to study her straightforward manner. Reserved and guarded, she still knew how to interact with others. Professional but not snooty. Simple yet dazzling.

Fifteen minutes into their first date, and he was already half gone.

Oliver tapped his finger on the corner of the desk as he stared at the paper with the Players address. "That's a profound discovery. Are you thinking that a former member was involved in counterfeiting or that this property was a station for printing money?"

Andi crossed her legs. "I'm certainly not insinuating anything illegal regarding this establishment. I simply followed the address, and it led me here. I'm hoping you can offer some insight. Relay any old stories you've learned in your time as director that may provide a link."

Oliver estimated them the way Beau did his opposing party. "Why the need to find answers? Why not enjoy your little discovery, use it as a conversation piece at dinner, and leave it at that?"

Andi's foot stopped swaying. "We all have a story. A past. Reasons for doing what we do. Someone stuffed that money in the wall of what was then the Winderfield Hotel for a purpose, and I want to know what that purpose was." She opened her tiny purse and withdrew a badge with her credentials. "The Smithsonian would like to know what that purpose is. Our tagline is 'Seriously Amazing' because the discovery of history is. It shapes us. It can define us. The more answers we have to the past, the better future we can create."

Oliver returned her discovery across the desk. "Look, Miss Andrews. This organization has had some adverse publicity lately. We're under investigation at this very moment over rumors that a former employee pilfered funds, and the last thing we need is more negative attention. If those bills are tied to a counterfeit ring inside this establishment, no matter how long ago, it might sink us."

"I understand." Andi clasped her hands in her lap. "Unless the ties between the money and the Players hold massive historical significance, I don't see why the organization needs to be mentioned in my article at all. Our magazine doesn't hold the reputation of slinging mud but of educating in historical facts.

"However, if there is a scandal involving the Players, it's plausible that it'll only boost the prestige of the club. Think of the public's response to overturned laws or banned books."

Oliver rolled his tongue inside his cheek.

Andi's foot continued its sway. "My first goal is to discover who the bills belonged to and then follow the trail from there. It may be a dead end, and it may be the greatest discovery of our generation. Wouldn't you like to claim you took part in that discovery?"

Wow, she was good. Maybe Beau could talk her into joining his campaign.

The air crackled with tension while the director considered her words. "Where do you suggest we begin?"

A minor victory. Oliver could always change his mind.

"An expert certified their age to be Reconstruction era through the start of the twentieth century. I wondered if the Players kept record of members during those eras."

The chair creaked as Oliver shifted forward, satisfaction lifting his face. "The Players didn't open until December 31, 1888. It's possible the counterfeiters circulated them prior to the club's opening and there would be no connection."

"Perhaps." Andi's patience was waning if the rigid grip on her purse was any sign. "I'd be grateful if you could provide a list of names from the club's opening through the year 1900. I can check those names against the guest register of the Winderfield Hotel during those same years. See if there are any matches."

Beau thought of another possibility. "The membership packet says this building was built in 1847 and was originally home to the Townsend family. Could be that the previous owners are tied to the bills, before Edwin purchased it for his club."

Andi brightened. "It's possible. I'll investigate that angle if this one doesn't provide results."

The phone rang, and Oliver tapped a button to silence the noise. "And what if the answers you find cause someone damage? You can't just pretend you didn't find them."

Her shoe slipped, revealing a slender bare heel. "I can't imagine the answers will bring harm to anyone two centuries later."

"Some secrets never stop hurting others."

Beau yanked his attention away from her foot and pinned it on Oliver. "Do you know something we should know?"

The director sighed. "I honestly know nothing of these counterfeit bills. I know, however, that sometimes it's best to leave the past in the past. Because of your family's long history and support of this institution, Mr. Quincy, I feel I can't deny you this request. However, it will have to be approved by the board. We meet on Wednesday. If they don't oppose, I'll provide the list as soon as I'm able. That's all I can promise."

"Understood." Beau rose and held out his hand. "We won't take up any more of your time."

Andi joined his side and handed Oliver a business card. "Please email the list to this address, if approved. Thank you for speaking with us."

Oliver nodded and turned to Beau. "The third floor is unlocked. Enjoy your evening."

Once they were in the hallway on the other side of Oliver's closed door, Andi whispered, "What does he mean?"

Feeling bold, he took her hand in his. "You, my dear, are about to get a tour that few have had the privilege to receive."

The brown bursts encircling the center of her green eyes appeared gold beneath the soft light of the sconces.

"We get to see Edwin Booth's personal quarters."

Her cheeks lifted with her grin. Tightening her hold on his hand, she reached across her middle and grasped his forearm with the other.

The stairwell to the third floor was narrow, not bothering Beau in the least. He welcomed the excuse to brush against her. When they reached the top, he turned the knob on the door marked BOOTH on a painted wooden plaque.

The hinges creaked. Stepping inside was like going back in time, minus the red velvet ropes blocking them from walking any farther than three feet into the room. A Victorian-style canopy bed draped in a hideous floral blanket was against the opposite wall next to a smaller single bed. No doubt there was an odd story regarding that. Beneath the crown molding that bordered the perimeter was a handwritten phrase.

Beau's voice echoed in the space. " 'And when the smoke ascends on high, then thou beholdst the vanity of the worldly stuff. Come with a puff, thus think and smoke tobacco.' "

"And thus obtain lung cancer." Andrea pressed against the velvet rope, still holding his hand. "What an odd quote for him to have painted on the wall. Do you know how he died?"

"A series of strokes."

"Tobacco related?"

"Maybe. I'm sure the stress of being known as the brother of the man who killed one of America's most beloved presidents factored in. Have you heard the story about how Edwin saved Abraham Lincoln's son from falling off a platform at a train station a year before his assassination?"

"I wrote a thesis on it in college. Strange how two brothers can be raised the same and share the same passions but handle life differently."

"The Brothers Grimm, Frank and Jesse James, the Kennedys."

"Cain and Abel."

"Makes me grateful I'm an only child." He played with her fingers. "You?"

"I have a brother and a sister. They're much older than me. I was a surprise."

She was that.

He pointed to the mantel where pictures of Edwin and his family sat next to a human skull encased in glass. "Story goes it belonged to a horse thief named Fontaine who knew Edwin's father, Junius. Also an actor. After sharing a jail cell, they hung Fontaine for his crimes with his last request being that his skull be shipped to the Booth home. Junius had the phrase 'And the rest is silence' engraved on it."

"Creepy." She lifted her chin. "You seem to know a lot about history. Are you a fellow antiquity geek, or did you cram last night to impress me?"

"Depends. If it's the latter, will I gain points or lose them?"

"Maybe Oliver is right—I don't always need to know all the answers. I'd like to retract my question and bask in your knowledge."

"Done. How about we have dinner?"

"Dinner makes this a date."

"So does holding hands."

She looked at their entwined fingers in surprise. It had felt natural to him as well.

He stepped closer. "We both need to eat, and I'm offering you a balcony table at the only restaurant that overlooks Gramercy Park."

She made a performance of thinking it over.

Beau's cheek grazed across hers as he leaned to whisper in her ear. "Stop resisting."

Soft strands of her hair tickled his lips.

Had she just shivered? "You make it harder by the minute."

Guilt swept in and settled like a boulder in his stomach. Would she still feel that way about him if she knew his dad was selling her home?

CHAPTER FIFTEEN

FRANKLIN

Pittsburgh, January 1867

The last place Franklin wanted to be on a cold January night was in a cemetery. He waited under a full moon for his Secret Service team, longing for the warmth of a fireplace. He wanted to be home with Margaret and Cora. Not leaving his family responsibility to two strangers he'd spoken to once in an interview before hiring. At least Miss Moreau, barely a day over nineteen, was good with Cora and had provided a glowing list of references for one of such a tender age.

But no one loved his girls the way he did. Even if Mrs. Albany, the new maid and cook, served the most delicious feast on this side of the country. It didn't matter that to get Margaret the care she needed he had to take these jobs far away. He'd abandoned them.

Not really, of course. He would be back, but that knowledge didn't lift the heaviness in his heart. Margaret needed him. When he'd lain in that field hospital in the Georgia mountains, floating in and out of consciousness, begging for the angel of death to have mercy and take him, she'd been his cornerstone. When the pain had become too much to bear, she had held his hand, administered medicine if any was available, and whispered uplifting scripture into his ear. By the time he was well enough to leave the hospital bed, he knew he wanted to spend the rest of his life with her.

Now here she was in her hour of need, and instead of being at her side, he was walking among the dead, needing to discover the gatekeeper to the counterfeiting ring so they could slow distribution. While the counterfeiters themselves could disappear quickly, their work could last for decades.

Footsteps crunched on the frozen grass. He spun, and through the puff of his breath, he witnessed John Hackney approach, hands buried deep in his pockets. He greeted Franklin. The mustache was new and so was the Irish accent.

"Walk with me." John brushed past him without stopping, leaving Franklin to catch up. "They know you're here. They followed me the entire way from Pickett Street. Don't look, but they're watching us from the shadows of the church across the street."

Franklin huddled into his coat and scarf, acting as if John hadn't just made such a revelation. He didn't know anything about what his friend had just revealed. "They" would be behind Franklin and John at this point, but with enough distance between them, they wouldn't overhear.

John sniffed and lowered his voice. "The operation is larger than we thought. I asked McBride for more men, but you were the only one he could spare. I apologize for taking you away from Margaret in her condition."

Franklin shrugged. This job kept his family far from Hell's Hundred Acres and starvation, so he couldn't really complain.

"Elijah Agnes is the gatekeeper. I've earned his trust and that of an old man who goes by Zeigfried. They agreed to let us in, believing we manage the ships for the Pittsburgh Steam Engine Company and will transport counterfeit and other cargo for a cut of the profits."

Franklin bowed his head against the wind. "Any idea what the other cargo is?"

Their footsteps sounded loud in the silence. John sighed. "Opium."

Franklin's steps faltered. Cold and rain always made the bones in his leg tender against the prosthetic. John's confession made him feel even worse. They wouldn't be hunting a group this time who wanted some extra money. These were dangerous criminals. Opium wasn't a drug to pass off lightly, and neither were its distributors.

"What's my job?" Franklin asked, wishing he could get on a train and go back home. Something about this case made him uneasy, but he couldn't pinpoint why. It certainly wouldn't be the first dangerous mission he'd gone into.

"You'll work beneath me. Managing the steam company gives us access to cargo lists, the ship schedules, the holds, and hundreds of employed former soldiers who might still imbibe. Veterans are their target until doors in the pharmaceutical industry open."

Targeting men just like Franklin. Men who'd sacrificed their lives for the betterment of this country, only to return broken and empty, needing some assistance but most too proud to ask for any. Opium would assist them right to their graves.

"I told them about your leg. Your story of returning home from the war. I left your family out but embellished a few parts and added that morphine was your demon. That's when they finally allowed me to bring you in. You're Ike McGovern. I'm Tank, short for Morton Tankersley."

"The ringleader?" Franklin's teeth chattered, more from anger than from the cold.

"I haven't met him yet. They're very protective of him. But I know his name. It's Moses. Moses Grande."

The fine hairs on the back of Franklin's neck and arms stood erect. Where had he heard that name before?

His heart thumped, and he stared at the moon, hoping the fixed mark would keep him on his feet.

Moses Grande. He searched his memory.

The image of a constable with a waxed mustache, dark eyes blazing, materialized before Franklin. He'd just explained to the constable who he was, where he worked, and where he'd been.

"So you say, Franklin Davidson. Or is it James Palermo? Or Moses Grande? You've quite a list of crimes."

His brother Edward had committed those crimes.

Franklin doubled over and heaved the vestiges of his supper. It couldn't be his brother. Yet it had to be. How many Moses Grandes could there be in the world? Ones who were criminals at that.

He wiped his mouth with his sleeve and stood, his stomach cramping.

"What's happened?"

"I'll explain later. For now, tell them I've had too much to drink."

Tears clouded Franklin's vision as they walked silently through the rest of the cemetery toward the seedy boardinghouse that was part of their ruse. He'd prayed fervently for months to discover Edward's whereabouts so he could make amends, but he hadn't meant like this.

Why, God?

How would he ever choose between his moral compass and his beloved brother?

Andrea
Manhattan, Present Day

Andrea's world was a flea circus compared to Beau's, a sideshow attraction in which the small of society performed entertaining acts for the elite. Solving the mystery of the clue in the crumbling wall was merely a distraction for him. An excuse to be around her. If only she fit into his aristocratic world of operas and benefit dinners and personal chauffeurs.

"Where to, miss?" The older gentleman with gray hair that matched the color of his suit met her gaze in the rearview mirror. Beau had introduced him as Jonas, an employee and family friend of thirty years.

"Greenwich Village, please. Winderfield Apartments." It would've been easier on Andrea's pride for them to part ways at the Players and she hail a cab home, but Beau insisted on being a gentleman and seeing her safely to her door.

It was both endearing and annoying.

Opposites in every way, a meaningful relationship would be difficult. Yet the chemistry was too strong to ignore. She liked him. A lot. She wanted to probe and explore the possibilities of a future with him, but it would only end in heartache.

For her.

She knew all too well the temptation beautiful women were to a powerful man. Or the ease with which powerful men slipped into temptation, was more accurate. Monogamy not recognized as a lifestyle. For the first time in months, the thought of Allen resurfaced, threatening to coil around her and squeeze. Logic told her not all men in esteemed positions were like Allen, but the scars of him were branded on her consciousness forever, and she never wanted to be so stupid again.

Besides, if Beau won the election in November, he'd move into the governor's mansion in Albany and forget all about the journalist who'd held his fancy for a few short days.

The car lurched forward, and Beau reached for her hand. "I enjoyed the evening. Thanks for coming out with me."

Prickles tickled her fingers. She liked his formal politeness. It was genuine and old fashioned and charming. "Thank you for dinner and for setting up a meeting with Oliver. Do you think the board will approve of him sending me a list of members?"

"I do. My donation will be hard to ignore."

"Please tell me the timing of your donation and my need for information was a coincidence."

"The answer is both yes and no. The men in my family have taken turns donating to the Players for the last twenty years, and this year is my turn. I admit, however, to having a check sent right away after learning of your failed attempt instead of waiting until the year's end like normal."

"You shouldn't have done that. You barely know me."

"I know enough to know it was important to you and that you're worth the effort." He ran a thumb along the back of her hand. "I'm also hoping you'll allow me the privilege of a second date."

She wanted to shout *yes!* but fear slammed the brakes. So did Jonas, as he pulled up to her building. "My apologies, miss. There was a dog."

"It's fine. Thank you for the ride, Mr. Jonas." She slipped her hand away from Beau's, hoping she didn't offend him. "How about I commit to a phone call while I consider a second date?"

"I'll take that. May I walk you to your door?"

"Please." She opened the car door and almost plowed into Myrna Zygart's shopping cart. The woman's face screwed up in anger, and she rattled something in Polish.

"My apologies, Mrs. Z. Our future governor is so handsome, it's hard to concentrate on my surroundings."

The gypsy studied Beau's long form exiting the car. "Future governor, eh? You plan to improve health care for the elderly?"

"Approving the new proposed health care bill is the first thing on my list." Beau tucked his hands into his pockets.

Mrs. Z's eyes narrowed to slits. "Crime? Inflation? Overpopulation?"

Beau nodded. "All the above plus public education and road conditions."

"You have my vote, then. Of course, a politician will say anything you want to hear."

"Not me." Beau rocked from heel to toe. "My slogan is 'We the people.' I'm a citizen of this beloved city, same as you. We'll work together to improve as many things as possible for everyone, despite income, race, or age."

The woman puckered her pruned face and patted his arm. "What pretty words you speak. Guess we'll see."

The front wheel of her cart shook as she continued down the sidewalk. A few feet away, she stopped and pivoted to Andrea. "One thing's for sure, he's handsome."

She winked a deeply wrinkled eye, making Andrea laugh.

"Are you blushing?" Andrea examined Beau's face.

"Guys don't blush. It's just hot out here."

"You are. How cute."

Beau shook his head, smiling.

The streetlamps flickered on with the cloak of darkness. The scent of rain hung in the air, but the humidity made it sticky. Moments like these made it easy to forget how different they were.

Beau looked around. "This is a nice complex. A simple but well-maintained exterior. Modern enough to fit in, yet completely old soul."

"You've described me well," she teased.

His face grew serious, and he acted as if he was going to say something then changed his mind.

"What is it?" Good news never came after a look like that.

He sighed. "I found out something the other day that, in fairness, I need to tell you before you agree to any future dates. I hope it doesn't change your opinion of me, because I'd really like to see you again."

Andrea's spirits fell to the sidewalk.

"My father invests in and develops land."

"I know. Davidson-Quincy Investment Corporation."

"Right. He informed me the other day that he's negotiating a large sale that would include this complex as an extra incentive."

"But…the owners haven't informed us of a sale."

"Legally, they don't have to. They're only required to notify the tenants of an eviction. It's fair that you know they plan to turn the complex into an upscale bed-and-breakfast."

"They can't!"

Beau looked around and patted the air with his palm to quiet her down. "It's not a done deal yet."

"But…it's a historic landmark. There are rules, right?"

Panic rose in her chest.

"Yes. They know those rules and can do what they desire while keeping within the guidelines. Just as your landlord and those before him were able to turn the hotel rooms into individual apartments as long as they kept the integrity of the building."

Likely one reason why the original plaster and baseboards continued to be a focal point.

Her chest rose and fell in outrage. "That means I'll be out of a home. All of us will." She glanced up at the windows glowing with light. With life. "I'm going to be sick."

She started walking away, but he caught her arm. "Please, Andi. Don't shoot the messenger."

"I'm not. I…" She exhaled. "This is such a shock. It took me forever to find a place I could truly feel at home after—" She dared not name the ghost of her past. "And now I'm going to lose it."

He rubbed her upper arms. She groaned. "I appreciate you telling me. How long do I have?"

"It's not official yet. They're looking at other property as well. Maybe we can put our heads together and figure out a way around this."

A blend of hope and misery reflected in her eyes.

"He's your dad. Why wouldn't you want to see the sale?"

"Just because we're family doesn't mean we always agree on business matters. In fact, we disagree a lot. We just don't do it in public."

He ran his fingertips up and down her arm. "I'll talk to him. Get more details. See if I can't sway favor to the other property. I just couldn't keep pursuing you with secrets between us."

Pursuing? The word was rustic and primitive and sent heated pulses throughout her body. His confession was a very un-Allen-like move, and it was killing all her preconceptions about powerful men.

"You are unlike any man I've ever met."

"Is that good or bad?"

She moved closer. "Definitely good."

"Does that mean I can call you?"

"I'll be upset if you don't." Because despite trying to fight it and the atom bomb he'd just dropped, she was entirely smitten with him.

His fingertips slid down her wrists to her palms, leaving a delicious trail of goose bumps before he let go. "I'll get you that list of members as soon as they send it."

"Good night, Beau."

He kissed her forehead. "Night, Andi."

No one called her Andi except the magazine staff. A masculine spin on a feminine name to earn her articles an extra notch of respect. Like Jo March. She liked the nickname coming from him.

Rain began to fall. She dashed inside her apartment, feeling as unsteady as if she'd just outraced a hurricane.

CHAPTER SIXTEEN

EDWARD

Outskirts of Pittsburgh, April 1867

*T*he old building was black as pitch, save for the lantern quaking in Zeigfried's feeble hand. Once a shack that held Confederate prisoners awaiting transport, its remote location and access to the river made it the perfect place for Edward to set up operation. "Mind holding it steady?"

"Sorry, Moses. I can't control the shakes." Remorse leaked from the man's eyes.

The feeling should jab Edward, as the reason for Zeigfried's shakes lay behind their actions here tonight. The former sailor had discovered the poppy years ago on an excursion to Asia to retrieve spices, silks, and other commodities. One time, and it made the man its slave.

But every man must make choices in life, and Zeigfried had chosen his path long ago. Edward refused to add that weight to his conscience.

As for Edward's own choices, well, he'd deal with those consequences after he was dead.

When all the lanterns were lit, Edward prepared the press. The others had yet to arrive, a fact that frayed his nerves. This was an important night. They all stood to profit. Instead, they'd probably lost track of time at the dockside tavern, consumed by a game of poker or taking pleasure in one of the rooms. Wouldn't be the first time. It was hard to find a man as dedicated as he.

"You seen Eurich?" Edward asked.

"He's standing guard with Tank. Just like you ordered. I'll help you, sir." Zeigfried's body shook like tree branches in a thunderstorm. Edward wasn't sure how the man stayed on his feet.

Zeigfried's help was not possible. The reason Edward's counterfeit was so successful was because of the pristine printing and operation. It was so close to the real thing, even the banks had trouble deciphering.

Before Edward could respond, Zeigfried said, "Want me to fetch McGovern?"

"Who?"

"The new man Tank brought in. Ike McGovern. He's been workin' with Eirich. First one b'sides myself to show up tonight. He's been waiting outside. A young man not tainted with age. He'll have a steady hand."

Edward cursed. He didn't like bringing in someone new, especially on an important night like tonight. "You sure the others aren't here?"

"Yes, sir."

Edward stilled the man by the arm. "Get this McGovern. And Tank. Then go fetch the others."

"Yes, sir."

"Zeigfried?"

The old man paused his exit.

"You might do something about that shaking while you're gone."

With downcast eyes, Zeigfried nodded then turned away.

Edward rolled ink onto the engraved plate, placed the paper on top, and then rolled a metal wheel over it to add pressure. After a few rolls, he lifted the paper away from the plate, starting with the corners. A stable hand was critical when lifting, as to not smudge the ink.

A thing of beauty.

Six hours wasn't much time to print, load, and clear the building before the authorities joined them. That was *if* he could still trust his informant at the station after the man's promotion at the jail. Though the informant stood to receive more by working with Edward versus not. New York's Chinatown proved to be the perfect haven for opium lovers of all kinds—those who imbibed for pleasure and those who profited from the imbibing.

He brought a lamp closer and fell into a rhythm of rolling the various colors of ink over the metal image with the passion of da Vinci or Van Gogh. Every color, every stroke, held significance, had a purpose. Down to the little details he'd carved that no one else would notice but would distinguish his work from other counterfeiters.

The Metropolitan Bank would find it difficult to decipher their true bills from Edward's. Only the likeness of Icarus spoke the truth with a miniature shield and bee engraved on his hat of wings. It had taken Edward weeks to carve that, making the tiniest of movements lest one mistake ruin the whole plate.

A shuffle in the doorway startled him back to reality. The romance of each line, curve, and dot had swept him away. Each shade of ink. The music of damp paper peeled from the engraving.

"Here he be, sir." Zeigfried stumbled sideways. A man Edward didn't recognize in the shadows of the space set Zeigfried to rights.

Edward's old friend would likely not see his next birthday at the pace his health was failing. Between the shakes and soiling himself at least once a day, Zeigfried reminded Edward of his father. Except Zeigfried was subservient.

"Agnes is here now." Another shake. "He's guarding the river. Buck's a no-show."

Zeigfried's cough nearly brought down the rafters.

Edward winced. He waited as the man gasped for breath then ordered, "No need to hunt him. Guard the entrance."

A chair sat against the wall by the door where Zeigfried could take a rest. Hopefully, his hacking wouldn't alert anyone of importance.

"You, hang this to dry." Edward peeled the paper from the plate and pointed at the clothesline where three papers hung over the rope, middles bowed and ends pointed to the floor. They'd lie flat again once they dried and were stacked into a bundle in the crate.

McGovern, as Zeigfried had called him, obeyed. Good. There was nothing more annoying than a recruit who acted higher than his station. There was something familiar in the dark eyes capped by sooty wayward brows. A thick beard covered his face but didn't mask the shape of the man's square jaw.

A slither of unease traveled up Edward's spine. Tankersley had brought him in. Edward trusted Tank with his life. Literally, in times past. Tank wouldn't double-cross him. Edward pushed away the sensation that he'd known this man in another life and continued his work.

Tank joined them shortly after, doubling the efforts of their operation. Minutes passed into hours. The night breeze stirred the black fabric they'd nailed over the broken windows. The papers swayed but not enough to disturb their position on the rope. Every five sheets, Edward would stop to clean the plate with turpentine. The pungent scent burned his nostrils and stung his eyes.

"This is the last of 'em." Edward peeled the paper off the plate and handed it to Tank. While Tank hung it up, Edward and McGovern carefully examined the others for dryness then stacked them in a crate barely larger than the printed sheets.

A commotion sounded from outside. Edward stiffened. "What was that?" Tank asked.

Edward crept to the window and peeled back the edge of the curtain. "Eurich's gone. Pack up."

McGovern began stuffing the rags and ink into a crate. "The bills," Edward ordered. Dry or not, they weren't leaving any evidence behind.

Tank yanked the drying sheets from the clothesline and tossed them in with the rest. Edward bent and started disassembling the press. The click of a gun's hammer sounded by his ear. He stilled, sliding his vision to see the metal barrel pointed at his head.

"Put it down. You're under arrest."

Edward lowered his hands and glowered at Tank for being stupid enough to trust an officer in disguise. But Tank's gun was pointed at Edward's chest.

Bile pushed up Edward's throat. "What is this?"

Tank lifted his chin. "I believe they call it a mutiny. Everything in this room is now property of the Secret Service."

Edward swore. He'd treated Tank like family since the day they'd met in an alley in Brooklyn, after he'd killed a man for abusing his own sister. For the past year they'd shared hunger, sorrow, booze, laughter. It had all been a ruse?

McGovern reached into a nearby crate and withdrew a set of shackles. Edward closed his eyes. A falsehood the entire time.

Fury built in his veins. He was tired of being on the bottom. Tired of everyone around elevating themselves so high above him they didn't need him anymore. He'd come too close to creating the life he wanted— all on his own—to spend the rest of his life in a jail cell. He would not go quietly.

As Edward came to a stand, he slipped his hand inside his coat pocket and withdrew his revolver. He pointed it at Tank's head. Two shots rang out, momentarily deafening his ear. Pain exploded in Edward's arm. He growled against it, watching Tank stumble backward and slide down the wall, his chest bleeding. The impact of Tank's bullet in his arm must have caused Edward's finger to spasm around the trigger.

Tank's eyelids fluttered closed.

"Drop it," McGovern yelled, Irish accent gone.

Edward cocked the hammer and swung to face his opponent. His arm burned as if someone held it on a hot stove. He blinked to clear the haze. He hadn't meant to kill Tank. But he couldn't stop now. His finger squeezed against the trigger.

"Don't do this, brother."

Time suspended in a thick fog. The stranger before him materialized into a face he recognized. He eased his finger off the trigger. "Franklin?"

Fury and regret flashed through eyes exactly like his own. How was this dirty, bearded Secret Service agent his brother?

The memory of that cold winter day in D.C. when he'd tracked Franklin to his new house, his new family, and his new job curled like paper on fire in his mind.

"Don't do this," Franklin said again.

For a moment, they were young boys again. It had been a few years since Mama had passed, and Franklin had walked into Edward's bedroom to find a bottle of arsenic traveling to his lips. A way to silence the pain.

Franklin had used the same words then.

But this time he wouldn't listen.

"You're in enough trouble already." Franklin approached one cautious step at a time. "Now you've done murder. Don't force me to uphold the law by killing my own brother. I don't think I can live with that."

"You always did value moral duty more than was healthy. How does that pretty wife of yours feel about being left behind while you play the gallant hero?"

"You leave Margaret out of this."

"Why? Because she's so frail and miserable she can't get out of bed? Don't look so surprised, Franklin. I have my sources. Seems your need to protect the weak didn't stop when you discarded me. She simply became your sacrifice."

"Let's not end it this way." Franklin's voice cracked with the plea. "I love you, Edward. I always have. All I've ever wanted to do is protect you, but you've chosen a path I cannot follow. The only way I can protect you now is for you to come with me willingly. Please."

Ah, yes. They'd circled back to the choices of men.

Edward hated disappointing his brother. Especially after Franklin had stepped in repeatedly to curb their father's rage so Edward wouldn't feel it days later. But Franklin had never understood the pain of being rejected, unloved.

They may have shared a crib, their appearance, and grief over losing their mother, but they would not share eternity. Franklin had made his choice. Now Edward would make his.

Grief mingled with his rage, pushing blasted tears to his eyes. "I never thought I'd see the day my hero would betray me."

Tank's cough gurgled behind him. The man's last, Edward was certain.

Franklin's gaze flicked to the agent on the floor. He winced. "I didn't want it to be this way. When I realized the trail led to you, I tried to get out. The other agents were already in the field. Then I thought—hoped—that with me on the case, I could at least offer you protection."

Tank moaned then fell silent.

"I realized ten years ago that I don't need your protection anymore."

"You need me more than you realize."

Edward's finger twitched. "I love you, brother. But in my hour of desperation, I will shoot you as surely as you will me."

Here they were, Cain and Abel. Had Cain's actions been born of passion or long meditated upon? When he'd looked into Abel's eyes for the last time, had he questioned his motives? Felt remorse? Relief?

Victory?

"Let's not one of us join Mama tonight," Franklin whispered, hand shaking. "Do the right thing, Edward. Father is gone. Start again."

In a cold, stinky jail cell?

Never.

Tension built like steam between them before the blast of a gun ended it all.

CHAPTER SEVENTEEN

BEAU

Manhattan, Present Day

*T*he board approved their request. Beau skimmed the list of members from the Players' opening on December 31, 1888, through 1900. Oliver's email had informed him that if Beau shared the information with Andi, it was his choice. The only stipulation the board made was that any information found involving the Players had to be shared with the board before publicizing. Beau had agreed, doubting they'd find anything of significance. From there he'd carved time in his schedule to have dinner with Andi the following Thursday so they could cross-reference his list to the list she'd obtained from the Winderfield Hotel's guest books.

He shouldn't be working on solving a pointless mystery right now with the election only two months away. Andi was too beautiful a distraction, too often pulling his mind from his campaign to text her or wonder what she was doing.

Wilson had been hounding him to stay focused. Beau explained to the man how hard he'd worked to convince Andi to give him a chance. He couldn't brush her aside now, like paperwork on a cluttered desk in the name of his ambitions. Cultivating their relationship would be difficult enough if he won. It'd be near impossible if he had to start at the beginning with her again. Now was his chance to see if what bubbled between them was real or fleeting.

Jonas parked at the curb in front of Andi's complex. "It'll likely take a few hours. I'll text you."

"Very well, sir." Jonas nodded.

A bouquet of fresh daisies in his grip, Beau opened the door and stepped onto the sidewalk, careful of little old ladies with shopping carts. All clear, he punched in the code to the main door Andi had given him and jogged up the stairs to her apartment.

Her door was open, sending appetizing smells into the hallway that made his stomach growl into the hallway. He knocked as he stepped inside. "Andi?"

"In the kitchen," she called, her voice muffled from the next room.

Her living room was clean and functional. Miley, his interior-design-driven and overbearing ex-girlfriend, had taught him this style was shabby chic—a blend of old and new with slight country flare. Not wanting any of his exes in his head tonight, he bent to observe the blue fish with gauzy fins staring at him from its position on the plastic plant in the water tank. Three small neon fish dashed around the tank as if looking for a place to hide.

Andi walked into the room wearing a frilly apron that provoked different thoughts he had to push from his mind. "Sammy, meet Beau. Beau this is Sammy Davis Jr. and the Supremes."

"You named your fish after singers?"

"I used to have a red betta named Billie Holiday, but she died. We had a great seven years together, though." She joined him at the tank, bringing the scent of basil and blueberries with her.

Beau smiled, drawn to her eccentric ways.

"I've only had the neon tetras for a few days, so they're still settling in." She untied the apron. It slipped from her body to rest in her hand, revealing a blue-and-white-striped dress that made her tan skin glow.

He stood to full height, captivated. "You are…"

She hid the apron behind her. "Unique? Odd? Peculiar? I prefer quirky."

"Lovely." He handed her the flowers. "Magnetic."

Bottom lip between her teeth, she grinned. "That's a bold word, Governor."

"I figured if I'm going to date a writer, I'd better brush up on my adjectives."

The attraction snapping between them was so intense he wanted to give in to it, but he knew that a relationship of substance had to grow beyond chemistry. He was a patient man, but Andi made it difficult.

She lifted the flowers to her nose, her eyelashes kissing her cheeks as she inhaled. "Hungry?"

"Starving." Beau cleared the heat from his voice. *She's talking about food, man. Get a grip.*

"I hope you like spaghetti." She closed her front door and gestured for him to follow.

He took a deep breath to clear his head. "My favorite."

The kitchen was tiny and outdated, but she'd worked hard to hide that fact with paint and decorations. A large window with girly curtains pushed to the sides offered a great view of a courtyard below. The hotel's engineer had built the rooms in a circle, leaving a good-sized oval of grass in the middle.

"I thought we could dine alfresco, if you don't mind. The yard is communal but shouldn't be crowded on a Thursday."

"Perfect. What can I do to help?"

"Food's ready. I've already set the table. Just fill your plate, and we'll carry them down the back steps."

"You get the drinks. I'll get the plates."

Steam lifted from the sauce-coated pasta as he scooped it onto plates and added garlic bread and small salads with dressing while Andi poured water into fancy glasses and grabbed napkins and silverware. Beau wondered how she'd handle all those steps in her thick-soled sandals, but she tackled them with the grace of a princess. The strings that ran from her feet to wrap around her ankles did something for him, and he found himself once again in need of a diversion from his thoughts.

"This one over here." She moved toward a wrought-iron table draped with a white plastic tablecloth that held a candle in the center. Industrial string lights draped from the building to posts placed throughout the courtyard, giving it a romantic summer aura. He understood the appeal the property had to investors, but he also hated to see good people like Andi removed from their homes to make a billionaire even more money.

Beau waited for her to sit before he did.

"What a gentleman."

"My mom taught me a few things that stuck before she passed away."

Her mouth grew serious. "I'm so sorry."

"Me too." The air smelled of warm tomato sauce and vanilla candle.

"Is this okay?" She looked around. Doubt lines marred her forehead.

"It's perfect." While he had no way of reading her thoughts, she was likely thinking this scenario would insult his privileged pride. All he wanted was to feel normal. And being with Andi felt as natural as breathing.

Her hand tensed in a fist atop the tablecloth. "Do you have any update regarding the sale of the complex? I really don't want to give all this up."

Ah, so that's what was bothering her. "Negotiations are on pause right now, as the investors have hit a snag with one of their other properties. Something about discovering dinosaur bones during excavation. It's bought us some time."

He uncoiled her fist, slipped his hand in hers to assure her it was fine to relax, and said grace. When he finished and picked up his fork, he caught her staring. "Did I do something wrong?"

"No. Of course not. You just surprised me, is all."

"Prayer and thankfulness were other things my mom taught that stuck."

"I wish I could've met her."

"Me too. She'd love you." The words *as much as I do* flashed through his mind, but he pushed them away. Love this soon was crazy, and a comment like that would only scare her off.

One of his favorite bedtime stories had been about the day his parents met. His mom's expression would turn wistful, her voice full of admiration when she recalled the first moment she'd seen his dad. Literal love at first sight. Beau was a practical man. It was doubtful so powerful a love would hit the same family two generations in a row.

"To your mom." Andi held up her water glass. The gesture touched his soul, and he tapped his glass with hers.

"To solving your mystery. And to keeping your little slice of heaven in the city."

"Hear, hear."

The meal was amazing. The company, even better. They talked about their childhoods, their awkward middle school years, and the first moment adulthood set in. They laughed in abundance, drawing the attention of the other courtyard patrons.

Beau rolled the sleeves of his dress shirt up to his elbows and relaxed in his chair, welcoming the evening breeze. "I told you we aren't all that different."

"Oh, but we are. However, the more time I spend with you, the smaller the great divide gets." She fingered the stem of her empty glass.

"Does this mean a third date is a possibility?"

"Beau, I'm not high society material. I don't fit into that world. As much as I want to agree to more dates, I can't shake the feeling we're both setting ourselves up for heartbreak."

"Governor is an elected position. A job, not the man. I may not even win."

"It may be a job, but it's one you'll carry with you everywhere. It'll become the man. The entire state will rest on your shoulders." She clasped her hands in her lap. "You'll win. I've no doubt."

"Behind every good man is a good woman."

"I'm just not sure I'm who you need."

Oh, but she was.

"Take my run for governor out of the equation. If I was, say, a sanitation worker or a banker or an artist, would you hesitate?"

She was quiet for a moment. "No."

He reached across the small table and touched her chin, guiding her gaze to his. "Then give Beau—the man—a chance. We can worry about occupations later."

When he released her, she dropped her chin into her palm. "Smooth talker. You'll make a great politician."

He laughed. "How about we see if either of us is any good at playing detective."

She went back to her apartment to retrieve the list she'd gotten from the library's archives department. Beau stacked the plates and glasses, pushed them to the side of the table, and moved his chair next to hers. Dusk had almost completely given over to darkness. The city's night sounds played quietly in the background. His phone pinged with a news notification, but he dismissed it. He wanted nothing interfering with this night.

Andi returned a few minutes later with a stack of papers, two highlighters, and a sweater. He stood and held the sweater in place while she slipped her arms inside. "There are a lot more names on my list than yours. I'll give you a name, you skim your list, and we'll highlight any matches. Sound good?"

"Aye-aye, Captain."

They worked for an hour with no exact matches, only two different men with the same last name. E. Davidson from her list and Franklin Davidson from his. Beau's last name was hyphenated upon his great-grandparents' marriage. There'd been no male heir to pass on the Davidson name. The task had fallen to Grandma Cora.

Was it possible these men were ancestors of his?

Andi clicked the lid of the highlighter off and on, looking thoughtful. "Are the matching surnames a coincidence? Maybe, maybe not. And what is the *E* short for? Who is this mysterious E. that rented my room on August 2, 1872? More importantly, are either related to the Davidson-Quincy clan?"

"That's a lot of questions. Neither name sounds familiar to me."

"You mean neither has a portrait painted by a famous artist hanging in the drawing room of the Davidson-Quincy mansion?"

Beau sent her a playful scowl. "We're not royalty. And we don't have a drawing room. We have a ballroom."

"Ugh, of course you do," she mumbled.

"Ballrooms were popular in the 1880s. It's not like we use it. Very often."

She smiled, but it turned into a yawn, signaling Beau they should continue this another time. He pulled out his phone and texted for Jonas to pick him up. "I'll help you clean."

Her pout was arousing under the glow of lights. "I thought for sure I had a story here. I really want that promotion."

"We'll keep digging. If it dead-ends again, we'll either find you another story or brainstorm a new angle for this one."

She tucked her arm under his and turned her head so they were inches apart. "You'd do that for me?"

"Absolutely."

"Why do you have to be so wonderful?"

He shrugged. "Another thing my mom taught me."

She kissed his cheek, heating his blood. "Help me carry everything back upstairs, and I'll worry about the dishes tomorrow."

"I can help wash." He had at least fifteen to twenty minutes before Jonas would arrive.

Standing, she looked down at him. "Be honest. You've never washed a dish in your life."

"I...can learn."

"Why do today what you can put off until tomorrow?" She tugged him to his feet.

"That's my campaign slogan. Don't steal it."

"Duly noted."

When the dishes were placed in the sink and the leftovers packed into the fridge, Beau checked her back door twice to make sure it was locked. Then he walked to the front of the apartment. "Thank you for dinner."

"You're welcome." She covered another yawn with her hand. "Sorry, I'm not trying to be rude."

"It's late. I understand." He reached for a lock of her hair and let it glide between his fingertips. Those sleepy eyes begged him to kiss her. But he was a patient man.

"Call me?" she asked.

"Gladly. Lock up." He brushed a thumb over her soft cheek and opened the door.

"Beau?"

He turned from the hallway.

"Do you think E. Davidson and Franklin Davidson could be related to each other?"

"It's possible. We can dig deeper next time. Maybe after a stroll through Gramercy Park?"

The fog of sleep cleared from her eyes. "You'd invite me into the park?"

"I would. Good night, sweet girl."

"Night." She closed her door, and he waited to hear the click of the lock.

He'd invite her into his entire world, if only she'd accept.

CHAPTER EIGHTEEN

Washington, D.C., August 1867

*T*he little two-story colonial brought a rush of emotion to Edward's eyes. Home. After all the boardinghouses and cramped rooms above taverns with lumpy beds and drafty spaces, home seemed too good to be real. Being so far removed from family these past years, some days he still had trouble believing he had one of his own now. A dream he'd never expected to obtain but was grateful he had.

Thoughts of his brother slowed his steps and weighed his chest. A piece of him—the piece the brothers shared from their first movements in the womb—was gone. Snatched away as quickly as an apple from a tree. The wound was still as raw as when he'd watched his brother close his eyes in death. Edward's life would never be the same.

How he longed to see Margaret. Such a beautiful and fragile woman. How would she react to his presence? Would she suspect he wasn't really her husband, or had the melancholy grown so dark she wouldn't notice? After all, they'd never met before. The telegrams he received from Mrs. Hackney these past weeks were vague enough to discourage hope, and the messages had ceased altogether after she'd finally received news of John's passing. He'd been an excellent partner in Edward's ring but an even better agent, his loss felt throughout the entire Secret Service.

The neighbor opened their door and shooed out a black cat. He nodded to the woman. She lifted her chin in disapproval then disappeared behind the closed door. His long absence no doubt encouraged controversy, but they didn't understand the limitations of a maimed man.

His leg had been hurting him something terrible, tempting him to seek solace from the pain.

Yet he hadn't. Thoughts of Margaret and Cora had kept him pointing north.

Who was he trying to fool? He wasn't a good man, even when he tried. He'd murdered his brother. His dearest friend. His confidant. His only protector. It didn't matter that he'd had no other option.

Mother and son were together again, and that gave Edward some measure of comfort.

He opened the door and stepped inside. The house smelled of lemon wax and beef stew. The rack by the door was bare. He shed his suit coat for relief from the summer heat and closed the door silently behind him.

Rays of sunlight burst through the windows and spilled across the rugs. The wood floors beneath gleamed. Not a speck of dust marred the furniture or mantels. Baby giggles sounded from a nearby room, so full of mirth, Edward couldn't help but smile. A moment later, a tiny girl crawled from the doorway of the neighboring room, hands and legs pumping like a steam locomotive.

"You can't escape that easily." A young woman wearing a brown dress overlaid with a white apron chased after the tot, producing more laughter.

When the woman noticed him, she straightened, her lips parted. Beautiful brown eyes rounded.

"I'm sorry to have frightened you." Edward tugged at his collar. "I'm Franklin Davidson, Margaret's husband."

"Yes…I remember." She crossed her arms, her gaze darting around the room. "Miss Margaret is napping. Cora and I were just passing the time."

Did the woman think he'd be upset to find her playing with the girl? He knelt in the baby's path, pain pulsing up his leg, and craned his neck to see the young nanny. "A wonderful idea. I apologize, miss, but I don't remember your name."

Pink dotted her porcelain cheeks. "Moreau. Madelaine Moreau. We've only met the one time, the day you hired me, and briefly at that."

The flow of her words held the hint of a French accent.

"I apologize again, Miss Moreau. My job keeps me very busy."

"It must. You look tired, sir, if I may say so. Cora and I can continue to play while you rest. Something much quieter. Mrs. Albany won't have dinner ready for another hour yet."

Cora, poised on hands and knees, stared at him with the clearest blue eyes he'd ever seen. So beautiful. So trusting. He smiled at her and was rewarded with her toothy grin. A feeling he'd never experienced before stirred deep within him.

He was a papa now. He'd known from the moment Franklin closed his eyes in death that he'd assume this responsibility, but now he felt it.

"As weary as I may be, I've been away far too long." He held out his hands.

Cora crawled into them.

She squealed when he picked her up and tossed her into the air. Miss Moreau's palms flew out, as if ready to catch the baby should she fall. Edward chuckled. He might not be talented at many things, but he could catch a child. His superior had granted him a month's leave after the latest raid, having arrested the leader and seizing thousands in counterfeit bills. He'd relish the time away and, in it, prove to this young woman—and himself—he was trustworthy of having a child.

Holding Cora against his side, he dove in and kissed her sticky cheek. More giggles. She clung to him, kicking her small legs. The baby smelled of milk and talcum powder. The scent of innocence.

Instant love overtook him. Is this how their mother had felt when her sons had been delivered? Certainly, their father hadn't.

"How long has it been since you've had a day off, Miss Moreau?"

Her smile was replaced by confusion. "A day off, sir?"

"That answers my question." He bounced Cora on his arm. "Take the rest of the day off, Miss Moreau. We'll see you in the morning."

Her wide eyes were as innocent as Cora's. "I, uh…I live here, sir. But I can see about staying elsewhere, if that's your wish."

Cora yanked on his tie. "I've no intention of putting you out, miss. Simply giving you permission to spend the next several hours however you like. Payment intact."

Her face brightened. "Thank you, Mr. Davidson, but are you certain? Of course you're certain. I apologize, sir. Thank you."

She turned in a twirl of skirts.

The sway of her bustle captivated him until Cora slapped his cheeks. Just as well. He had a wife upstairs he'd love to spend the night with if she'd have him. That part of him had lain dormant far too long.

Cora babbled incoherent words as he climbed the stairs. The air was thicker up here. Almost smothering in the late summer heat. Wet hit his cheek. Cora pulled away, taking her slobbery lips with her.

That indescribable emotion rose again, threating to choke him. She was so precious it hurt. Had he ever witnessed anything so pure? He'd certainly never held such purity in his hands.

The first room he passed was simple and tidy, with nothing more than a bed, a chest of drawers, and a washstand and pitcher. Miss Moreau's, he presumed. Next was the nursery. The last and largest room held a four-poster bed draped in gauze. The rumpled blankets were empty underneath. He stepped inside to find Margaret, thin and pale, sitting in a chair next to the window, staring out the tiny shaft of light that emanated from the side of the heavy drapes.

"Hello, darling." He waited for her to answer before stepping inside.

"You haven't called me that since our wedding night." Every word was lackluster and uniform. She kept her attention riveted to the window.

"Then I am the greatest of imbeciles."

Cora grunted and pushed at him, wanting down. He patted her back in a steady rhythm.

Margaret chuckled, the sound rusty from disuse. Taking it as permission, he approached his new wife. Bruises marred the skin beneath her eyes. Had someone hurt her?

Alarmed, he stepped closer, only to realize they weren't bruises but signs of poor health. Her lips were dry, and her fingers trembled.

The vibrant, youthful woman was gone.

Edward swallowed his disappointment as he knelt beside her. He traced his fingertips over the back of her hand before capturing her fingers in his. "My darling."

No warmth seeped from her expression. No returned endearments. She simply studied him, one inch at a time. As if she'd forgotten what he looked like.

Or as if she was already noting differences.

Her mouth fell open. "What happened to your ear?"

Concern for her turned to alarm then embarrassment, but at least she was showing emotion.

Her hand touched the offending appendage, and he clasped it. "It's nothing to worry about. I...I..."

"What is it?" The delicate skin on her forehead wrinkled. Her hand tightened around his.

Cora stilled, staring up at him as if sensing the gravity of what he was about to reveal.

He swallowed, barely able to let the words pass his throat. "My brother, Edward, is dead. I killed him."

His voice broke in true grief over killing Franklin and ending his own identity.

Margaret gasped. "Why? How?"

Edward shook his head, hoping it would shake away the horrific memory of that night. He sucked in air. "An informant led us to a counterfeiting ring that Edward was leading. John Hackney had been working with him for months and had earned his trust enough to let me in. I wore a disguise. Edward didn't recognize me until it was time to make an arrest."

He wiped at the moisture in his eyes. "We exchanged words. Gunfire. I didn't want to shoot, but he left me no choice. I was fortunate his bullet only skimmed my ear. It took several weeks to heal. The doc did the best he could. I'm sorry if this changes your love for me."

Her clammy hands turned his face to the side as she inspected his ear. Nothing to see except scarred and mangled skin, but it had completely healed years ago. Cora joined her mother's probing by yanking on his earlobe.

"No." Margaret's stern voice scolded the child.

"It doesn't hurt anymore," Edward said, propping the baby on his raised knee.

Margaret's voice wobbled. "Something so trivial could not change my love for you."

Her words washed over his aching soul like cool water bubbling in a peaceful brook.

He swallowed. "John died that night too. Edward killed him." He rested his forehead against Cora's.

Margaret pressed a hand to her stomach. "Poor Angelica. I should write to her." She guided his chin back around. "I'm grateful to be out of New York City and Hell's Hundred Acres, but I imagine this job is its own kind of hell. God knows how I worry while you're gone."

"Do you?" He lifted one corner of his mouth in a grin. "I thought…"

"That all I do is stare out the window and cry?" She huffed. "I do. But I—I want so badly to stop."

Despite her confession, her face had returned to the window.

His thumb grazed her upper thigh. "Maybe I can coax you away from that window. Give you something new to focus upon."

Her gaze snapped to his. He continued the ministrations on her leg, searching for answers in her eyes. Her head tipped to the side. "You're different."

His thumb stilled. His pulse ticked harder, but he transformed the nervous energy into agony. "Losing my brother, pulling that trigger… it changed me, Margaret. Life is fleeting. Precious but fleeting. We shouldn't waste it, my darling."

He continued tracing circles on her thigh.

She squirmed. "You missed Cora's first birthday. I suppose a celebration that includes you this time would make for a pleasant distraction."

He nodded, removing his hand. All in good time, he supposed. "That's a wonderful idea. I'll ask Mrs. Albany to prepare a cake for tomorrow night."

Though losing his brother and closest friend would dampen the celebration in his spirit, it was time to move forward with life and his blessing of a family.

CHAPTER NINETEEN

ANDREA

Manhattan, Present Day

*T*here was no better place to work than a library. The quiet movement of patrons, the low *thunk* of books being stacked and shelved,
worlds of knowledge and possibilities that waited inside each one for
someone to open and explore. The archives department and the micro-
film machine were as familiar to her as her smartphone.

The genealogy department was her favorite, as it was never as congested with patrons as the other areas. She'd come today not only to
find more information on the New York City Board of Water Supply,
but to discover the identities of Franklin Davidson and the elusive
E. Davidson. She had no clue how old Franklin was when he became
a member of the Players, so searching for a genealogy record would
be difficult. Quick mental math gave her an estimate of where to begin,
as odds were lower that he was an old man enjoying the club's benefits.
She started with the census of 1840. She clicked on the census record
and typed in what little information she knew.

A tree with continuously falling leaves appeared in the middle of the
screen while the program scanned vital records from across the United
States in an attempt to find matches with Franklin's name. If the man
wasn't one of Beau's ancestors, then he could have emigrated from anywhere, making the search impossible. The thought struck her that she
might not find what she needed at all, wasting her entire afternoon. She
rolled her neck from side to side to stretch her knotted muscles.

Phone silenced, the screen lit with a text.

Beau.

They hadn't seen each other in five days because of his rigorous schedule. Watching him on television giving his campaign speech made her heart long for him even more. It also sprouted a tumbleweed of fear and doubt in her stomach that had been blowing around ever since.

He was an eloquent speaker. Grace, coupled perfectly with athleticism, made him unstoppable, and oh so desirable. Beau could easily win this election and move on to become president someday.

Andrea was not first lady material. She was the Erin Brockovich of historical writing, not Barbara Bush. And yet she was powerless to stop her growing feelings for him.

She opened the text.

DINNER PLANS?

Disappointment cut deep as she replied.

WAITING TABLES. TOMORROW?

Dots danced in his reply bubble, letting her know he was typing. Serving was the last thing she wanted to do after his invitation.

CAN'T. FULL DAY. BREAKFAST SATURDAY?

Vital records popped up in rows on her computer screen. She typed, IT'S A DATE.

YOUR APARTMENT? I'LL BRING THE FOOD.

PERFECT.

MEATS OR SWEETS?

A LIGHT MIX OF BOTH. I'LL PROVIDE COFFEE, JUICE, AND MILK.

Several seconds passed without a reply, so she set her phone aside and skimmed through the vital records. There were several matches in every state. A popular era for the name Franklin. This might take days. She'd start with New York and branch out from there.

Two hours passed before Andrea stumbled across a record that stood out. Augustus and Eugenia Davidson from SoHo, New York—then known as lower Manhattan since it was south of Houston Street—had two sons at the time the census was taken. Franklin and Edward. Unfortunately, it didn't provide the ages of the children or the background of the family. However, this might solve the mystery of what name the *E* was short for on the hotel registry list.

Next, she searched for birth records for Franklin and Edward using Augustus' and Eugenia's names as parents. Almost immediately, she found Franklin's birth record. Edward appeared to be nonexistent. Perhaps he was stillborn, so they didn't record his birth? But if that was the case, he wouldn't be listed on the census as a household member.

She rubbed her forehead and yawned. No birth record meant she was at a dead end with her mysterious E being short for Edward. It would take decades to search through every E name that had ever existed.

The man sitting to her right held a finger to his lips. She realized she was clicking her pen against the table. She mouthed an apology. Staring at the ornate ceiling of the library wouldn't provide her answers, but it helped her think. She recalled each piece of her discovery from memory. The denomination of the bills didn't appear to hold significance. But the address of the Players did. What if the E stood for Edwin?

She jotted the thought in her notebook. What if Franklin Davidson and Edwin Booth were working together to create and distribute counterfeit money using her apartment as a hideout, and joined their names on the registry as an alias?

Convoluted but not impossible.

To be sure there wasn't an actual Edwin Davidson, she ran a search but found nothing. Still. . .16 Gramercy Park South and the Players were linked, she knew it. She just had to find out how.

⁂

Beau
Manhattan, Present Day

Beau arrived at Andi's on Saturday morning carrying boxes of pastries, fruit, sausage and bacon, and hard-boiled eggs. When she opened the door, the aroma of strong coffee awakened his senses. Then his sight zeroed in on her in fitted jeans, which jolted him even more. Her gray T-shirt had an image of a typewriter that said I'VE GOT THE WRITE STUFF. Boy, did she, with that sexy knot of hair on top of her head and a few tendrils grazing the side of her face, drawing attention to those amazing eyes.

He wanted to forget breakfast and spend the morning kissing them awake, but he'd bide his time. Patience was getting harder to maintain with each passing day.

She motioned him inside. "Whatever you brought smells so good."

He leaned in to kiss her cheek, catching notes of something fresh and pure that reminded him of a mountain stream. "You smell so good."

"You're just trying to coax me into agreeing to hang on your arm at the Met Gala."

Beau helped himself to the kitchen. "Not true, but I would love to have you on my arm all night. Have you decided?"

She watched him unload the boxes onto her small countertop. "That's a highly publicized event. What message will our being together send?"

Vulnerability radiated off her like sunrays. He abandoned the bags and reached for her soft hands. "What is it that makes you hesitant about us?" He touched her cheek. It was even softer than her hands. "I'm not gonna hurt you, Andi."

She swallowed, working her throat against that thin strip of leather she wore as a necklace, doing crazy things to his body. "The first time— and last time—I gave my heart fully to a man, he broke my heart. It took a long time to find *me* again, and I don't want to give that up."

"You should never have to. A relationship should be a blending of two people who bring the best of themselves to each other, not lose themselves for each other."

"Simply said, but not always simply done."

"Can I coax the story out of you over an eclair?"

"I try to avoid the telling." She pulled away, reached for the coffee-pot, and poured two mugs full. Seconds passed as she stared into the liquid. "Allen was head over cybersecurity at the Pentagon. I was fresh out of college, naive, and very stupid. He was ten years older and saw me coming like a bright light in a dark tunnel."

Beau lifted the lids on the boxes, attempting to remain casual but already wanting to find this Allen and work him over with his fists.

She pressed a palm to her stomach. "We dated for several months. Things were starting to get serious. Long story short, he was married."

Words stuck in his throat and rubbed like sandpaper.

"I didn't know, of course. Never even suspected." Her voice wavered. "Once I discovered it, I was physically sick for days. Couldn't eat. Couldn't sleep. Knowing that I'd infiltrated someone's marriage, even accidentally…"

"I understand. I'm sorry he put you through that." Beau wasn't a vengeful man, but in this case he'd like the opportunity to make an exception.

"Me too." She sipped her coffee then stared into it as if memories played at the bottom of the cup. "That's what men in powerful positions do. They bend the rules, mold others to fit their needs. They live it up and enjoy the fruits of other people's labor. Have their cake and eat it too."

"We're not all that way," he said quietly.

"My brain knows that, but convincing my heart is another matter."

He pulled her close and tucked her head beneath his chin, hating the weight of betrayal she carried. "I promise I'm not married. I've never even been close to it."

She barked a laugh. "That's good."

He rubbed circles on her back. "I won't rush you into anything. I just ask that you please let me prove to you I'm an honest man. I don't have demons chasing me or secrets lurking in my closet."

"I'll try to trust."

Her breathy words had him lifting her face to his. He had never felt so strongly about a woman so quickly before. The reactions his body and heart had for her were, at times, overwhelming. He lowered his head to hers.

"Bacon."

He paused. "Huh?"

She cleared her throat. "Did you bring bacon?"

He stood to full height and moved toward the boxes, knowing a rejection when he got one. "I did. Nothing better than bacon for breakfast."

Except kissing.

They filled their plates and carried them to the tiny table for two sitting against her lone kitchen window overlooking the courtyard. He'd talked to his dad about not including this complex with the sale on Fifth Avenue but was told if he couldn't provide a better offer for the apartments, then negotiations would proceed.

Beau had always been more humanitarian than businessman, and real estate had never been his passion, much to his dad's disapproval. In different circumstances, he'd not get involved in his dad's business dealings. But if Andi was losing her home, it became personal enough to fight for.

"Are you angry with your eclair?"

"What do you mean?" He took a bite.

"You're scowling at it. What's on your mind?"

If he confessed she filled every space in his mind, he'd scare her off, so he offered a diversion. "I spoke with my dad about the sale. He's willing to reconsider if I can offer something better. I'm looking into other available properties that would best fit their agenda."

Her palm rubbed against her sternum. "Thank you. I know that's a lot of extra work you don't need right now. Just know that I won't hold you responsible if the deal goes through. Some blessings in life have expiration dates. This may be one of mine."

"I'll do everything I can to make sure it's not. How's your research going?"

The overcast sky danced shadows across her face through the window as she updated him on her findings with the census and her theory that Edwin Booth and Franklin Davidson worked together.

He licked remnants of the eclair's cream from his finger. "My family has deep roots in New York, going as far back as the Revolution. I inquired about our ancestry and discovered that Franklin Davidson is my great-great-grandfather. His daughter, Cora, my great-grandmother, married a copper mining magnate from Michigan and carried on the Davidson name, as she was Franklin's only heir."

Andrea's bacon thumped against her plate. "You think your great-great-grandfather is the same guy I'm looking for?"

"I do. Our ties to Gramercy Park go way back. Great-grandma Cora inherited our home upon Franklin's death."

"Is there any record of an Edward or any name that started with an *E* in your family?" Coffee dribbled down her chin, and she swiped it with a napkin.

"No luck. Sorry."

"What do you think of my theory about Edwin Booth and Franklin Davidson joining their names as an alias?"

"I think it's crazy." He winked. "Our family record says that Franklin was a Secret Service agent, honored for his integrity and years of service. Those were the days before they protected the president. Their job comprised tracking down counterfeiting rings and securing the false money. I'd say it's more likely that the *E* is really an *F* smudged with age and he was using his hotel room to secure the bills he found while undercover."

Her eyes glittered with the excitement of possibilities. "But why hide the bills in the wall? And even if that was necessary, why not take them out once he'd solved the case?"

"Maybe he wasn't able to." He picked the leaves off a strawberry. "Or maybe he forgot he'd put them in there."

She fiddled with her necklace.

He could sit and watch her all day. "I'm going to be out of town for a few days next week, but I promise to help you find out more when I get back."

"I'll go."

"With me to Boston?" The idea had merit.

"No. To the Met."

"Best news I've heard all week."

He would never grow tired of seeing her smile.

This silly mystery consumed too much of his time, but it gave him an excuse to be near her. If that was all the reward they received for their efforts, it would be worth the trouble to him.

CHAPTER TWENTY

EDWARD

Washington, D.C., Christmas 1867

$\mathcal{E}$dward rubbed his palms together as Margaret opened the little box, unsure of his gift.

"Oh." The word came on a sigh. "Franklin, I…"

Her chin wobbled. Then her face lit in the first genuine smile he'd seen since her pregnancy. The same day he'd observed her and Franklin from across the street.

The dark cloud that hovered over her every waking minute had slowly begun lifting. Now it was as if the sun burst through. He'd been waiting for this day.

"They're beautiful." She ran her finger over the ruby earbobs with reverence. "I've never owned anything so fine."

"They aren't the finest, but you'll improve them." Edward leaned back against the chair, relishing the heat from the fireplace and the sight of his family surrounded by gifts. He'd longed for Christmases like this after Mama died, but his father had been too busy wallowing in his own grief and thinking of ways to blame Edward for his loneliness. The brothers would make gifts for one another and exchange them quietly in their room. Then they'd spend the evening trying to divert their father's rage away from Edward.

If Franklin had never infiltrated Edward's counterfeiting ring, where would Edward be this morning? Robbing folks of their newly opened gifts? Seeking pleasure in an opium den? Printing more counterfeit?

Margaret held up an earbob and watched it sway. The red gem

sparkled in the light. "How on earth did you ever afford these?"

She had a beautiful smile. He only wished she'd share it more often.

"My position affords us many luxuries, darling. Something good has to come from all my time away."

"But enough for these? This cut is the caliber of earbobs Queen Victoria would wear." She clasped the earbob in her closed palm and lowered it to her lap. "You should have spent the money on yourself. Purchased that amber-crested cane you've been eyeing in the haberdashery window. You work so hard."

"I'll purchase the cane someday. When it's needed."

She placed her hand on his knee. "Your leg has been bothering you of late. I can tell. The cane might relieve some pain."

"I'm fine." He didn't intend for his words to sound harsh, but it was Christmas, and his shortcomings were the last thing he wanted to dwell on today. He smiled to soften the blow. "Let me see how those look on you."

Cora balanced on her feet and tottered toward him, stopping to bend and grab a bow Edward had discarded at his feet. She dropped onto her bottom and crammed the bow into her mouth. He extracted the slobbery fabric while Margaret put on the earbobs. When Cora began to cry, he balanced her on his knee and bounced. She jabbered and laughed.

"How do I look?" Margaret turned her head from side to side. Ringlets of hair framed her face where they'd fallen from her coif. The earbobs swayed and glittered with the movement, fascinating him.

"Now the jewelry looks complete."

The color in her cheeks darkened. The brisk walks outdoors he'd insisted be a part of her daily regimen had cured her pallid skin. He'd demanded he be allowed to work in the Secret Service office for a while to help Margaret make a full recovery. Her youthfulness was evident once again.

Without thinking, he leaned over and captured her lips with his.

She stiffened and pulled away.

"We're husband and wife, Margaret."

"Yes." She fiddled with her hair, her dress. Her gaze landing everywhere but on him.

Since his arrival from the Pittsburgh raid in August, he'd kept his lips confined to her forehead and cheeks only and slept in the spare bedroom, giving her time to feel comfortable. Most days he was a man on fire, burning like the logs in the hearth. His patience was waning.

His fingertips ran a slow trail up her neck and stopped to cradle the earbob. Her eyes slipped closed. She shivered. "Franklin, Mrs. Albany is in the kitchen, and Miss Moreau could join us any moment."

"And neither should think poorly of a man who desires his wife."

The color in her cheeks darkened even more. She eyed the doorway, lowering her voice. "You've never spoken so boldly before. What's overcome you of late?"

If he had to explain the ways of a man, then his brother had done a poor job of educating her to the benefits of marriage from the start. Something he'd remedy as soon as she'd allow him.

"Da-da." Cora clapped her hands.

Edward stilled then looked at the girl.

Cora gave him a toothy grin, drool running down her chin. Her chubby hands clapped. "Da-da."

His heart went from smoldering to mush. He faced the fire so it wouldn't reveal the tears clouding his vision.

Margaret stood, taking advantage of his distraction. "I'm going to check with Mrs. Albany about dinner. Thank you for the earbobs."

She bent and kissed his cheek. Her new dark red dress swished against the floor, moving in ways that set him to broiling again.

The meal of roasted pheasant with chestnut stuffing, parsnips, carrots, and figgy pudding was the best he'd had in years. He raised his glass of mulled wine and toasted to their successes. Mrs. Albany had gone home to her husband after dinner had been served. Miss Moreau was free to retire after she cleared the dishes, so Edward challenged Margaret to a game of chess.

She might have made a fantastic nurse during the war, but she was a disgrace at chess. He tried to help her throughout the game, but she never seemed to grasp the concept. Not that it mattered. His position across the board allowed him to study her, talk to her, flirt with her.

When Cora grew tired of playing with her new toys on the floor beside them, she curled up in a ball and fell asleep. "I should get her into bed," Margaret said.

"Our game isn't over."

"I'm a dreadful opponent." She giggled. "I'm boring myself."

"Then I'll help you tuck her in."

He bent and scooped Cora into his arms while Margaret collected the lamp. Treading carefully, he followed Margaret up the stairs to the nursery. He tucked Cora into her plush cradle and covered her with a tiny quilt. His knuckle grazed her velvety cheek.

"You're good with her," Margaret whispered. "You connect with her in a way that I cannot."

Unfortunately, some parental instincts didn't come naturally. His were blossoming, despite Cora not being his biological child.

"You'll learn with time. Dr. Fullerton says some women's bodies and minds change after delivery. But your light is growing brighter."

She looked down at her feet. "I'm trying. I want to."

Clasping her hand, he led her from the room, taking the lamp with them. The bed he'd been using in the spare room was too cold to inhabit tonight. At Margaret's closed door, he set the lamp on the hallway table and cradled her cheeks. The reflection of the flame glinted off her ear-bobs. "Merry Christmas, darling."

"Merry Christmas. I hope you enjoyed your gifts as much as I did mine."

"I did very much." He pressed closer. "There's one thing I'd hoped to receive, though, and have not gotten."

Her breathing became shallow, her eyes pools of desire. "That is?"

"You, my dear." He ran his fingertips down her bodice.

Her eyes fluttered closed. "Franklin, I…"

He leaned his mouth to her ear. "You have no idea how many hours in the day I spend imagining what you look like beneath all those layers of fabric."

Her mouth fell open. "You already know."

"It's been long enough, I can't remember." He watched the war between want and fear rage in the depth of her eyes.

"I've felt only sadness for so long. I'm not sure how to feel anything else."

"That could end tonight." He kissed her deep and slow. At first her movements were stilted, but then she melted beneath his roving palms.

A door at the end of the hallway squealed. Edward opened his eyes, continuing his ministrations. Miss Moreau stepped from her room. Consumed by his actions, Margaret didn't notice the nanny stirring behind them. Without breaking stride, he gazed at Miss Moreau, who startled upon seeing them. She spun and retreated to her room.

He pulled away and allowed Margaret to catch her breath before diving in for more. She pushed at his chest. A glaze of intoxication covered her eyes. It had little to do with the wine. "You've never kissed me like this before."

He ran his thumb over the buttons at her neckline. "There's a great many things I haven't done but plan to remedy with your permission."

The delicate skin where her jaw met her neck tasted like oranges.

"Will you stay with me tonight?" Her hands gripped his upper arms as if she'd fall over without their support.

Wasting no time, he blew out the lamp. Pressing her as close against him as her huge dress would allow, he kissed her again and groped for the doorknob behind her bustle. The door gave way faster than he intended, and they stumbled into the bedroom. He lurched forward to keep his balance and prevent them from falling. Pain shot through his ankle. The squeak of metal sounded beneath his pant leg.

She pulled her face away. "What was that?"

He kicked the door closed. "I believe Miss Moreau is awake."

"You don't think she saw us, do you?"

"No." Before she could give the situation any more thought, he let his hands distract her from any suspicion as to who he really was.

CHAPTER TWENTY-ONE

ANDREA

Manhattan, Present Day

The evening was as close to a fairy tale as Andrea would ever get. Designers had transformed the ceiling of the Met into an astrologer's paradise of twinkling lights covered by a layer of black organdy. Artwork and sculptures of renown hung from easels and wall pedestals, showcasing *The Beauty of Night*.

It *was* a beautiful night.

Euphoria settled deeper into her bones with every touch and caress Beau offered. Whether they were sitting, dancing, or chatting, he was always holding her hand or guiding her by the small of her back. Nothing sleazy or possessive, but protective. Declarative. As if he was afraid she'd disappear into the crowd and he might never find her again.

While dawn would soon sweep the magic into a distant memory, for now she'd sit in the foreground and soak in every detail of Beau working the room. Confidence radiated from him, coupled with the fine layer of arrogance that came from having money and power. His was a controlled power, and his authenticity overshadowed the arrogance enough to make him irresistible. It was clear he understood humanity and desired to do his part to improve it. Everyone seemed to love him.

Seeing Beau in his element only solidified how inept she was in his world.

"Oh no. Not you too." Maribel Quincy, the cousin Beau had introduced Andrea to earlier, poised on a chair beside her. Her royal-blue gown shimmered, a perfect complement to her olive skin. "I've yet to meet one of Beau's dates who didn't look at him as if he were some mythical god in the flesh. I'd hoped you were different."

"And here I thought I was playing it cool." Andrea leaned an elbow on the linen-covered table. The gown she'd rented was lovely but homespun compared to the mega designers worn tonight.

"Don't scold yourself too harshly. It's a natural reaction experienced by every female on the planet and, unfortunately, there's no cure. His brilliance is sickening."

"He is brilliant, isn't he?"

"And very much smitten with you. Congratulations. You're the envy of every woman in this room, single or otherwise."

The *otherwise* swept Allen through her memory, which soured the moment.

"Too bad the powers that be injected all the charisma into his DNA instead of dispersing it evenly throughout the family." Maribel sipped champagne from a glass flute. Sapphire and diamond earrings swayed from her earlobes. "Or maybe it stems from the Davidson blood. My grandmother always told me the Davidsons were a force to be reckoned with."

"I take it you and Beau don't share a grandmother?"

"We're second cousins twice removed or something like that. It's complicated. Something our family excels at."

"I think it's safe to say most families excel at complicated."

"True. But our issues are infinite and costly." Maribel threw her head back and downed the last of her champagne. Her throat worked against a bejeweled necklace so expensive it could feed a third-world country. "Tell me, where did you two meet?"

Andrea gave her the short version of their first introduction.

"Hitting on his waitress? I've never known Beau to do something so elementary. Now, what's this I hear about a mystery you two are trying to solve?"

Andrea didn't appreciate being cataloged as elementary, but Beau had warned her that Maribel was harmless despite her heiress dramatics. Unsure how far his cousin could be trusted, Andrea's first inclination to be vague was overpowered by the thought that Maribel might be able to shed light on their family history that Beau could not. Besides, it wasn't like she'd found much of consequence anyway, so Andrea told the story.

"Now I've hit a dead end." A yawn threatened to break free. Andrea hadn't stayed up this late in years. The crowd was thinning, and she hoped Beau would be ready to leave soon. "I found a census record listing both Franklin and Edward as brothers, but there's no birth or death record for Edward."

Maribel frowned, the lines on her forehead the only flaw on her otherwise perfect body. "That is strange. I've never heard mention of an Edward. Franklin's daughter, Cora, married a man named Matthew. He was my great-granny's brother, but their relationship circles us back to complicated. I don't know exactly what happened, but whenever she would speak of Franklin, she'd always mention the two faces of January. She also had dementia and passed away when I was six, so my recollection might be a little skewed. That phrase always made me picture two faces appearing in a pile of snow. It kind of freaked me out."

"Understandably."

"One time, she—"

A hand outstretched in front of Maribel's face, cutting off her words. "Maribel, would you do me the honor of giving me the last dance?"

Wilson Kennedy, Beau's campaign manager, helped Maribel to her feet before she could answer. The woman swayed, but Wilson held her steady. That obviously hadn't been her first champagne of the night. His stiff smile turned to disapproval as his gaze swept over Andrea.

It wasn't her fault Maribel was tipsy.

The strains to "The Way You Look Tonight" played as couples joined on the dance floor. Where was Beau? She rolled her ankles to encourage circulation back into her aching feet. She felt as if she'd walked two miles around the room as he introduced her to everyone he knew.

"Would the lady like the last dance, or would she like to beat the crowd home?" Beau's low voice rumbled against her ear. Heat pooled in her belly.

She opened her mouth to speak, but a yawn escaped instead.

Beau laughed. "Home it is."

The warmth in her middle spread to the rest of her limbs as the idea of what a home together might look like. As much as she'd love to feel his arms around her once more, she took his offered hand and woolgathered all the way out the door.

Traffic was thick for the late hour. Onlookers and paparazzi clogged

Fifth Avenue. Hadn't they gotten enough pictures when the guests had arrived? Jonas was waiting with the car, and it wasn't long before they were pulling up to her apartment. Beau leaned forward and placed his hand on the back of Jonas' seat. "I'm going to walk Andrea to her door. I'll try not to take long."

As he spoke, Beau's other hand skimmed the sensitive skin on her wrist, sending ripples of desire through her limbs.

Jonas glanced in the rearview mirror. "Take all the time you need, sir."

Though his words were kind and professional, the weariness that frayed the edges spoke of his longing to be asleep as soon as possible.

Beau left the car first then assisted her out. Fatigue laced with euphoria and a ballgown made a gal unsteady on thin heels. His hand grazed the bare skin on her back and came to rest in the curve of her hip. She wasn't ready for the magic of the night to end, and it seemed as if he felt the same.

He punched in the code to the main door and waited for the unlocking mechanism to click. The smell of Chinese food wafted from Mr. Yevitz's door. He always ordered Chinese on Saturday nights.

She lifted the length of her gown to maneuver the stairs while Beau held her elbow. "I enjoyed watching you in your element tonight. You were sensational."

"You look sensational. Every man there had his eyes on you."

"Ha! I doubt that." She remembered what time it was and pressed her lips together.

Should she invite him inside? She didn't want the night to end, but she also didn't want to give him the wrong idea. How silly. They were both adults. And she knew how to set boundaries. Plus, she wanted to share what Maribel had told her.

"I don't doubt it at all," Beau whispered.

The fabric of Andrea's dress swooshed against her legs as she released it to unlock her door. She opened it and gestured him inside so their conversation wouldn't wake her neighbors. "They were only curious who I was."

"Mine. I hope." The hushed tone of those two small words made her body hum like a plucked guitar string. He gravitated toward the vibration.

The door closed.

If only it were that simple. While she'd loved seeing him in action tonight, it only solidified how inept she was in his world.

But he'd made it so easy, hadn't he? Leading her along, making introductions, filling the awkward exchanges when her anxiety made her fumble for words. He'd detected when she'd needed breathing room and whisked them to a more private area of the building, never mentioning her inadequacy. After a respectable amount of time, he eased them back into the spotlight.

Could being a part of his world be something she could learn?

"What are you thinking?" He brushed his thumb along her cheek.

Her eyelids fluttered at the contact. "That once you kiss me, the entire world is going to change, and I'll no longer know how to navigate it."

"That's what GPS is for."

"I'm serious. I—"

He touched her forehead with his. "I'll not pressure you. We can either play it safe by keeping things the same, or we can chase our dreams together. The decision is yours."

She'd already lost her heart, so keeping things the same wasn't really the safer option. She tossed her purse on the couch next to Sammy's tank then circled her arms around his neck. "I don't want to wake up on some distant morning and wonder what I threw away any more than I want a broken heart."

Tingles shot up her spine with every movement his fingers traced in the hollow of her back. "Does this mean I can kiss you?"

"That would be a yes," she whispered.

His lips brushed over hers. Soft. Reverent. Cautious.

He was all energy and serenity and light.

Her fingers curled into the hair at his nape. Her other hand tugged him closer by his tie. He angled his head and dove deeper, sending her into a delightful numbness. Now he was electricity and heat, and she was an absolute goner.

Beau
Manhattan, Present Day

Beau sat at his dining room table and stared in blissful shock at the picture accompanying the news headline. Davidson-Quincy Stuns

THE MET WITH DATE. A picture of him with his arm around Andi on the velvet carpet, gazing lovingly at one another, made his chest swell with pride. The image was so perfect he wanted to hunt down the photographer and obtain the original. Maybe he would. The gleam in her eyes and the flush in her cheeks made him believe she was falling in love with him. He hoped it was true. Not only because a married politician brought a sense of stability to any campaign, but because he was already falling in love with her.

She was the first woman he'd ever had to win over with something besides his family name or bank account. She was making him prove his worth as a man, and Beau was ready for the challenge. Their kiss the night before banished any lingering doubts.

Wilson walked up beside him and scowled at Beau's tablet. "I don't like her. She asks too many questions."

"So you'd like her if she only asked a minimal number of questions? That statement is ridiculous." Beau scooted from his chair, forcing Wilson to take a step back. "Besides, it doesn't matter if you like her. I do."

"Clearly, if one comment has you ready to pull out your sword and take off my head. I'm simply concerned. I caught her asking several invasive questions regarding your family history. I'm afraid she's dating you more for a story that will advance her career rather than genuine feelings. I've seen it before."

If her kiss last night was any proof of her authenticity, her feelings for him were strong and very real. Beau pointed to the tablet on the table. "If that were true, she wouldn't be looking at me like that."

His campaign flyers the printer had delivered that morning still needed his approval. He made his way to the boxes stacked on a side table. "Before we started this campaign, you investigated every family member past and present and found nothing that could smear my name."

Beau opened the box and pulled out a card-stock flyer the size of a manilla envelope. After approving the front, he inspected the back. He wished they'd used his other headshot instead. "I haven't kept anything from you regarding this little mystery of hers, and you found nothing damaging in her background either, so there's no reason to treat her like a criminal."

Beau took a calming breath. "Did you set up a luncheon with the surgeon general?"

"Monday at noon."

Beau studied the flyer again. "I approve."

He tossed it back in the box.

Wilson notated something in his book. "Did you get the list of contributors?"

Beau checked his paperwork. "I must've left it in my dad's office."

He jogged down the hallway, hearing his mom's gentle scolding when he was a young boy running through the house. Then there was the time she'd handed him a pair of dress socks and they'd pretended to ice-skate on the freshly polished hardwood floors.

After that, she'd gotten sick.

He shook off the bittersweet memory and pushed open the office door. The space still smelled like his dad's aftershave and Cuban cigars. He'd presented his alternative idea for preserving the Winderfield last night, and Dad had seemed intrigued. If Beau couldn't work it out to save Andi's home, he'd help her find another she liked equally well, even if he had to pull a few strings to make it affordable.

The desk was empty except for a laptop and a small stack of books. Where was that list?

Beau rounded the desk and looked in the drawers beneath the books. He hoped it hadn't gotten rolled up in the city map his dad had spread across the desk when Beau had interrupted the night before.

He fingered through the items in the drawers, coming across the section of his family history. It had been so many years since Beau had looked at any of the stuff, he'd forgotten there was a section of their study that documented their genealogy. Could he find something here that would help Andi?

There were books and ledgers and photo albums. When his hand grazed a small wooden box, he opened it to see what was inside. A military medal lay on a velvet cushion. A dingy fabric ribbon of Stars and Stripes secured by an eagle sitting on crossed cannons, gripping a large star in its claws. A woman who resembled Lady Liberty was engraved in the middle of the star, shielding off the enemy. The inner lid of the box held a handwritten notation that had faded with age.

Franklin Davidson, Fifth New York Infantry

Battle of Chickamauga

Under heavy fire, voluntarily carried information to a battery commander that enabled him to save guns from capture. Was severely wounded but saved two of his comrades.

His great-great-grandfather had been a Civil War hero.

"Oh good. You found it. I meant to show that to you last night. Looking for this?" Dad entered the office wearing a gray suit and navy tie. He held up the paper Beau had been searching for.

"Yes. Where'd you get this medal?" Beau set the box on the desk.

"When your girlfriend started poking around the family history, I had Malcolm retrieve some items stored in the attic. This confirms our family's stellar reputation. We were never counterfeiters. Now you can set her mind at ease. And Wilson's."

"Andi has never accused our family of counterfeiting."

"Pet names? You two must be serious."

"It's her pen name. I like using it. Less formal." Beau reached for the list his dad held out. "How did you hear about her discovery, anyway?"

"Wilson has expressed his concern. Multiple times." Dad lifted the books off his desk and slipped them into his briefcase. "There is no record of an Edward Davidson. I've checked twice. Franklin Davidson dedicated his life to combating counterfeiters. Perhaps she can attribute her criminal accusations at another Davidson family."

"She isn't accusing anyone of anything. Wilson is entirely too paranoid."

"I can hear you." Wilson's voice filtered from the other room.

Dad's mouth turned down at the corners. "We're paying him for his expertise and thoroughness. Too many times I've seen a politician's secrets emerge to ruin his career."

"Meet her, and you'll see she's not in this to ruin me."

Dad studied him from across the desk. "You're serious about this one." A statement not a question. "Very."

"My sources tell me she lives in the Winderfield. No doubt that's what's driving your passion to save it."

"No doubt."

Dad rounded the desk and put his hand on Beau's shoulder. "Son, I want you to find a good woman like your mother and live a long and happy life together. In fact, I encourage you to do so. Just be careful. Make sure her motive for you lies deeper than what she can gain from such a match."

His dad's warning rattled in his ears all the way back to the dining room. Beau shook it off. Andi had already proven her motive. After all, he was the one who'd begged her for a date. Besides, nothing they unearthed in this silly mystery would damage his image.

CHAPTER TWENTY-TWO

Washington, D.C., May 1868

*O*f all the vices a man could have, women were the hardest to manage. Edward squirmed as Margaret tightened his tie and adjusted his collar. He wasn't sure what all the fuss was about. It was a simple dinner at home, not a night at the opera. Smiling was her daily habit now, the warmest of her responses given when he returned home from a case. She'd grown a little heavier the past few months, the change more flattering than not.

"Will you wear it tonight?" Her palms slid down the lapels of his coat, her purring voice attempting to coax him into fulfilling her wishes.

"Wear what?"

Her cloying simper smoothed his irritation.

She went to the bureau and withdrew a box. As her steps neared, she opened the lid. "Your Congressional Medal of Honor."

A medallion of an eagle sitting atop crossed cannons, a large star in its claws, hung from a ribbon of Stars and Stripes. Reward for Franklin's services at Chickamauga. More than one comrade within the Secret Service had asked Edward to regale the tale. He always waved them off. He hoped Margaret didn't want him to recall any details, because he didn't have any.

"I'm not wearing that to the dinner table." The medal honoring his brother's goodness and bravery was a jab to his jugular.

"We're not dining out?" The hope in her expression fell. "But I didn't have Mrs. Albany prepare dinner."

"Why ever not?" He took a step back, his irritation jumping to the forefront.

He didn't have time for dramatics, and he hated anything that proved he was ignorant of details regarding Franklin's life. Dinner needed to be served so he could make his meeting on Dixon Street by ten. If he was going to continue to afford all the things he wanted to provide for his wife and daughter, he needed to be there tonight.

Sadness overtook Margaret's countenance. He cursed himself for putting it there after all the progress she'd made.

"Answer me, Margaret."

He adjusted his new gold cuff links, losing patience.

She fiddled with her gloves. "Today is our anniversary. Did you honestly forget?"

He bit back a curse. How could he have forgotten? It was the first thing he'd sought the answer to after moving in.

"My darling." He held out his arms. "I'm terribly sorry."

When she didn't step into them, he went to her. "I've been busy lately. Too busy. Of course I remember the day we wed. Vividly. I'm sorry I failed to realize the anniversary of that day was today."

Edward rubbed a path along her stiff back while she laid her head on his chest. She was such a small thing. Frail. Much like Cora but in a different way. How he wished he knew how she'd met Franklin. Courted. Spent their wedding night. Judging by the enthusiastic way she responded to Edward now, he guessed that evening to be formal in nature. Just like his brother.

Edward loved Margaret. How could a husband not? Especially when she'd birthed sweet Cora, with her toothy smile, sparkling blue eyes, and a laugh that would buoy the saddest of hearts.

"I don't understand," Margaret said against him.

"Hmm?" He traced the embroidery at the waistline of her new dress.

She leaned away enough that he could see the red rims around her eyes. "You've been different ever since Pittsburgh. In some ways, it's glorious." Her cheeks turned rosy. "But in others, it scares me."

He kept his body relaxed, mouth placid. "It saddens me to think I've scared you, my dear, but I'm delighted to put that stain into your cheeks."

"Franklin, be serious. You've forgotten our anniversary. You didn't recognize Angelica when she came calling, and John was your partner for two years! And yesterday you wouldn't eat the sweet potato pie. That's always been your favorite."

"I admit to being an imbecile regarding our anniversary. I'm a man. Sometimes I make mistakes. That's all I can say. As for Angelica, between the gray stripe in her hair and her widow's weeds, she looked entirely different."

He eyed the clock on the wall. Murder wasn't something he was fond of, and it had been hard to converse with the woman and chat about old times when he'd watched her husband die a slow and miserable death. It had been almost as hard as watching Franklin. Tank—John—had become his closest confidant, only to betray him. He'd left John's body to rot in that shack until the authorities discovered it. His brother…bile rose in Edward's throat when the icy stare of death materialized in his memory. He'd wanted to give his brother a proper burial next to their mother, but the river became Franklin's resting place.

Guilt was another thing he wasn't fond of. He shoved it away.

Margaret waited for further explanation.

"As for the sweet potato pie, I haven't been able to eat it since that night in Ohio when a stomach ailment made me wish I hadn't gorged myself on the boardinghouse cook's famous recipe."

He tickled her ribs then picked up the small bottle of tonic the doctor prescribed and handed it to her.

She frowned at it and sighed but uncorked the neck and took a sip.

He slipped the closed bottle into his pocket and drew her back to him, holding as tight as he could without crushing her. "Put away your fears. All your concerns have reasonable explanations. Including my hunger for you."

She buried her face even deeper into his chest, embarrassed by his boldness, but he could feel her smile against his chest. Then her fingers tightened on the fabric. "Do you suppose this means I'm turning insane?"

"What?" He gripped her upper arms and held her away. When she wouldn't look at him, he guided her chin up, forcing her to look at him. "Why would you say such a thing?"

She sighed. "When Dr. Fullerton comes to check on me, he often asks if I hear voices that aren't really there or if I fear things being different from what they really are. He says more ailments of the mind are being discovered every day, especially in females, and to let him know immediately if my melancholy turns into something more sinister."

The doctor had said as much to him also, and Edward had wanted to throw the man out by his neck. There was nothing wrong with Margaret besides some wallowing in sadness, but he'd found the patience to help pull her from it.

"You are not insane. You are my wife. You are beautiful, and your mind is healthy. I don't deserve you."

He meant it.

A little sob escaped, but she cut it off with a wobbly smile. She threw her arms around him and squeezed. He patted her shoulder. They'd never have time to dine at the hotel and make it home before he had to leave. He'd send word to Monroe that the mission had been compromised and they'd have to meet another night. Reconstructing this evening was more important. Because if she discovered he was really Edward, he'd lose everything.

"Franklin," she whispered.

"Yes, darling?"

She pressed her cheek against his. "Let's stay in tonight."

Her lips met his and grew bolder by the second. He doused the lamps, bringing the room to total darkness. Her request had just solved both their problems.

CHAPTER TWENTY-THREE

ANDREA

Manhattan, Present Day

*A*ndrea had fifteen minutes to change out of her uniform and meet
Beau. Thousands of people attended the Broadway Flea Market and Auction this weekend, packing Gant & Company for Saturday brunch. She'd promised to meet him at the end of her shift so they could attend together. The event was a great opportunity for him to mingle with the public, and she was after a rare antique to add to her eclectic collection. What, she wasn't sure, but she'd know it when she saw it.

"Your blouse on fire?" Caylee exited the stall next to the one Andrea was entering.

"I'm meeting Beau." The door slammed shut. Andrea winced. Her fingers made quick work of the remaining buttons on her shirt.

Water flowed from the sink tap. "I can see the headlines now—'From Server to First Lady.'"

"You're so dramatic." Andrea shoved her blouse into her bag and slipped on her sweater.

"Speaking of dramatic. . .yours truly has a second audition for *Paradise Square*, a smashing Civil War tale depicting the horrors and hope of the lower Manhattan Irish slums."

"Civil War? That's a lot of history for someone who claims to hate it." Andrea pulled on her jeans.

"This is different. This is history come alive on the stage to entertain and enlighten. To captivate, to—"

Andrea opened the stall door, one hand on her bag, the other on her hip.

"Okay, it's really just a chance for me to prove my talent, but I'm hoping that if I can psych up the potential audience, then maybe I'll get psyched about it too." Caylee caught Andrea's gaze in the mirror, her shoulders wilting.

"If you're not feeling it, don't do it."

"I've been auditioning for months, and I've never been called back for a second before. I *have* to feel it."

Andrea put her arm around Caylee's shoulders and squeezed. "You'll be wonderful. If you need help with your lines, let me know."

"Thanks."

Caylee's blunt bob was kelly green now and matched the colored contacts she wore behind red cat-eye fashion glasses. She was more anime than Irish slum wench. "You are strong. You are valued. You are loved. You've got this."

Caylee rolled her eyes at Andrea's arm muscle pose. "You say I'm dramatic? Tell your gorgeous governor I said hello."

"Will do."

Andrea slipped into her jacket, tied her boots, grabbed her bag, and weaved through the dining area to the front door. The crisp autumn air held the wonder of color and scent. She loved fall. The cooling temperature swept away the stuffy atmosphere of the metropolis. Everyone seemed to breathe deeper, and the anticipation of the coming winter was palpable.

Beau rounded the sidewalk at the end of the block, carrying two sleeved cups, his open coat flapping with each step. He grinned as they both closed the distance. His lips and the tip of his nose were pink from the cold. Oh, how she wanted to remedy that.

"Pumpkin spice latte, extra whip." He handed her a cup.

"You remembered."

"Of course. I'm an outstanding boyfriend."

He grabbed her scarf and tugged her closer, lowering his mouth to hers. He tasted like trust and love and a hint of mint. She groaned in pleasure before pulling away. "What a greeting."

"Yeah, I'm pretty outstanding at those too."

He winked.

Being with him filled the empty spaces of loneliness she felt sometimes. He made the pieces of her that felt incomplete whole. Allen had made her feel that way too, but she couldn't keep comparing every man to him. Not all men carried dark secrets that could turn the world upside down.

Farther down the sidewalk, Jonas waited with the car. By the time Beau and Andrea reached it, Jonas stood by the open back door. "Hello, Miss Andrea."

No matter how far her relationship with Beau went, she didn't think she'd ever get used to having a private driver who opened and closed her door. "Thank you, Jonas. How is your daughter?"

Surprise, then pleasure, lit his eyes. "She's well, thank you. She loves the job and is settling in nicely."

The night of the Met Gala, Jonas had told her about his daughter's new degree in marine biology and that she'd accepted a position in the rehabilitation center at Sea World in San Diego. He missed her terribly but was happy to see her achieve her dreams. Andrea suspected his hefty salary with the Davidson-Quincys all these years was what had enabled him to send her to Boston University for six years.

"Glad to hear it." Careful to keep her cup balanced, she slid inside the car and scooted over for Beau.

Jonas closed the door, checked for traffic, and then walked to the driver's side. Beau stole another kiss but pulled away when Jonas settled behind the steering wheel.

It took twenty minutes to drive the two miles to the theater district. Throngs of people lined the streets. Hundreds of vendors were in attendance, and rumor had it there were a few celebrities too. The money the auction raised would go to a charity that helped fight childhood cancer. Andrea couldn't wait to dig through the rare and unique items the flea market was famous for.

The scent of roasted nuts and hot chocolate floated through the air. Beau kept possession of her hand as they weaved through the booths. He had such a way of making her feel safe and cherished. It was hard to ignore other women sneaking appreciative glances at him or pointing him out in recognition. He shook hands with people throughout the afternoon, always introducing Andrea as his girlfriend.

Despite the activity of the flea market and all the bodies moving around them, he gave her his full attention, making her feel special and needed and appreciated. She fell deeper under his spell every day. She prayed the result wouldn't be a broken heart.

The south end of the flea market was full of vintage toys used as props in Shirley Temple movies, the original *Little Rascals* episodes, and animation memorabilia from the birth of cartoons. One booth held a few Victrolas with wax cylinders, old stage clothing, posters, and postcards. Andrea flipped through the postcards, enjoying the black-and-white landscape scenes and stern faces of the Victorian-era models.

One postcard caught her eye, and she studied the ornate dress that rivaled anything Scarlett O'Hara wore. The woman's young alabaster skin practically glowed against a gown Andrea guessed to be a shade of red or purple. She stood on a stage arranged with pillars and flowers, and the longing way she gazed at someone in the audience struck a tender and familiar emotion inside Andrea.

That woman had been in love.

Beau came up behind her and wrapped his arms around her middle, inspecting the image too. She flipped the postcard over and held the looping cursive message closer to her face, reading aloud. " 'To my darling Paul. Had this terrible war not started, I'd have never met you. Soon I shall become Mrs. Cheskonova and we will live a life of passion and purpose in these hills as the rest of the world crumbles around us. Yours and yours alone, Beatrice Everwood.' "

"Was she someone famous?" Beau asked.

"She was an opera singer." A man who worked the booth approached. His knit cap barely covered a pair of large ears. He wore fingerless gloves. "That image has always held me captive too."

He winked. "She was approximately twenty-five in that picture. She and her mother traveled from Boston to San Francisco after her father struck it big during the gold rush. By the time they reached the West Coast, he'd died from cholera. Not wanting to succumb to prostitution the way many women were forced to do to survive out west, the mother married a man headed for Utah Territory so they'd be cared for. She died a few years later during childbirth, and the man shortly afterward from a heart condition.

"With the silver boom, towns were popping up overnight, along with playhouses. Miss Everwood exchanged her singing talent for room and board in a safe neighborhood."

Andrea ran a finger along the scalloped edge of the postcard. "Wow, you've done your research."

The man grinned, deepening the lines around his eyes. "Actually, I was just curious, so I googled. Poor thing had overcome so much just to meet with a tragic end."

"What happened?" Beau asked.

"A miner came to town hoping to strike it rich. Paul Cheskonova. They immediately fell in love. He spent everything he had buying a successful silver mine and workers that didn't really exist. He went to work in someone else's mine so he could save enough for them to marry but died from mercury poisoning while on the job. Miss Everwood committed suicide three days later."

"Oh, that's terrible." Andrea stared into the eyes of a woman 160 years in the past. Though the clothing and hairstyles were different, the heartbeat and complex emotions that made them women were the same. Andrea's heart reached out to this forgotten woman.

Beau's phone rang, and he pulled it from his pocket. "I've got to take this. Be right back."

He kissed her cheek and left the booth.

"I'll take ten dollars for the postcard if you promise to take good care of it." The proprietor casually leaned his arms on the table, as if he were doing her a favor.

Ten dollars was ridiculous for a postcard, but Andrea was so entranced by the woman and the story, she paid the price. Besides, the money was going to a good cause. Perhaps if she couldn't solve the mystery of her counterfeit money, she could take the unrequited love of Miss Everwood and write an article worthy of a promotion.

The proprietor thanked her for her purchase and moved on to the next customer. Andrea slipped the postcard into the zippered compartment inside her bag, closed the flap, and left the booth to find Beau. He leaned against a lamppost several feet away, lines bracketing his mouth. His smile was grim as she approached.

"Get him comfortable. Be there soon." Beau dropped his cell into his back pocket. "I'm sorry, but I need to go. My dad's gallbladder is inflamed again. He's in a lot of pain. I expect the doctor to schedule surgery any day. He's been battling this too long."

"I completely understand. I hope he feels better soon." She wrapped her arms around him. "You go. I'll be fine."

"I'm not leaving you here alone." He linked his hands behind her back.

"I've lived here long enough to have learned what places to avoid and how to remain safe on my own. You go take care of your dad."

"I'm not leaving you here alone." He bent and placed a gentle kiss on her lips. "Jonas is on his way, and we'll see you home. Mrs. Sloven is with my dad. She'll make sure he's as comfortable as possible."

They started walking. "Who's Mrs. Sloven?" she asked.

"Our maid and longtime friend."

"Of course you have a maid. You have a butler, a cook, and a personal driver. I should've known you had a maid."

He chuckled and led them across the street, where they waited for Jonas. She told him about her purchase of the postcard. A gust of cold wind whipped around the building they were standing against, making Andrea shiver. He buttoned her coat, gazing into her eyes as his fingers worked over the buttons. Desire radiated from his expression, causing her a different kind of shiver.

"I'm sorry your counterfeit bill mystery hit a dead end, but I'm grateful it brought us together."

She scrunched her nose. "You're only saying that hoping to obtain my vote."

"Not so." He nibbled her bottom lip. "You are voting for me, though. Right?"

"I…mmm." Her legs were turning to gelatin. "What are we talking about?"

A horn gave a short blast beside them, making them both jump. They'd been so engrossed in each other they hadn't noticed that their ride had pulled up to the curb. Her face heated, and Beau laughed as he opened the door. She slid inside, and he settled in beside her.

She listened as Jonas updated Beau on his father's condition. Beau apologized once again for cutting their date short. "Stop," she said. "I understand. Take good care of your dad, and call me later."

Jonas parked in front of her apartment. He feigned interest in the architecture while Beau stole one last, long kiss. She got out of the car and waved as they drove away.

The apartment entrance smelled of warm beef and vegetable juice. Someone was cooking chili. Andrea's stomach grumbled. Now that she was solo for dinner tonight, chili would be the perfect companion to an evening of research.

She retrieved her mail from the box, ascended the stairs, and unlocked her door. The living room was dim except for the light in the fish tank. "I'm home, loves." She turned on the light, kicked off her sneakers, and hung her coat on the rack. "Well, Sammy, it's just you, me, the Supremes, and comfort food tonight. I'll be working on a project, though, so try not to distract me with too much conversation."

The fishes' movements grew more excited as they watched her reach for the container of food, familiar with the drill. She sprinkled some flakes on the water then went to the kitchen in search of her own meal. Cooking for one was always a little depressing, especially when she was supposed to be spending the evening with Beau, but she made the best of it by giving herself permission to eat the rest of the carton of double-fudge ice cream in her freezer.

An hour later, seated in the comfy chair at her desk, she opened her laptop and inhaled the scent of the steaming chili at her side. Using the Smithsonian's employee-only database, she searched for information regarding Beatrice Everwood. She retrieved a list of places the woman had lived, her career accomplishments, awards, and details of her death and burial. Next, she searched for Paul Cheskonova but found nothing.

Google was her next source. The name brought up a million different things, so she specified her search using the dates that Beatrice would've been in Utah Territory. Paul's name was attached to a large cargo shipment, presumably with items he'd need for his new mine that didn't exist. He was also mentioned in an article in the *Deseret News* as being engaged to the "enchanting Miss Everwood—Utah Territory's siren of the stage." Minus the scam, the couple seemed to have a fairy-tale romance.

The internet also suggested related searches, such as American theater in the West, Native American history, and Wild West wanted posters. Fascinated by early criminology, she clicked on the wanted posters for fun. Dead or alive rewards were offered for the usuals like the Jesse James gang, Billy the Kid, Butch Cassidy and the Sundance Kid, and Sitting Bull. Then lesser knowns filled the screen. Cassandra Blackburn, wanted for murdering a string of suitors. Jonathan Wheelright for horse thievery. Adolphus Dickerson for forgery, selling property already owned by another, and selling land and mine claims that didn't exist.

Could this be the man who'd swindled Miss Everwood's fiancé?

Andrea clicked on the image for more information. The photograph showed a man around the age of twenty-five with dark hair and dark eyes glaring back at her, his mouth twisted in sedition. He was handsome in a bad boy sort of way, despite the deformity of one ear. The type beneath his picture claimed his real name was Edward Davidson but that he went by several aliases, such as Adolphus Dickerson, John Montgomery, Moses Grande, and James Palermo. The authorities believed him to be heading east.

She leaned back in her seat, staring at the man, her last few bites of chili forgotten. Goose bumps trailed up her arms. Could this be the Edward Davidson she'd been looking for? What were the odds?

She pulled out Miss Everwood's postcard from her bag and propped it against her laptop screen. She stared into the woman's eyes. "What are you trying to tell me?" she whispered.

Beau had said his great-great-grandfather Franklin had been a Civil War hero. She had found a census record of a brother named Edward, but the trail had grown cold after that. The man in the poster before her couldn't be younger than twenty-five, so it was plausible that Edward had somehow ended up in Utah Territory during the war, especially since his name hadn't appeared on any military registries from either side.

"Is this the guy who swindled your man?" she asked Miss Everwood, glad no one else was around to think her insane for speaking to a dead woman's picture. Her next step needed to be finding a picture of Franklin. To see if there was any resemblance to this Edward.

She commanded the computer to print the image while she dialed Beau's number. Four rings later, he answered. "Miss me already?"

"Of course I do. How's your dad?"

"Sleeping." Beau yawned. "It's a good thing you called. I lit a fire in the study and was almost out myself. I can't sleep, though. Too much work to do."

Andrea pulled her feet into the chair and curled an arm around her legs. "I won't keep you long, just wanted to share some good news."

"Hmm…you've decided to come over and distract me from writing my speech?"

She giggled. "In researching my tragic opera star, I'm certain I've found our elusive Edward Davidson."

CHAPTER TWENTY-FOUR

EDWARD

Maryland, November 1868

*I*f they walked any longer, Edward's feet would freeze to the snowy ground. His arms had stiffened at his sides minutes ago, and he'd lost all feeling in his face. Sure, they'd seized another ring, put away the criminals, and he'd made a few thousand on the side, but if he lost his extremities to frostbite or his life to pneumonia, it would all be for naught. If only the axle on their carriage hadn't split, causing them to travel on foot. Leland held the reins of the horses, his hand probably frozen to the leather straps by now.

Did Franklin have a will in case of unexpected death? If so, who was the lawyer? He'd have to check the study for documentation when he returned home or get the information out of Margaret without raising suspicion. He certainly didn't want to leave her or Cora destitute upon his death.

The docile, petite woman flashed into his mind, warming him a little. He'd noticed her attractiveness the first day he'd seen her from across the street, the day his brother had helped her from the carriage, swollen with child. She'd beamed at Franklin, love spilling from her eyes as bright as the sun. In that moment, he'd wished it was him she loved so fiercely. Now it was, and some days he wasn't sure what to do with it.

One thing he was sure of, if they didn't reach a town soon, he might never see his sweet girls again. Was his brother waiting for him on the other side, waiting to take vengeance?

Minutes felt like eternity as they trudged through the accumulating snow. Wind ravaged Edward's face. There were four of them, which made pilfering counterfeit from the raid more difficult, but they trusted Franklin, which meant they trusted *him*, so no one scrutinized his movements regarding the money.

He was also careful to never use the same tactic twice, and therefore he avoided any suspicion from his superior.

Piano music floated in the air. Someone pounded a lively tune over that rise. His companions looked at each other and grinned. Edward thought they did anyway. Hard to tell with ice crusted in their beards. Or maybe their lips were frozen in that position.

It was impossible to determine how long it took them to follow the music into the town of Dorchestshire. Thankfully, they'd entered on the side of town where residents were still awake. They all needed a stiff drink to warm their blood and a bed to sleep away the chill.

The tavern crowd was thinner than Edward guessed it would be, and his group took an open table closest to the fire, while Leland paid a man to take their horses to the livery. Edward was so cold he could barely feel the heat of the flames. The man behind the bar observed their every move, as if he'd need to run at the slightest provocation. None of them cared at this moment what crimes the man committed. They weren't in any state to give chase. Hopefully, none of them would suffer lasting effects.

"What'll it be?" The man's Irish brogue filled the room.

Fritz opened his mouth, but nothing came out. He cleared his throat a few times then ordered the strongest whiskey for them all. Four glasses clinked on the bar, followed by the pouring of amber liquid. The man gestured to a woman Edward hadn't noticed had been standing in the back corner. She took the tray of drinks and served them, bending low to expose her cleavage to each man.

Again, as if any had the stamina.

"We're looking for a place to lodge the night," Essenhause said. "We're chilled to the bone."

The wench smiled, revealing grayish teeth. "No better place than right here." Her gaze flicked to the man behind the bar, who nodded. "We can provide you with rest after your entertainment."

She turned her face away, and a soured expression flashed across her features so quickly Edward would have missed it had he not been watching her carefully. He knew most of the women in these places didn't wake up one day to choose the career. The decision had been born during a primal moment of survival, all other options expended. Usually caused by the loss of a husband.

He never wanted Margaret or Cora to have to make such a choice to survive. He'd secure the means to protect them from the grave as soon as he returned home.

"No thank you, miss." Essenhause tipped up his glass. Winced. "Lodgin's the only necessity we'll be needing. We'll pay extra if we have to."

The man behind the bar nodded, and the woman returned to her corner. Her stiff shoulders relaxed. She reminded Edward of a woman from his past. Another soiled dove. Too much whiskey made him mean like his father, and when she'd refused to take his money on her night off, he'd forced her to take it.

That night he'd crossed the line from criminal to monster. A monster like his father. Though he'd vowed never to unleash that part of himself again, his efforts failed. He rubbed his chest where it ached at the memories of his brother.

Rounds of whiskey emptied at the table for the next two hours. Customers came and went. Edward must have dozed off, because the next thing he knew, Fritz was shaking him. Leland spit heated words at the man behind the bar as the rest of them climbed the stairs, trying not to fall back down. The bar man argued they throw a few coins at the "girls" they'd refused, but Leland's level head and sharp tongue won.

They paid for the largest room and bunked together. Edward dropped onto the chaise by the fire, Leland made a pallet on the floor, and cousins Fritz and Essenhause took the bed. Edward was on his way to oblivion when something smacked his chest.

"Forgot to give this to you earlier with all the commotion." Leland released the paper. "The news came from headquarters when I wired Smith about the raid. Congratulations."

Leland kicked off his boots and dropped to the pallet.

Head pounding, Edward lifted the note. His vision was too blurry. The room too dark. He put a hand to his throbbing forehead. "What's it say?"

"It's a telegram from home. You're going to be a papa again." Leland lay down and closed his eyes as if that news was the most natural in the world.

Edward sat up, the whiskey fog clearing. He'd fathered a child?

Well, of course he had. He and Margaret practiced the ritual often enough. But…a papa? The idea had never crossed his mind, which was ludicrous. Sure, he was already a papa of sorts. He had Cora and adored her more than anything. But this child would be his own flesh. His own blood. He and Margaret had created a life together.

Happiness made him burst with energy, and he wanted to shout the news. The others had already fallen asleep. Edward lay back down, watching the flames flicker in the hearth and wanting desperately to go home and stay home for the first time in his life.

Maybe this twisted path he'd created would bring him everything he wanted after all.

Andrea
Manhattan, Present Day

Andrea's brain kept bouncing between Beau's televised speech, the mysterious Edward Davidson, and her customers. Serving was the last thing she wanted to do, knowing that Beau needed her support on his big night. Hundreds of citizens packed the Medgar Evers College stadium, along with dozens of reporters covering the constituents' addresses, and Andrea tried to keep up with the live stream from her phone whenever she could steal a free moment.

Edward Davidson's trail had grown cold once again. After leaving Utah Territory, he'd vanished as if he'd never existed. Even his aliases had dissolved. Had he died traveling east? Murdered, captured by Indians, or infected with disease? Cold cases were common in those days, especially in areas of lawless land. Had he simply taken on a new pseudonym? How else did a man with no birth record show up on a census, appear years later on the other side of the country, and disappear with no record of death, but his belongings and signature showed up decades after his disappearance?

Of course, she had no proof the signature in the hotel's registry was his. Or that the counterfeit money had belonged to him.

She was normally proficient at connecting puzzle pieces, but this mystery eluded her. What was it she was missing?

"Order up!" The chef's sharp French accent startled her from the deep waters of her thoughts.

She arranged the plates on her tray, gave a small grunt as she balanced it on her palm, and exited the swinging doors to the dining room. Two more parties had been seated in her area, making them the thirtieth table she'd waited on tonight. After serving the food and taking drink orders for new guests, she stacked their menus and headed for the hostess stand.

Caylee smiled at a middle-aged couple dressed as if they were meeting the queen and assured them a table would come available within the half hour. Her blunt-cut bob had grown to her shoulders now and had been dyed a lovely shade of lavender. Andrea stacked the menus behind the stand and started to walk away when Caylee caught her arm.

"Would you be able to pick up two tables for Mary? She's only been here two weeks, and the rush tonight has her overwhelmed. I found her in the bathroom a few minutes ago, nearly hyperventilating."

Andrea's feet were weepy themselves, but she'd noticed Mary struggling as well. "Sure."

"Thanks." Caylee looked at the iPad. "Tables 46 and 54."

Andrea gave a quick salute and turned away. Caylee grabbed her arm again.

"I got the part."

Andrea smothered a squeal. "Congratulations!" She hugged her friend, despite it recking of unprofessionalism. "Well deserved."

"They called right before my shift. I'm working in a blissful fog."

"Enjoy every moment." She squeezed Caylee's arm and left to retrieve water glasses for the new tables.

"Welcome to Gant & Company. My name is Andrea, and I'll be your server this evening. Are we celebrating anything special tonight?" She set a water glass in front of the man to her right, who smiled as he lowered his menu.

"It's my birthday." He picked up his glass and took a sip.

"Mine too." The other man lowered his menu next. Andrea did a double take.

Both men chuckled.

"You threw me there for a second," she said.

"We do that on purpose." The man on her left shrugged. "It's a lot harder to pull off now that we're not kids anymore."

Andrea tucked the empty tray under her arm. "Judging by those mischievous grins on your faces, you two have some entertaining stories."

"A few," the man on her right said, perusing his menu.

"We may have gone Hayley Mills a few times growing up." The other twin handed Andrea his menu. "I'll take the chicken Florentine with asparagus, please. Lemonade to drink."

She removed her order pad and wrote the request down. "Hayley Mills?"

"You know, the movie *The Parent Trap* where the twins switch lives?" He fiddled with the clasp on his watch.

"You switched places? That's hilarious." She looked at the man at the opposite end of the table.

"Guilty." He smiled. "The consequences were always harsh, though. Especially once Mom found out."

"Yeah, Dad thought it was funny until Mom got involved. She'd ground us for weeks. I'll have the Cajun pasta with a Coke."

She wrote the order down. "I'll be back with your drinks and garlic bread."

The kitchen was alive with bodies and smells and steam lifting from the grill. She typed her new orders into the kitchen computer then delivered meals for table 16. Once she had drink orders filled, she grabbed a basket of garlic bread and returned to the twins.

She set the Coke in front of the man on her right and the lemonade on her left. They looked at her, then the drinks, then switched the glasses. Heat filled her cheeks as she presented the basket of bread. "Sorry for the mix-up."

They snickered.

"Actually, we should be sorry," one of them said. "We switched places on you."

"Couldn't resist the trickery?" she teased.

"Couldn't resist the beautiful brunette in the corner," the other man said.

Andrea followed his finger to a group of women celebrating a bachelorette party on the other side of the room. The redhead wore a white sash that said BRIDE-TO-BE. Cocktails, in all colors and sizes, decorated the table, along with little gift bags and party trinkets. The group had been giggly and louder than their usual patrons. Andrea hoped they tipped well.

She returned her attention back to the men. "I heard her say earlier that she's still looking for a good man. If that's you, try talking to her before she leaves."

Before Beau, she never would've considered a restaurant as a place to land a date.

The man's hand clenched around his glass.

His brother laughed. "He's more the creeper, wallflower type. I'm the outgoing one, but I'm taken."

"Ah. Well, let me know if you need anything. Your food should be out shortly." Andrea rushed to the kitchen to check her phone.

The live stream was still playing, though her phone was on silent mode. A female reporter filled the screen while she asked a question. Then the camera focused on Beau and his rival, Timothy Greene. Beau opened his mouth to speak, but Timothy interrupted. The man passed Beau a smug grin, and Beau's jaw turned to granite. Aggravation welled inside her. She should be in the audience right now, throwing rotten tomatoes at the man, instead of serving food to strangers.

My, had her mentality changed in the last few months since meeting Beau. She'd gone from opposing his offers of a date, to dating him, to wishing her job away so she could sit at his feet and admire him. Fight for him. Hold him.

"Order up!" Chef Fontaine yelled.

Using phones while on the clock was against policy, but if she kept it brief, no one would tattle. Andrea slipped her phone into her apron pocket and continued making her rounds, praying God would give Beau confidence, grace, and the right words to say. She slipped in a thought of gratitude for bringing Beau into her life as well.

An hour later, the twins argued over whose turn it was to pay the bill. The evening rush was dying down, and the candidates' speeches had concluded. She couldn't wait to talk to Beau to see how it had gone.

Andrea held up a finger. "Would it be easier if you both paid for your own meal? I'll even throw in a piece of cake for each of you to take home."

"Easier, yes." One brother ran a finger along the band of his watch. "But he should buy because he lost our bet on the Colts-Packers game."

The other man frowned. "True, but I also replaced all the faucets in your house last week."

"Sounds like you're even, then." Andrea smiled. "I'll go get those pieces of cake."

Good grief, if they were this complicated as grown men, they must've been terrors as children.

She paused halfway through the kitchen doors.

Twins.

Maribel's strange comment about the two faces of January that night at the Met Gala hit Andrea like an arrow to a bullseye.

Could that be her missing link between Franklin and Edward Davidson? Could they have been twins? Then again, Beau claimed there was no family record of Edward, which blew that theory.

Maybe she wasn't thinking enough like a Secret Service agent. To succeed at their job, they studied real money so intently it was easy to spot a fake. According to her research, counterfeit engraving plates held a symbol or mark only they knew to look for. She needed to examine the money closely to see if she could find some such mark. She'd also scour for any legal documents attached to Edward's name in hopes she'd discover some record of him between the census and the counterfeit bills. See if the man popped up anywhere else. Then perhaps she could connect the dots.

Was it possible for Franklin and Edward to be twins without a birth record for both? Sometimes with home birthing, documents failed to get recorded. Or human error at a courthouse intervened.

If they had been twins, she hoped for their poor mother's sake they were less complicated than the twins leaving with free cake.

Andrea had two weeks to turn in her article and prove that she deserved the promotion. So far, all she had was the tale of an opera singer's unrequited love, a handful of old useless money, and the list of Players Club members from the late nineteenth century. The pieces might all connect to form an intricate and complex puzzle, or they could be entirely different stories that merely appeared to fit together.

An early October Sunday evening alone meant she could layer in her coziest of cozies, drink all the hot chocolate her heart desired, light candles for ambiance, grab her future with both hands, and solve this mystery.

She really didn't want to go behind Beau's back and creep into his family's background without his prior knowledge and consent, but he was busy with his campaign and last-ditch efforts to win the hearts of voters, and she didn't want to interfere. He'd already told her it was unlikely he could see her this week with responsibilities to his children's charity, news interviews, podcasts, and a project meeting at his dad's company. It was highly probable that her investigation would hit another dead end or the results wouldn't produce enough magnitude for a promotion-worthy story anyway, so bothering Beau was pointless. If she discovered something, she'd tell him afterward.

It wasn't like she'd be using illegal methods to gain the information. This case was old enough that the details would be public. It just might require special *Smithsonian* employee access to get it from files dated and stored that far back.

See? Nothing to feel guilty about at all.

Already wearing fleece-lined leggings and a long-sleeved shirt, she slipped into her knit oversized cardigan and fuzzy slippers. She added her Edgar Allan Poe–themed writing gloves because they gave her the illusion they'd add sparkle to her writing.

She settled in her firm but plush office chair in front of her laptop, took a sip of hot chocolate for fortitude, and placed her fingers on the keys. Examining the counterfeit bills had gotten her nowhere, and she'd already researched the Davidson-Quincy family tree and census records. Tonight she'd start hunting other common records such as medical, military, purchase, and ship records.

Since Edward had no known trail, she'd start with Franklin.

Results: Franklin had no documented medical conditions. There were two boat records in June 1872 attached to his name that documented crates for various home furnishings from England and France that Andrea was certain was for his newly purchased home in Gramercy Park, as the deed she'd found was from six months earlier. As for military records—

Bingo!

She stared at the image of a faded Union army paper listing Franklin's father, Augustus Davidson, and Franklin's brother, Edward, as next of kin to be notified in case of death. Edward had to still be living then, or Franklin wouldn't have listed him.

Her fingers worked overtime in search of a military record for Edward but found none. A draft in July 1863 forced every able-bodied man who wasn't already enlisted with the army to join and fight unless they paid a three-hundred-dollar fee to the government for exclusion. Another draft was called in 1864, as young men became of age. So why was there no military record for Edward? Chewing her bottom lip, Andrea rocked in her chair. Beatrice Everwood stared at her from the postcard Andrea had clipped to her bulletin board.

She sprang from her chair, jostling the brown liquid in her mug. "That's it, isn't it?"

Good thing only the fish were in her apartment to witness her conversing with a postcard.

Taking down the postcard, she stared into Beatrice's eyes. "There's no military record of him because he was in Utah Territory, evading the war and taking advantage of innocent investors."

Her gaze flew to the wanted poster tacked on the board. His description mentioned walking with a limp. Such a condition wouldn't have gained him access into the army, even during a draft. While his brother was valiantly fighting to end slavery, Edward was building a legacy of his own by scamming other men out of their hard-earned money.

Every family had a black sheep. She was certain she'd just met Beau's.

CHAPTER TWENTY-FIVE

EDWARD

Washington, D.C., January 1869

*W*as this his brother's way of punishing him from the grave?

Edward's footsteps grew heavy as he ascended the stairs to their bedroom. Margaret had lost the baby. *They'd* lost the baby. The elation he'd lived in for the last six weeks ignited, leaving nothing but ashy remains. The telegram informing him to return home immediately lay wadded in his pocket. Miss Moreau had met him at the door to prepare him for what to expect when he saw his wife.

The home smelled of orange, cloves, and cinnamon, remnants from the Christmas season. Margaret had been fine when he'd come home for a brief visit three weeks ago. Cheeks flushed, smile prominent, a small mound beneath her skirt. Delighted by the pearl hair combs he'd purchased in Boston. How had it all been snuffed out so quickly?

At the top of the stairs, Cora's chatter filtered through the door of her nursery. Soundlessly, he peeked inside, watching her play with the new dolls he'd bought her for Christmas. She was growing quickly, able to recite colors and the alphabet. Though she mumbled the letters *L* through *P*. Cora had seemed just as delighted about the baby as her parents. Had anyone told her?

He wouldn't disturb her just now. If he did, it might be hours before he could assess Margaret without interruption. He needed to see his wife.

His stomach churned as he muted the noise of the closing door and padded down the hall to their bedroom. Margaret wasn't truly his in the eyes of the law, but he'd accepted the responsibility of becoming her husband when he'd taken over Franklin's life. In truth, Edward loved her. Sometimes temptation stole the better part of his soul when he was away, but it wasn't anything uncommon to man. Would Franklin have been so weak, months being away from his wife? Undoubtedly not. His brother had been the closest thing to a saint.

Edward gently rapped a knuckle against the door. When Margaret didn't respond, he turned the knob and stuck his head inside. She lay on the bed, staring up at the ceiling with red-rimmed eyes. The gray winter day let enough light through the window to bathe her in an eerie pallor. Miss Moreau had informed him that Margaret had attempted to take her own life upon delivery of the mutated infant that had been no bigger than a child's hand.

The door closed behind him, and Margaret gave no indication she heard the loud click. He worried his hat in his hands, still stiff from the cold. A chair rested beside the bed, the place where Mrs. White next door, Miss Moreau, or Mrs. Albany sat vigilant when not cooking a meal.

"I came as soon as I could." He rested his hat on the end of the bed and sat. The chill embedded into the fibers of his coat leached into the warm air.

No response. No movement, save the lone tear that dripped down her cheek.

He reached for her hand. "I'm sorry, Margaret."

More genuine words he'd never spoken.

She shivered from his icy touch, and he pulled his hand away. He rubbed the grit from his eyes and blew out a breath. "We'll get through this. We will. There will be other children."

Unmoving, she continued staring at the ceiling. Another tear, followed by another, rolled into her ear. "I'm not sure I want to, Franklin."

The statement pushed him against the chair. Was she saying she didn't want to try for more children, or that she didn't want to get through it? That she wanted to give up and die? "I know it's a devastating loss, but—"

"It wasn't easy living in Hell's Hundred Acres. Sometimes the house was suffocating. You were miserable trying to find work with your injury. Your father could be unbearable with his grousing, and I couldn't leave the house unattended for fear someone would mistake me for a prostitute. But we were happy. Things were hard but happy. Passed from one orphanage to another as a child, I finally had the family I'd always longed for."

He was ashamed to be ignorant of the details of her upbringing and sorry she'd been subjected to his father's temper. "Look what all you have now. I found work. You're safe to leave your home anytime you want. You have nice things. A beautiful daughter. Life's not hard anymore."

He winced at his own stupidity. He'd not meant to suggest that losing a child wasn't hard. Or that her journey from melancholy to happiness hadn't been hard. He was simply trying to get her to see all the good things she had in hopes it would stoke a desire to continue living. He'd always desired a family of his own too.

"But it is." She turned her neck and pinned him with a gaze so hollow, so intense, it made his blood turn to ice. "It's just a different kind of hard."

The finality of her words told him she believed no hope existed. That no matter what he gave her, no matter what he did for her, he'd never be enough for her. A desolate feeling he was all too familiar with.

He fingered the ribbon securing the braid splayed across her pillow.

The image of the little house on Wooster Street flashed through his mind. Followed by his mother smiling down on him while he touched that ribbon, the horrible grief of losing her, his father's rage, the pain of his fists, the kindness of his brother, the fear in Franklin's eyes that night in Pittsburgh, the blast of gunfire. The pool of blood.

He buried his face in his hands, trying to block out the memories. He'd never been good enough for his father, his classmates, his employers, or, in the end, his brother. Now he wasn't good enough for Margaret.

Why didn't anyone want to stay with him forever?

The blanket rustled. He lifted his head, hoping she'd moved to reach out to him, but she'd gone back to her fascination with the ceiling. The walls pressed in on him. He stood and fled the room, the chair teetering from the sudden movement. He couldn't think. Couldn't breathe. He needed to escape this pit of guilt and rejection and all the accusations yawning wider at his feet.

He paced the parlor, running his fingers through his hair. He couldn't fall apart like this. Not here. Not where someone might see.

So set was he on locking himself in the study, he didn't see Miss Moreau until he'd nearly knocked her over. Her slender form filled his grasp as he reached to steady her. "I apologize, Miss Moreau."

Her brown eyes widened in surprise. His face was inches from hers. Her body was hard against him, her lithe curves glorious beneath his palms. He needed comforting, and he needed it badly.

He could not give in. Not now.

He dropped his hands and stepped away as if she'd scalded him.

"How is she?" Miss Moreau whispered, not meeting his gaze.

"Her spirit has faded to nothing."

Crossing her arms, she took a step back. "I'd hoped that once you returned…"

What, that his presence would magically fix things? It never had before. In fact, his presence always made things worse.

If he couldn't seek solace in Miss Moreau, he needed something just as heady.

"Thank you for your services, Miss Moreau. Once you have Cora settled into bed for the night, you may have the rest of the evening off. I'm sure you could use the reprieve. I don't expect Margaret's condition to change, but if it does, I'll be here."

She nodded. "Dr. Fullerton said to fetch him if there's any difference at all. He left a list with detailed instructions on her care, medications, and what to watch for. I put it on the desk in your study."

"Thank you, Miss Moreau."

She took two steps before pausing. "Are you certain of this, Mr. Davidson? You just returned from Delaware. I don't mind helping with Miss Margaret."

"I'm certain." The temptation of her, following Margaret's rejection, was too great a load to bear. He'd rather see the young woman leave than lose his self-control. "Knock before you leave, and I'll keep vigil with Margaret through the night."

He brushed past her to the study. The door slammed harder than he'd intended. He looked around the room, the bookshelves, the desk, the lamp. Where had he hidden it?

He rummaged through books, knocking them to the floor. He shuffled and upended one desk drawer at a time until he finally found the opium bottle he'd hidden for emergencies such as this. Imbibing was something he rarely took part in, not wanting to become like those he provided the poppy for.

But he was too desperate in this moment to be strong. He needed escape from the agony.

After stoking the fire, he lit a lantern and took a long drink from the bottle. A drop spilled over the side and across the emblem of a shield and bee stamped there.

Demon after demon danced before him as he coupled the opium with sips of whiskey. His limbs grew relaxed, and his mind took him to places he wished he could experience. He shed his coat and tie, loosened his collar, tugged off his shoes. The brace stabilizing his foot had been paining him for days. He removed it and then his socks, tossing it into a corner. Propping his foot on the chair, he drifted in and out of consciousness as daylight faded to darkness.

Through the haze of sleep and the black of night, the demons came faster. Growing more evil.

Screams of the innocent he'd wronged filled his ears. His cheek burned where the wench he'd attacked had dug her fingernails into his flesh. Tank stood in the background, pointing his finger at Edward, laughing, as Edward realized his friend's betrayal. His father ran into the room and raised his fist with unwavering malevolence. But the face contorted into Franklin's, and his brother beat him without mercy.

Everyone Edward loved turned their backs on him. Mother. Father. Franklin. Tank. Margaret.

Everyone except Cora. Her sweet smile, her dimpled cheeks and hands, allowed him light in his dark world. She would not turn her back on him. She was too young to know better. He wouldn't allow her the opportunity.

He thrashed in his sleep, fighting the legion threatening to drag him underground. They groped at him with their strong hands. Bashed him with his own memories. The sound rattled his ears.

Edward jerked awake. The house was quiet around him, save for the crackle of embers in the fireplace. He concentrated on slowing his racing heart, his rapid breaths, when a frenzied knock sounded on the door. That must have been what had awakened him.

"What is it?" His tongue stuck to the roof of his mouth.

"Sir, I apologize for disturbing you. May I enter?"

Miss Moreau. He ran a hand over his face and looked down at his disheveled appearance. He buttoned his shirt, straightened his tie.

"You may enter." His head was pounding.

His fingers finished running tracks through his hair when she stepped inside. "Cora has a raging fever. She…" Her gaze roamed the length of him then took in the mess of the room. "I don't know what's wrong with Cora. She's been fine all day. I've done everything possible to help her myself, but I believe she needs a physician."

She fiddled with a button on her sleeve. "When I couldn't rouse you, I asked Margaret what to do, and she bade me to get the doctor."

He squeezed his eyes then blinked them hard. He needed to sober up and quick. "It is night. I shall go."

The room swayed when he stood. He gripped the chair's arm in time to keep himself from falling.

Miss Moreau frowned at the empty whiskey glass on the table then at him. Her lips pursed. "You're in no condition. I shall go. You sit with Miss Margaret."

The young woman was gone before he could remind her of her station. Just as well. He wasn't in any condition to be hunting down the doctor when he didn't even know where the man lived. He dropped back into the chair, rubbing his temples and cursing himself for his weakness.

He must have fallen asleep again, because he awoke to a woman hissing his name.

Margaret.

Her nostrils flared. "Have you no regard for your daughter? She's in her bed shaking with fever while you sleep, as if nothing is happening."

Edward shook his head to awaken his brain. "You've decided to start caring? Yesterday, you were ready to board the death train and leave us both forever."

Her intake of breath was like a slap in the face. He shouldn't have said that. He was a mean drunk, like his father.

"Of course I care." She splayed a hand against her middle, as if protecting the life inside no longer there.

Her face crumpled. A sob leaked from her mouth. He was such an idiot. He stumbled toward her, desiring to make things right.

She clamped a hand over her mouth, and her eyes grew as big as dinner plates.

He followed her gaze to the floor. From the glow of the hallway sconces and the lamp illuminating the study, his bare feet revealed his clubfoot, the appendage curled in on itself. Gnarled and twisted. Shouting all his secrets.

She shook her head and backed away. When he stepped toward her, she screamed behind her hand.

Shame drenched him like a heavy rain. He was sick of being defined by his deformity. Tired of the horrified looks. The taunting. The agony.

He reached for her, wanting her to see *him*, to accept *him*. Hadn't he loved her despite her faults? Why couldn't she do the same?

She continued backing away, her chest heaving. "You're not my husband. You're…you're…" She gagged. "Edward."

Something inside him snapped like a twig under too much pressure. "I am Franklin Henry Davidson. Your husband."

Her hands dropped to her side, her lips shiny with tears. "He told me about you. About your childhood and your crimes and your…foot. He told me you were a dangerous man and might come here to take what you wanted."

"I am your husband." He took a tentative step closer, unsure what he should do next.

She caught the next sob in her closed mouth. Her head shook with vehemence. "No, you're not."

Margaret closed her eyes as if wishing to block out reality. "It makes sense now. Your changed interests. The way you forgot our anniversary and how we met. How you haven't recognized some of our friends. Your motivation for material possessions."

Her eyes opened. "The way you've handled me," she whispered.

"I didn't hear you complaining."

She'd backed herself into a corner. Literally. With walls surrounding her and the back side of the staircase above her, there was only one way to escape, and he blocked her path. "Is he dead? Did you kill Franklin?"

"Edward is the one who's dead. I made sure of it."

She continued staring at his foot. He'd let her get her fill. It wasn't like he'd allow her to tell anyone about it. It was a shame, really. They could have been so good together.

"Calm yourself, darling. You're in no state to think rationally with everything you've been through. In the morning, after you've had a good night's rest, you'll see the absurdity of all this." He opened his arms for her. "Come. Let's check on Cora."

Margaret trembled. "You're not going near her. You're not her father. You're not my husband."

Disdain leached from her voice and wrapped around Edward's ankles, pulling tight. Now that she knew, all he'd worked to build would vanish. He would not allow that to happen.

He lunged for her. She screamed and reared back, knocking her head against the wall, as she couldn't retreat any farther. He grabbed her by the wrists and wrenched her against him. She cried for help, but there was no one to hear except for a toddler upstairs ridden with fever.

Margaret fought against him, biting and screaming. She was a lively one when she wanted to be. "You're a monster!"

He yanked her arms behind her back and pulled. She dropped to her knees with a moan, face red, cheeks wet. The ribbon tied to the end of her braid began to slip. He rubbed it in his fingertips then yanked it from her hair and tucked it into his pocket. "I love you, Margaret. Don't make me do this to you."

"I hate you! I hate you!" She threw her head back and wailed. "You killed my husband."

He braced his inner elbow around her neck and applied pressure. He snaked his other arm around her waist. Her screams quieted. "I am your husband. Whatever you think you saw is only the runaway imagination of an insane woman."

She shook her head in the little space he allowed her.

"No? You don't believe your own husband?" Keeping a grip around her neck, he let go of her waist and withdrew the small bottle from his pants pocket. The liquid jostled inside the bottle as he flicked the cork off with his thumb.

"You'll have no choice but to trust me." Grabbing a handful of her hair, he ripped her head back and poured the liquid past her lips.

She sputtered and coughed but swallowed the remaining opium. She should calm soon.

"Mommy?" Cora's timid voice called from the middle of the stairs behind them.

Edward shoved Margaret. Her palms slapped the floor as she braced herself. He cleared his throat and infused a lightness to his tone. "The doctor is on his way, darling. Go back to bed, and Daddy will be there in a minute."

Margaret crawled from the corner. She tried to speak, but with the mixture of pressure he'd placed around her neck and the effects of the opium, nothing she said was coherent.

"Why was Mommy screaming?" Cora's little footsteps thudded on the stairs.

"Do not come down here." Edward's voice boomed through the room. "Get back to bed. I'll be up in a minute."

Cora whimpered, and a second later, her footsteps thudded above them then silenced.

Margaret stumbled to her feet, using the wall as leverage. "Don't…hurt my baby."

Her tongue sounded as if it had swollen double in size.

"I would never hurt our daughter."

She babbled something else, but Edward dismissed it and stalked back to the study to put on his boots. His chest heaved with adrenaline. He would not be rejected again. Would not fall to the bottom again. This time, he would rise to the top and stay there. And no woman—whether or not he loved her—was going to interfere with his future. Even if it meant helping her end the life she no longer wanted.

He left the study just as the front door opened. Stepping over Margaret, he rounded the corner and intercepted Miss Moreau and Dr. Fullerton at the stairs.

"Thank God you've come." He limped toward them and pulled the doctor by his arm. "It's my wife. She came down after Miss Moreau left and attacked me. She keeps screaming that I'm not her husband. I'm afraid she's going to hurt herself."

The doctor paused when he saw Margaret crawling on the floor. She must have fallen after Edward walked away. She groaned and groped the air for something solid to hold on to. The doctor helped her up. As her eyes met the physician's, her slurred words became more frantic.

"It's all right, Mrs. Davidson. Let's get you seated." Dr. Fullerton steered her toward the parlor.

"My husband." Margaret's eyes crossed, and she blinked hard. "He killed him. Look at his foot. He killed my husband."

She pointed at Edward. Her hand dropped to her side, no energy left to keep it upright. The opium was working its magic. He'd probably given her too much, but it was better than too little in this case.

Horror passed over Miss Moreau's face, likely regretting the day she ever took this position.

"This man is your husband." The doctor lowered Margaret onto a chair, patting her hand.

"No." The word came out as more of a grunt. "He has his foot. He's not my husband. He killed my husband. He'll kill my daughter."

Edward's mouth hung open. "I would never harm little Cora."

He meant it as fiercely as the words left his lips.

Margaret continued babbling, half sobbing. The opium was making it difficult for her to communicate her thoughts clearly, which made it easier for Edward. She grew more agitated with each minute that passed until the doctor rummaged through his bag and removed a bottle and a needle.

Morphine.

The combination of pain medication and opium might very well kill Margaret, but if it didn't, it would give him time to come up with a plausible story. If the authorities demanded proof of his missing limb, he'd cut it off to keep from being discovered. Hopefully, it wouldn't come to that.

Within a few minutes, her babbling transitioned to moans, her glare silently threatening Edward in a hundred different ways.

Dr. Fullerton put the supplies back into his bag and scratched his aging cheek. "Mr. Davidson, it breaks my heart to suggest this, but I believe Margaret may benefit from an asylum."

"Asylum?" Edward hadn't had time to conjure up a punishment so clever. Here the doctor was handing it to him on a silver platter.

"I would never mention it unless I thought it absolutely necessary. You've both been my patients since you moved here from New York. I know well who you are. I've examined your leg myself. Her accusation is not coming from a sound mind. I know of Margaret's struggle with melancholy and of her attempt to take her life just yesterday. She needs more help than either of us can give, Franklin."

The doctor frowned at Margaret. "She's gone mad."

Miss Moreau turned her face away, fist pressed to her mouth.

"I apologize for my forthrightness in such delicate company." The doctor touched Miss Moreau's elbow. "Why don't you go up and stay with Cora while Mr. Davidson and I discuss this."

She nodded, looking at Margaret one last time. They heard her cries all the way up the stairs.

When Miss Moreau had disappeared, the doctor repeated his recommendation.

Drool dripped from the corner of Margaret's mouth, her glassy eyes fixed on Edward. The groaning had transformed into a demonic rage as she fought the effects ravaging her body. She had more spirit than he'd given her credit for.

Edward pressed a thumb and forefinger to his eyes and looked away. "I can't do that to my wife."

He made his voice crack.

"I understand, Franklin, but there's nothing to be done outside of an asylum. She could be a danger to her family, the staff, and herself. She needs observation, medication, and monitoring night and day."

Edward paced, displayed emotion to rival a Shakespearean actor, and attempted to reason with the doctor. After a while, he accepted the doctor's advice. Margaret had passed out a few minutes ago, her color going deathly pale.

With Edward's permission, Dr. Fullerton sent his carriage driver for nurses at the asylum.

With Margaret asleep in the chair, the doctor sent Miss Moreau downstairs to monitor her while he examined Cora and Edward gathered some of Margaret's things. An hour later, a knock sounded at the door, and the asylum nurses stepped inside. A large, burly man followed behind in case of trouble.

They woke Margaret trying to carry her to the barred carriage that awaited outside. Shadows in neighboring windows shifted as they watched Margaret Davidson being hauled away. "No. No!" Margaret screamed. "He's not my husband. He killed my husband!"

Unwanted tears streaked down Edward's cheeks. He was sorry it had come to this. Truly. It had never been part of his plan. He loved Margaret. But he couldn't allow her to ruin him.

"Where are they taking Mommy?" Cora ran down the stairs, face flushed with fever. She stumbled, and Edward snatched her up before she fell and broke her neck. He could never live with himself if something happened to Cora. Margaret was dispensable. Cora was not.

He held her tight against him.

The little girl buried her hot forehead in the crook of his neck. "Is Mommy going to heaven to get the baby?"

Someone had told Cora of the baby and its passing.

"Yes, sweetheart. She's going to heaven." Might as well tell her now, as it would be the last time she ever saw her mother again.

He'd make sure of that.

"I will miss you, Mommy," Cora called. Her trust, her innocence, was so pure it cracked Edward's heart wide open.

Margaret sobbed at Cora's declaration. "Don't let him hurt my baby!"

His wife continued screaming as they stuffed her into the back of the barred carriage. Mr. and Mrs. White watched in horror from their open front door. Cora yawned then rubbed her eyes with a chubby fist. A deep breath later, Cora went limp in his arms.

Edward turned his back to carry her to bed. The door closed behind him, concluding the horror of the night.

CHAPTER TWENTY-SIX

Manhattan, Present Day

A week was too long to go without seeing Andi. Experiencing her smile. Touching her soft skin. Hearing her laugh. She brightened his world, and whether voters elected him as New York's next governor in three weeks or not, he needed her in his life. Daily.

He shifted on the stone bench, arching his back in a stretch. Leaves rustled above him, a few dancing to the ground. His eyes burned from checking emails and scrolling through social media the last two hours. Had Caylee been unable to convince Andi to come?

Maybe the purple-haired actress hadn't been the perfect accomplice. Andi had planned to spend the afternoon doing research in the library, but Caylee was supposed to intercept her at her apartment, hand her a clue, and talk her into a short scavenger hunt that would lead from her apartment to Gramercy Square where Andi would find a box holding a key.

The key to Gramercy Park.

He hadn't forgotten that she wanted to see inside, and with all the reporters and paparazzi stalking his every move, the gated park was currently the perfect place for privacy. Andi wanted to believe the conspiracies that centuries-old secrets were imprisoned in the garden, including rumors that Edwin Booth's statue was really a headstone to his grave that lay beneath.

None of it was true, of course. Upon the park's completion, the gates were put around the garden to give the community a sense of privilege and grandeur in hopes of attracting the social elite to the square. Who didn't love being one of the few to hold enough power to enter forbidden territory?

White flashed in between the branches of a shrub. A moment later, Andi emerged around the corner, beaming like the sun on this clear October day. Beau stood. Her pace quickened to a near jog. He held out his arms, and she launched herself within his grasp, her squeal ringing his ear.

The softness of her body against his sparked an appetite that was hard to suppress. The scent of pumpkin spice clung to her, and he wanted to bury his face in her hair and stay there all day. She pulled away, grinning. "I missed—"

He silenced her with his lips. The stress and sleepless nights of politics and speeches and charity functions drained from his muscles. Andi was his favorite season. She was everything that completed him contained in a graceful, five-foot-six frame. He wanted the privilege of doing this every day for the rest of his life.

Slow down, Governor.

She broke away, smiling against his lips. "Hi."

Birds chirped. A horn sounded in the distance. Trees and shrubs surrounded them, and it was as if they were the only ones in the city. He kissed her again. "Hi back."

Her laugh was breathy. "You make me dizzy."

He was only getting started.

"Then let's sit."

"Let's walk. I've always wanted to see this place, and it may be my only chance."

Not if he had anything to do about it. Maybe thoughts about their being together for the rest of his life were premature, but the foreseeable future was safe.

He locked her fingers in his, and they strolled down the path, stopping every few feet for her to admire a plant or a garden decoration. She brought a pink flower with a white center to her nose. "It's been so long since I've been in a garden. I'm surprised the frost we got the other night didn't kill them off."

The way she took such pleasure in something so simple had him wanting to buy her a private greenhouse so they could both enjoy this view all year long. It had been a light frost, but soon it would put to sleep the last of the summer colors and everything within the gates would be a mix of reds and golds and browns.

"The Gramercy Park Block Association will start decorating for Halloween next week. Pumpkins, ravens, fake spiderwebs, and Macbeth-style skulls will fill the entire garden."

"All that for the enjoyment of the homeowners?"

"And their guests. The festivities kick off the official start of Halloween. Of course, to gain clearance, you'll have to pass a drug test, and a criminal background check, give a sample of DNA, and sign over the rights to your firstborn child."

She elbowed him in the ribs.

"It's a fun day for all ages. Come with me. Invite your parents."

She stopped beside a bush whose leaves had turned a fiery red. "I'm sure they'd love to come, but are you sure?"

Was the woman seriously asking if he was serious enough about their relationship to meet her parents?

He palmed the sides of her face. The breeze stirred her hair across his knuckles. "I'm certain. Not seeing you this past week almost drove me crazy. I can't tell you how many times I almost walked out on Wilson and his endless list of tasks. Knowing you're close helps me focus."

"Your 'behind every good man is a better woman' thing?"

"Exactly. If I'm going to do this well, I need someone by my side to keep me grounded, encouraged. Someone to make sure I take time to relax." He brushed his thumbs along the velvety skin at the corner of her lips. "Someone to offer a good distraction."

When her eyelids fluttered closed, it nearly did him in. He leaned in and gave her the softest kiss. "I know we've only known each other a few months and how hesitant you've been to start a serious relationship, especially with someone in my position, but I need you, Andi. You're my person."

Her hands sandwiched his against her face. "How's a girl supposed to say no to that?" Her gaze roamed his features. She swallowed. "I'll talk to my parents."

The next few minutes were a blur of kisses before he finally broke away. "Come on. I'll show you the man you really came to see."

He led her around a bend in the path.

"Oh, Beau." Her feet slowed to a stop.

Trees fading into autumn splendor framed a spectacular view of the Empire State Building against the backdrop of blue sky. She rested her head on his shoulder. "It feels like we're tucked away in our own little world."

She begged him for a picture with the cityscape behind them.

"Can't. The park association has a list of strict rules, and one of them is no photography. They enforce these rules with hidden cameras throughout the garden."

"You mean to tell me you pay as much as you do for access and upkeep, and you're not allowed to take pictures?"

"Or walk pets, play sports, leave children unattended, bring furniture, have music, drink alcohol, or feed the wildlife."

"Wow. And you think I'm crazy for believing there's a reason they keep these two acres monitored like Fort Knox."

"No, I think you have an overactive writer brain. There's a difference."

She made a face at him, and they walked the remaining twenty yards to Edwin Booth's monument. A sycamore offered little shade to the bronze man bowing his head, fist clutching his cloak as if playing a part onstage.

Andi studied the statue from all angles, as if by doing so she could learn every facet of the man when he'd existed. "I feel sorry for him."

"Why? Because he's dead, yet his legend still lives on?"

She narrowed her eyes. "Because he had to carry the shame of what his brother had done. Imagine the heaviness of that. The very sibling you grew up with assassinating one of the country's most beloved presidents and forever shaping American history. The pain, the mortification, the banishment poor Edwin must've gone through. I think he's holding his heart here for more reasons than a performance."

"Cue the writer's imagination. Enter backstory." He grinned wryly. "It's a statue that was made long after his death. It doesn't feel anything."

"I realize that. But one human to another, I can't imagine the pain of living through that."

He toyed with the ends of her hair. "Your empathy and compassion for others is one of my favorite qualities about you."

"Really? What are some of your other favorite qualities?"

"A politician never reveals all his cards at once."

"I guess I'll have to reconsider my vote, then."

"You wouldn't!"

She shrugged. Winked. "Speaking of brothers, I found something last week that I wanted to wait and tell you about in person."

"Regarding what?"

"I found your great-great-grandfather's Civil War military record that lists a brother named Edward as his next of kin to be notified in case of death."

Unease squirmed in his gut. If that was true, how was there no record of Edward with the family? Had the brothers been estranged? Had there been some tragic event? But that still didn't explain the missing record.

"While Franklin was fighting valiantly for our country, Edward was in Utah Territory scamming anyone evading the war who was wealthy enough to purchase land."

She pulled a folded paper from her pocket and handed it to him. It was the wanted poster she'd mentioned several days ago. He scanned the drawing—the dark, slicked-back hair, wide-set eyes, square jaw, serious mouth. The man's features eerily resembled his own aging father's.

"How can you be sure the Edward in this photo is the brother listed on Franklin's military record?" he asked. "Maybe he just shares the same name."

And maybe she should stop poking this bear.

"I can't say with one hundred percent certainty, as two of the Secret Service photographs I found of him are too grainy for recognition when enlarged, but I'm pretty certain." The skin between her brows bunched. "Does your family have any photos of Franklin somewhere? We could compare them side by side."

"Not all brothers resemble each other."

"Please, Beau. Call it crazy or intuition, but I suspect they may have been twins."

He shook his head, peeved. "There's no record of twins in my family, or an Edward Davidson, despite what the military record says. What good will it do to dig up the past?"

"But—"

"What if all your theories prove true? Then what? You write your article on the good and evil of the Davidson-Quincy family?"

What if Wilson was right about her only dating him for a story, and he was too blinded to see it?

"You'd likely earn your promotion, Andi, but it could destroy me."

"Look at me." She gripped his upper arms with gentle force. "I'm not in this to hurt you or destroy your family. I care about you too much for that. Something happened to Edward while he was fleeing east after being discovered, and it's plausible that Franklin used his brother's name as an alias when he'd go undercover with the Secret Service. A way of hiding his identity but also bringing some honor to Edward's name. I believe that's why E. Davidson appears on the hotel record."

She returned her attention to Edwin Booth's statue. "Imagine growing up in the same household, taught the same way, sharing thoughts and memories and love, only for the demon of betrayal to rip it all to shreds. I think Franklin was just as torn about his brother's actions as Edwin was with John's. There's honor in that."

Beau glanced at the concrete path, the plants, the sky, his mind reeling. How had this day shifted course so quickly? "My question still stands. Then what? You publish it? To what good?"

Her posture curled in as she crossed her arms. "For the good of history. To solve the mysteries of the past and educate those living in the present. Your family practically helped build New York City. What better way to disprove the accusations that your age and privilege disqualifies you from becoming governor than to prove that you come from hardworking, patriotic stock? That you understand the people in all their facets."

He threw his hands out. "Have I not done that already?"

If not, three weeks wasn't enough time to convince voters.

Up to this point, he'd kept his doubts and anxiety bottled and stored in a small compartment to keep his head on straight. She'd just blown it all wide open.

"Of course you have. You've done a fantastic job." Andi rested her forehead on his chest. "I'm making a mess of this."

When she craned her neck to look at him, a breeze blew small strands of her hair against her cheeks. He was too angry to brush them away.

"What I'm trying to say is, I'm in awe of who you are and the magical way you understand people of all ages, nationalities, and social standing. You have more than proven yourself, and I am so proud of you. Truth is, I want to solve this mystery for me. I've been attempting to stand on my own and prove myself since Allen upended my life, and this is my chance. This is all I have."

She looked down at her feet and kicked at a stray rock. "I don't believe in fate or coincidences. I believe I found those counterfeit bills in my room for a purpose."

Was that purpose to take him down? Because if all her theories proved true and the information got leaked to the media, it would blow his aphorism of truth to smithereens.

Seconds of strained silence passed before she reached for his hands. "I promise I won't use any information I find to hurt you or your family. I promise to tell you everything I've discovered before any of it goes to publication."

Here he'd cleared his entire day to invite her inside the gates, his heart, his life.

He couldn't allow her to expose his family. Make him look incompetent or untrustworthy. No matter how deeply he'd fallen for her.

He also couldn't fault her for wanting to forge her own path. If things didn't work out between them—and he really wanted things to work out—she'd need her success. Her independence. Heck, if there was anything his mother had taught him, it was that a woman needed some of that even after she was married and settled.

Compartmentalizing his concerns with his sour attitude, he wrapped his arms around her back. "You're going to continue solving this mystery whether I offer my blessing or not, aren't you?"

She chewed her bottom lip. "Yes."

"Then we'd better continue sticking together." That way he'd have a chance to defend his family if needed.

"Thank you, Beau." She stood on tiptoe and pecked the side of his mouth.

Keeping hold of one hand, he turned them toward his house. "Come on. Let's see what we can find."

CHAPTER TWENTY-SEVEN

EDWARD

Manhattan, February 1870

$\mathcal{E}$dward inhaled the familiar scents of New York City. Snow. Horse-flesh. Woodsmoke. Refuse reeking from slum alleys. The pungent spices of Little China. The earthy smell of Little Italy. In the last fifteen years, he'd traveled across the country and toured all the East Coast, only to circle back to where he'd started from. Now that Secret Service head-quarters had relocated to New York City, a modest home on an average street was not enough for him. He would give Cora the very best of Fifth Avenue or, if possible, Gramercy Park.

They were all each other had now. She was his daughter, and Cora would have every opportunity he had not.

"Slow the carriage, please."

The driver shifted the team to the side of the road and halted.

Edward stared across the East River at Blackwell's Island. The wind coming off the water stung his face and burned his eyes. The horses danced in impatience. If he left Margaret in Washington, there would be enough distance between them to suppress threats to his identity. Sometime over the past month, however, she'd figured out that if she acted normal and mentioned nothing about her husband's twin brother or murder and helped around the asylum, they'd believe her to be cured and would have no reason to keep her locked away.

If she was released, it would finish him.

But if he moved her to Blackwell's Island Asylum, he could keep up with her progress. Here he could manipulate her condition to prevent her from ever leaving their doors. It pained Edward to consider it. He'd loved Margaret and all they could have had together. But not enough to risk his future.

Yes, he would have Margaret transferred to Blackwell's Island.

"Walk on." Edward settled against the seat, pulling the bearskin blanket farther up his torso.

The driver flicked the reins, and the horses moved, jerking the carriage. He would begin looking for a house immediately and a new cell for Margaret.

There was no longer a foundation for a murder accusation, as Edward had gathered all family accounts of his birth as well as the hospital's record. Sneaking into the records department and removing it had been one of the easiest crimes he'd ever committed. The next night in his study, in front of a blazing fire, he'd burned it all, barefoot and braceless just to spite Margaret. Cora had sat beside him, singing a happy tune and playing with her jacks while he tossed document after document into the flames.

Miss Moreau was no longer in his employment after rejecting his advances. He'd be seeking out a new nanny as well. Thank goodness Mrs. Albany had insisted on staying full-time now that her husband had passed.

His vision of a proper family had burned that night too. He should have known better. Family had been taken from him on the day of his birth, when his father had seen his clubfoot. Where his mother's love had knitted them together for a short time, his father's disdain had ripped them apart. He belonged in no family.

So be it. Other than Cora, he didn't need anyone or anything. He was master of his own life. His own destiny. He would rise from the ashes and become one of the city's most respected and revered men.

⁂

Andrea
Manhattan, Present Day

Beau's home was unlike anything Andrea had ever seen outside of a magazine or museum. Pale gray walls surrounded furniture and decor strategically placed to give each room a calm and airy feel. Neutral drapes hung from massive windows. Live plants made the rooms breathe. The patterned wood floors were masterpieces in their own right. Mirrors and crystal chandeliers reflected light in all the right places.

But it was the study that held her spellbound. Every reader's, writer's, lover of knowledge's dream. Mahogany bookshelves ran floor to ceiling on three walls. Padded seating curved with the wall of windows, exposing a breathtaking view of Gramercy Park.

She ran her fingers along the keys of the old typewriter placed there for ambiance more than functionality, no doubt. "How do you make yourself leave this room?"

Beau chuckled. "The way I do any other room, I guess. I get hungry."

"Who needs food when you can feast on the written word? And this view!" She stepped up to the glass and let the sunlight bathe her face.

"A bit melodramatic, isn't it?" He sidled up behind her. "My earliest memories of this room were sitting right here with my grandma Mary and playing jacks."

He pointed to a spot in the corner where the sun pooled on the gleaming floor. "I remember vividly because she couldn't stand up after our match. I was too little to be of any help getting her to her feet and had to call for help. I was afraid she'd die on that floor."

"A bit melodramatic, isn't it?" She leaned against his chest.

"I was four. She was close to ninety, and I was terrified I'd doomed my grandma by asking her to play jacks."

"I bet you were the cutest boy to grace the Davidson or Quincy family."

"I was." He tapped her hip. "I think the family files are over here."

She followed him to a bookshelf on the other side of the room. A small golden plaque that said GENEALOGY graced the outer edge of a shelf. "Is every section so well organized?"

"My great-grandma Cora's doing." He scanned the titles.

"I'm sure she was lovely."

"And thorough. If there's anything dark or untoward about our past, she'd have it documented. Don't be disappointed if your search comes up empty. My campaign manager—and opposing party, for that matter—have scoured our lives for dirt without success. We're as pure as the first fallen snow."

"I'm glad."

She meant it. Even if it sabotaged her article. A truly good man was hard to find these days. And she had other stories she could fall back on in hopes of gaining the promotion, like the birth of the New York Public Water system and tragic tale of Miss Everwood. Though she doubted either would secure the position.

"Cora was Franklin's daughter, correct?"

"Mmmhmm." He pulled down a Bible that had belonged to Cora and flipped open the front cover. "See? The tree goes all the way back to the revolution. No record of an Edward Davidson."

She glanced at the yellowed page. "She was married in June 1890. One month before her father's death. What a sad way to begin a marriage."

He slipped a black-and-white photograph of a beautiful alabaster-skinned woman in front of her.

"Is this Cora? She was gorgeous."

"She was. If that's not too weird to say about my grandma."

Andrea snickered.

"Poor thing." She pointed to a line in the Bible. "She lost her mother at four years old. Complications from childbirth."

"I've heard Grandma Cora suffered from something they called 'the vapors.' Nowadays, they call it a panic attack."

"I can't imagine losing a parent. And at such a young age."

Beau grew quiet, and she wanted to kick herself for such an insensitive comment. "I'm sorry. I only meant—"

"No harm done." He rubbed a quick circle on her back then slipped the Bible onto the shelf and continued skimming the titles. "They say, Grandma Cora was cautious, missed no detail, and took nothing for granted. That even when she grew as old as the crypt keeper, if her grandkids wanted to play pirates, she played pirates."

Andrea waited while Beau continued searching for whatever he was looking for. It was surreal knowing that she was in one of the oldest homes in Gramercy Park with one of the wealthiest men in New York City. It was a privilege. Being part of Beau's life was a privilege. Despite their vast differences from the beginning, Beau had quickly made it seem as if he were an ordinary man and that they'd known each other their whole lives.

She refused to take that for granted.

"You're doing it again." Beau removed another book.

"Doing what?"

"Mentally retreating." He walked to the desk and sat, patting his knee. "Our differences are a source of strength for each other. Not a downfall."

Embarrassment flooded her. "How did you know what I was thinking?"

One side of his mouth curled. "Your eyes get large like a deer right before a car plows into it. You also fiddle with your necklace."

Her left hand dropped from the thin metal chain around her neck. She sighed and perched on his offered leg. "Actually, I was thinking about how wonderful you are and how no matter what we do or don't find, being with you is something special I won't take for granted."

His right hand curled around her hip. He leaned for a kiss then flipped open the book.

To her surprise, it was a scrapbook of newspaper articles, cards, letters, and brittle photographs. "This is amazing." She stilled his hand from turning the page. "Is that what they called a calling card?"

"According to the notation, it's a calling card from Matthew Quincy, my great-grandfather."

"To think, nowadays we'd just text the person and tell them to open their door."

Beau smiled. He turned the page, rubbing a thumb along the small of her back as he did. Her arm went around him, and she massaged the hair at his nape.

"Here's one of her old dance cards." He pointed to the list of names nearly faded with time. "My great-grandfather is on there three times."

"How sweet! I hope it was a marriage of love and not convenience like so many were back then."

"The family has always said they adored each other. Competitive and passionate about everything they did. They consulted each other about everything."

"Sounds wonderful. I wish I could've known her."

"Me too. I've heard she was meticulous about keeping journals, but I've never seen them. They maybe didn't survive the test of time."

He flipped through more pages until he reached the section dedicated to Cora's father, Franklin. Small strips of hair ribbon—gifts from her father's travels—cards, and newspaper articles were tucked into the pages. Beau paused when they reached a page dedicated to his time in the Secret Service.

A newspaper clipping from 1868 had an accompanying photo that showed five men lined in a row, kneeling in front of a building marked U.S. TREASURY. The article stated that Abraham Lincoln had commissioned the Secret Service before his assassination to stabilize the fledgling economy after the Civil War, as one-third of the circulated money in the country was counterfeit. After Lincoln's death, Andrew Johnson worked closely with the Secret Service in his mission as president to rebuild a tattered nation.

The five men pictured had just taken down a large counterfeiting ring in Ohio, capturing criminals wanted for murder, desertion, counterfeiting, and land frauds. They'd also seized several large crates containing opium. Though opium use was not illegal, the drug's addiction had become a growing problem.

"Franklin was a hero."

Beau leaned back in the chair, shifting her closer. "I told you we're pure."

She pulled the wanted poster from her pocket and unfolded it. "Do you have any close profiles of Franklin?"

He yawned. "You're welcome to look through anything you like. Wake me when you're done."

While he leaned his head against the chair and closed his eyes, she scoured three more pages before landing on a wedding photograph of Franklin and his wife, Margaret. Andrea's hands shook as she held the pictures of the men side by side. The two faces of January.

"Twins."

Beau woke, knocking her into the desk. "Sorry. What do you mean, twins?"

"Look."

Nearly identical. Edward's face was a little thinner, his eyebrows thicker, one side of his mouth drawn in a sneer. All those characteristics that could've been false due to the artist's depiction, but it was the description of his right ear that gave it away.

Her backside was growing numb from sitting on Beau's knee, so she shifted positions. "The description on the wanted poster mentions a clearly deformed right ear. Both of Franklin's ears are perfect. Both men—well, they were boys at the time—were mentioned in census records. They're twins."

"Wow." Beau's facial muscles tensed in concentration. "Then why is there no birth or death record of Edward on file with the government or with our family records?"

"I don't know."

But she was going to find out.

She flipped another page to a headshot of Franklin dated 1880. Age lines and gray, thinning hair marked the only differences from his wedding photo. His head was angled, hiding his right ear. One lapel of his suit sported his military medal and the other a pin—a shield with antlers on the sides and a bee in the middle.

Familiarity buzzed at the edges of her memory. Where had she seen that before?

Beau voiced aloud his concerns of this information and his confusion as to why the family had kept it hidden. She heard his words, but her mind wouldn't let go of the familiar emblem. "Any idea what this pin is about?"

Beau took a closer look. "That's our family crest. Why?"

She should've thought of that herself.

"No reason." Except she'd seen it somewhere before.

Then she remembered. It was the same design on the blue bottle at the relic shop. The one Grant Caudalie said had been used for storing opium. Franklin Davidson had been part of a Secret Service raid where they'd seized opium. He'd either adopted the same emblem as their family crest after raiding those opium bottles, or he'd had the emblem stamped into the bottles to mark them as his.

Goose bumps skittered up her spine.

She needed to get ahold of that bottle.

CHAPTER TWENTY-EIGHT

EDWARD

Manhattan, June 1872

*C*ora's six-year-old hand was small and soft in Edward's calloused palm. The girl was nothing but delightful, believing he held the world in his hands. In many ways, he did.

"Where are we going, Papa?" Big curious eyes, so like her mother's, gazed up at him with absolute trust.

"I have a surprise for you."

"Another one? You give the best surprises, Papa." Her full cheeks lifted in a grin that brushed against the ringlets cascading from the side of her little hat. Now that Cora was no longer a tot, Mrs. Albany fulfilled both roles of cook and governess. She was responsible for the young girl's dernier cri, for he knew nothing of feminine fashion.

Except that he enjoyed a décolletage on an attractive woman, single or otherwise.

When it came to Cora, no expense was too much. He'd paid handsomely for padded bustles with looped overskirts, large bows in bright colors, and sleeves and collars that Cora claimed made her itchy. Her button boots were no bigger than Edward's hand, but she managed to run and play in them like any energetic child.

Cora gripped one side of her dress and mimicked the sashay of the magnificent woman in front of them who was clinging to her lover's arm. Edward was grateful his curse hadn't transferred to Cora during development. Not that he'd taken any part in conceiving her, but he'd heard such deformities could transmit within families.

What if the child he had created with Margaret had been like him? What would he have done, knowing all of society would shun the child?

There was a theory that some infants died in the womb from improper development. That divine Providence interceded to make it whole versus allowing it to suffer on earth. If that was true, then he was glad his and Margaret's baby had died. Edward hadn't been spared the suffering, and he wouldn't wish that on any child.

Sure, the highest of social circles accepted him now. He was respected among society alongside the Astors and the Guggenheims. After all, he was Franklin Davidson—war hero, Secret Service agent, successful entrepreneur in medical advances. If only they knew he'd killed his own brother, stolen a portion of seized bills during every raid, and replaced it with his own counterfeit so he could continue circulating the money he'd stolen by trading it for opium and then selling the opium to Curtis and Perkins in Bangor, Maine, to be used in Mrs. Winslow's Soothing Syrup for fussy babies and children.

Duplicity at its finest.

Those men were no different simply because they'd been born into privilege. They'd evaded war, paying the government fee. They cheated on their wives. Left debts unpaid. Gambled. Played dirty with their investments.

No different than he.

Leaves rustled overhead, their shadows dancing on the road between the reflection of sunlight. Cora hummed as she made a game of hopping on the patches of light. She would begin her studies with a tutor this fall. For now, it brought him joy to see her simply live in the moment.

He paused before a wrought-iron gate. Cora quieted and gazed up at him, as if sensing the seriousness of the moment. "Is this a graveyard, Papa?" she whispered.

Edward chuckled and patted her head. "No, my dear. This is home."

He opened his palm.

She gaped at the brass key. "We're going to live outside with only these clothes? Like carpetbaggers?"

A cough covered his humor. "No, Cora. This is a garden. A very special garden. Our new home is on the other side of it."

To his chagrin, her tiny ears had been listening more to the conversations with his business associates than he'd realized. She'd misused the term, obviously thinking carpetbaggers to be gypsies.

Those meetings with his associates ensured she had everything a young girl needed to succeed and grow into a desirable woman of society. However, she would also need training in how to act like a lady, which meant less time spent in male company.

She bounced on her toes. "Is it a magical garden?"

"In many ways, yes. Only the most prominent families in the city can access this garden. And the Davidsons are one of them."

"What does prominent mean?" She wrapped her fists around the gate's bars and yanked.

"It means special." He dangled the key before her eyes.

She danced on tiptoes, waiting for him to unlock the gate. "Are there bunnies inside?"

"If not, I'll buy you a bunny to put inside."

Her hands smacked together in excitement.

"Cora Elaine Davidson, welcome to Gramercy Park."

The key turned in the lock. The mechanism squealed before releasing its hold. He let Cora open the gate and smiled when she rushed inside. For the next twenty minutes, he followed her as she smelled every flower, inspected every plant, and skipped down every path.

Her dress fanned out around her as she spun in a circle. She stopped abruptly, and her hand went to her forehead, likely to quell the dizziness. "Will Mommy be coming with us to our new house?"

Edward stuck out his chin. She hadn't mentioned her mother in several weeks, seeming to accept that her mother was in the hospital and never coming back. Even the night terrors had quelled.

"No, darling. Mommy isn't coming."

She frowned up at the trees. "Okay."

He grasped her hand, and they walked to the gate on the opposite side of the garden. "Let's go see our new home."

Cora's mood lifted again. A continuous waist-high wrought-iron fence surrounded the brownstones on the other side of the square. Only one of those homes had twin lampposts outside. The home of James Harper, father of *Harper's Bazaar*. Apparently, the man had a shop in the back that used a horse to work the printing press. Edward hoped the press didn't operate too loudly.

Edward had purchased the home next door to Mr. Harper, with

Dr. Valentine Mott—New York's greatest surgeon—occupying Edward's other side. Edward expected the man to have a tight rein on his nine children.

As the city moved and breathed around them, they paused at the steps leading to the front door of their new home. Edward lifted his face to the sky. If only Margaret could see them now, despite her threats and accusations. She'd see all he could have given her.

If only his brother, Franklin, were watching, envying all the things he never would have been able to give his family. He'd know that turning his back on Edward was the wrong thing to do when they could have built this empire together. Fulfilled their childhood dreams. Together.

If only their father were alive, so that while he watched them enter their new home he could choke on every demeaning comment he'd ever thrown at Edward.

Perhaps his mother was watching. Was she proud of him?

Likely not.

The ribbon threaded through the end of the key was worn from his constant touch. The ribbon he'd taken from Margaret's braid the night she'd been taken to the asylum. The ribbon that reminded him of his mother's.

It might have taken him years using methods unconventional, but the Davidson name had finally come to mean something in this city.

Andrea
Manhattan, Present Day

While Edward Davidson's death eluded history, Franklin's and Margaret's had not. The wooden chair creaked beneath Andrea as she settled against the back, the sound echoing in the silent library. She stared at the screen, a ball of anxiety expanding in her stomach. Discovering the answers to this tangled mystery wasn't just a want, it was a need. Historical investigative journalism wasn't just her occupation, it was who she was. Sorting out facts, laying them out, connecting the dots, and exposing them was important. Facts helped people make informative decisions. Thorough research and disclosing details kept surprises from jumping out to strangle a person. Like Allen's hidden lifestyle had choked her.

Facts helped keep people safe.

But facts wouldn't keep her warm at night. Or provide her with love. Secure her future. Give her children someday.

She rubbed her tired eyes, a part of her wishing she'd never found that stupid pouch in the wall. Except, without the pouch, she never would've gotten close to Beau, which still left her alone with her reliable companion —facts. And the blue opium bottle bearing the Davidson-Quincy family crest she'd paid a ridiculous amount for. Grant Caudalie had smelled her desperation coming from twenty blocks.

Beau and the counterfeit bills were synonymous with each other, whether she liked it or not. However, pursuing one meant losing the other, she was certain. Which made this even more difficult.

She'd easily discovered through public records that Franklin had died at forty-nine in his home on July 11, 1890, from a failing heart, his daughter Cora by his side. Cora's mother, Margaret, had died years earlier in 1873 at the age of thirty-one, her death certificate signed by a doctor named T. I. Calloway.

The New York City Department of Records and Information Services database also offered related searches to any name that appeared on a record, and the program was alerting Andrea that Doctor T. I. Calloway was listed on 132 other death certificates from the Almshouse Ledgers, specifically Blackwell's Island Asylum.

To click or not to click… She fiddled with the small pendant on her necklace, moving it back and forth along the chain as her thoughts raced.

Zip. Zip.

What were the odds that the same doctor who treated patients at the country's most notorious insane asylum also treated the cream of society in Gramercy Park? Slim. Members of society often had personal physicians and would frown upon using someone who worked in places that might expose them to the diseases of the lower class.

Unless Dr. Calloway transferred to Blackwell's Island after Margaret's death. But would a doctor who'd worked in the best of conditions among the social elite transfer to such a terrible place? And wouldn't the doctors of the asylum specialize more in mental conditions than a typical physician?

Then again, she'd read books on Nellie Bly, and those mental health doctors weren't specialized in anything other than using their patients like lab rats to perform horrific experimental treatments that often led to brain damage or death.

Oliver's words from that night at the Players echoed through her mind. *"What if the answers you find cause someone damage? You can't just pretend you didn't find them. . . . Some secrets never stop hurting others."*

He had a point. Did it really matter what someone had done two centuries ago?

Her finger hovered over the button to close the program.

But she couldn't let this go.

Zip. Zip.

Why couldn't she let this go?

Because the world was not a reliable place. She couldn't rely on Beau for a happily ever after. She needed her job, especially if things with Beau didn't work out. Working for *Smithsonian* magazine wasn't just a writing outlet, it was her calling. History was beautiful. History was ugly. But every breath given and taken, every jot and tittle ever recorded, made the nation what it was today. History needed to be taught, it needed to be examined, and wisdom needed to be gained from it.

Or was her passion to expose and share the truth a distraction from dealing with her own issues? Did she use it as a diversion to point attention away from herself?

In some ways, she supposed she did. Something to self-examine. However, she couldn't deny the career opportunity provided a great platform. If she gained this promotion as writer-at-large, she could promote the magazine to a new level. Use that platform to create programs for schools, libraries, and other public outlets.

Collaborating with the Smithsonian curators to build new displays was her calling. She couldn't let a man, no matter how wonderful he was, convince her to give that part of herself away.

If that meant wading through the swamp of family secrets without Beau's approval, so be it. She wasn't in this to hurt anyone. Only to gain the truth. Beau had built his campaign on truth. Here was his chance to prove his authenticity. If he meant what he touted, then he'd understand. If he didn't, she would still have her job.

Only he never asked her to give up her calling. In fact, despite his reservations about it all, he'd worked beside her to find the answers.

Oh, she was losing her mind.

Inhaling a deep breath, she moved her cursor to the bar of related searches and clicked on T. I. Calloway before she could talk herself out of it.

One hundred thirty-three handwritten documents appeared, scanned by city employees a decade ago after being awarded a preservation grant to preserve asylum and Almshouse records. Andrea looked through seventy records before her gaze locked on Margaret Davidson's.

Blackwell's Island Asylum—B.3.

No. 74.   New York.   April 1, 1873

This certifies that Margaret E. Davidson, born in Pittsburgh, Pennsylvania, on May 16, 1841, died at 4:17 a.m. on Blackwell's Island.

Cause of death: unknown

Institutionalized by her husband on February 12, 1873, after being transferred from St. Elizabeth's Hospital in Washington, D.C.

Diagnosis: hysteria and insanity

Andrea's heart raced. Had Beau known about this? Was this why he was apprehensive about her poking further? He'd said his campaign manager had done a thorough investigation on his family. Surely it had revealed such records. Then again, this was 150 years ago. Maybe Wilson hadn't checked that far back.

She took a screenshot that she could print off and show Beau later. She'd honor her promise to tell him everything she discovered. Her word was good, and he meant too much to her to do otherwise.

However, this discovery added another question to her list. If the Davidsons were from New York City, why had Margaret originally been institutionalized in D.C.?

Unfortunately, the records from St. Elizabeth's Hospital weren't as organized in the database as the Almshouse site, but Andrea was able to obtain Margaret's medical record after several attempts.

Patient has suffered from melancholy since the birth of her first child. Upon the miscarriage of her second child, her condition has grown worse according to her husband and family physician, Richard J. Fullerton. Patient admitted upon the request of her husband and by the authority of her physician for madness leading to hysterics. Patient continues to claim that her husband was murdered by his twin brother and that he assumed his identity. No record of a twin brother found.

Andrea's vision grew fuzzy at the edges. Margaret Davidson was either truly insane or Andrea had finally discovered the truth behind why Edward was so elusive.

CHAPTER TWENTY-NINE

BEAU

Manhattan, Present Day

*B*eau's dynasty was crumbling at the hands of the woman he'd fallen in love with.

He leaned his elbows on the table and rubbed his throbbing temples. His dad paced the length of the dining room windows. Wilson and his assistant, Lizzy, were at the kitchen island, scrambling for a way to keep the scandal hidden.

"How much do you think it'll take to keep her quiet?"

Beau looked at his father, who'd aged ten years overnight. He swallowed the rising bile. "Andi doesn't work that way."

"Everyone has a price. The hardest part is finding out what it is."

Beau had hoped his affection and devotion to her would be enough. How naive he'd been. He wasn't successful by showing the world who he was as a man, but by proving what he could do for the world. His image was too important to let her attack it.

"Did you know about Grandma Cora's mother?"

Dad stared out the window without replying.

"You knew." Beau blew out a long breath, anger simmering. "Nearly every detail of our family's history is in that study, documented and organized with fancy little plaques as a shrine to the Davidson-Quincy empire. There isn't one word about anyone being institutionalized or Franklin having a twin brother—or any siblings for that matter—and now I can't help but wonder what other dark secrets are being hidden."

Papers shuffled, and the low hum of conversation in the kitchen filled the silence.

Dad joined him at the table, smoothing a hand along his tie. Hard and composed as always. "I knew that my great-grandmother had been institutionalized, but I never knew what for and, frankly, never cared to know the details. It was so long ago, and they locked women up for almost anything back then. No one in the family ever discussed it. I only learned of it because an older cousin let it slip one night thirty years ago after too much to drink."

Dad rubbed at his side where his gallbladder tortured him. "Medical records are sacred, but on ones that old, the statute of limitations has expired. It hasn't been until the last ten years or so that the city made them public after being awarded preservation grants. Wilson discovered the information on Grandma Cora's mother but felt it unthreatening. Those records can only be accessed if one is seeking them specifically, and Timothy Greene's team wouldn't think to check medical records from the Civil War."

Post–Civil War, but that detail wasn't worth correcting.

"No doubt, at this point they'll use anything and will be thrilled to get ahold of this." Beau rubbed his hand down his face. "My campaign is founded on truth. On the stellar reputation of the Davidson-Quincy family—the honest and hardworking patriarchs of this city. After Wilson leaked that story about Timothy Greene and his ownership of an Asian factory that dumped hundreds of gallons of toxins into the ocean, they'll run with this information on Edward Davidson and stop at nothing to take us down."

Dad sighed. "Then it can't get out. You're twelve days from Election Day, and we've worked too hard these past years to let some gold-digging journalist who works for an insignificant magazine ruin your career."

Beau could say confidently that Andi wasn't a gold digger, and *Smithsonian* magazine wasn't an insignificant periodical. "If she was intent on ruining my career, she wouldn't have told me about this in the first place. She'd have blindsided me with it right before the election and gotten her fifteen minutes of fame."

A truth that did nothing to quell the misery running through his veins.

"Don't be foolish. She's only telling us now because she knows she can get far more out of it than fifteen minutes."

Was Dad right? Had Andi been playing him this whole time?

His head pounded like a sledgehammer on concrete while he recalled their time together. He'd pursued her. Practically had to beg her to go out with him. She'd never asked him for money or gifts and had demanded she purchase her own meals, though he never let her. She'd been too hesitant about their different worlds to be in this relationship for gain.

Or was it all an act?

"The Winderfield Apartments," Dad said.

Beau looked up from his hands bracketing his temples. "What?"

"Your insistence on negotiating that property away from the Woodrow Corporation to add to your own portfolio was to benefit her, correct?"

"Mostly."

"Done." He slapped his hand on the table, startling Beau and gaining the attention of the guests in the kitchen.

"What do you mean, done?"

Dad stood with a triumphant lift of his chin. "The Winderfield property is yours. I'll rush the payment and have the paperwork to you by tomorrow morning. Secure her silence by allowing her to keep her home. Offer it rent-free for life if you want to. I don't care what you bribe her with. Just get it done."

He walked away then paused. "Whatever you work out, get her signature on a contract."

Beau sat, stunned. Only a few times in his life had his father torn down the wall to order Beau around like an employee versus a son. Theodore Davidson-Quincy was on the warpath today, and by the time the battle was over, the landscape would look completely different.

"I don't see how this fixes anything." He could just imagine that conversation, how'd she react. How he'd react.

His father tugged on the lapels of his suit coat. "It gives you the upper hand, my boy. You'll own the building and any remaining secrets that may still lie inside. If she doesn't agree, you can throw her into the street."

※

Edward
Manhattan, Greenwich Village, April 1873

The handle of the carpetbag seared Edward's hand. The burden was weighty and venomous, ready to strike at a wrong move. He glanced around at the few guests traversing at the late hour and approached the hotel clerk for a room.

"How many nights will you be staying with us, sir?" The fat man's mustache twitched.

"Just the one, please." Edward rested the carpetbag at his feet.

Cora's seventh birthday was tomorrow, and he would be done with this business and back home when they delivered her pony.

The clerk placed the guest book in front of him, then the quill and ink. Edward dipped the quill and ran the tip along the glass rim to dislodge any excess. Hand poised on paper, he drew a scratch to begin the letter *F* then paused. Considering his actions, he backtracked and looped his script into an *E*.

He hadn't used his real name in almost a decade. No one should recognize him in his current disguise, but there was no chance that they would connect him with the name E. Davidson. After all, there was no record of such a man, and he'd exhausted the other names he went by.

A strange despondency settled over Edward. He'd thought of himself as Franklin for so long, he hardly considered his former life anymore. While he didn't miss the tribulation that followed the Edward Davidson name, he did miss the freedom of his own identity.

He even missed his brother.

Sadness stirred in his gut.

The clerk smiled as he took the guest book, revealing crooked teeth between ruddy cheeks. "Thank you, Mr. E. Davidson. We hope you enjoy your stay at the Winderfield Hotel."

That would depend on the softness of the bed and where he could stash the contents of his carpetbag. He thanked the man, took the key, lifted the bag, and went up the stairs in search of room 14. The scent of lye soap hung in the air from the laundry room.

The new hotel was antonymous to his usual haunts along Gramercy Square and Fifth Avenue. How different his life was now from his childhood. Instead of poverty, he had wealth. In place of persecution, respect. Apart from loneliness, there was Cora. How that child had woven her tapestry of love and devotion around his heart.

When he considered her motherless upbringing and compared it to his own, he loathed himself for being the one responsible. Often when he and Cora would go on walks or play games in the study, she'd ask about Margaret. Her longing for female company did not escape him. While Mrs. Albany treated Cora as if she were a grandchild, she was no replacement for a mother.

He'd considered taking another wife. Now that he was an eligible bachelor with a home in Gramercy, single women of society practically threw themselves at him. Especially the ones already past marriageable age. But he could not risk a wife discovering anything that might reveal his true self.

So, Cora would grow without a mother and he would spend most of the nights he had left in life alone, seeking comfort for his needs when he was away with the Secret Service. Even then, his excursions would be limited. Franklin's good name had a reputation to uphold.

Room 14 was simple, with only a small sitting area, bed, bureau, and washstand. A small round mirror hung above the bowl and pitcher. A fresh towel, folded, hung on a hook beside it. He could use a good shave and a stiff drink. A cleansing of his marrow.

His reflection in the mirror struck him hard. At thirty-two years of age, he looked at least ten years older, with thick patches of hair graying at the temples and swollen skin beneath his eyes. He looked like his father. His choices were catching up to him. Aging his body. A body that would one day die and release its soul into the hereafter.

Wherever that might be.

Every Saturday evening when Mrs. Albany served dinner, she reminded him that a proper upbringing in society must include Cora's attending of Sunday services. That a child's education needed a balance of reading, writing, arithmetic, and Bible studies. "Then I'll have her tutor include Jonah and the whale in her next lesson," he'd told her the last time she'd beat him over the head with it.

"Hogwash. No respectable family will accept that excuse. She must attend services in person and be seen. Do it for her benefit, her future, Mr. Davidson."

Maybe the old lady was right. While he had no desire to search the depths of his mortal being and repent of his wrongdoings, he wouldn't deny Cora anything that might enrich her life.

He tossed the carpetbag onto the bed and opened it to reveal its contents. Stacks of bills secured with leather bands stared back at him. Something inside him shifted. Shame? No, it couldn't be. This allowed him the means to provide the best for himself and Cora. There could be nothing wrong with that. But the need to make peace with *something* prodded him far too often.

Shoving the feeling aside, he scanned the room for the best place to hide the money. Counterfeit, all of it. Seized from his last raid in Virginia and swapped with his personal counterfeit made from the very plate he'd engraved himself and used the night of his brother's death.

As time went by, the less he remembered his brother's betrayal and the more he remembered the time of their youth. Playing stickball in the alley. Sleeping outside on warm summer nights to escape their father's drunken rages. Dreaming of what they wanted to be when they grew up. Franklin's gentle hand when tending to Edward's wounds.

Tears pricked his eyes. Franklin's dream had been to become a husband and father.

Edward had stolen that from him.

The horrid emotion stabbed him again. There was no peace for a man who'd murdered his brother. The unforgivable act marked him as it had Cain. God had turned his back on Edward too. *"Vengeance shall be taken on him sevenfold."*

Until then, he'd do whatever he had to do to provide a grand life for Cora so that when vengeance caught up to him, she'd be well cared for.

He pulled out the washstand and knelt, feeling along the wall where it met the corner. The baseboard was harder to pry away than he'd expected, making a clean split four inches in length. Nothing he couldn't repair. He notched out the plaster with his chisel and tucked the bills into the wall, along with a cloth pouch of counterfeit and the Townsends' address at 16 Gramercy Park South. Edward had learned through his connections that the family's newest butler had a secret background in theft and forgery. Much too convenient for Edward not to take advantage. If the money in this wall was found before he or one of his men could retrieve it, it would lead the authorities to the other side of the square, where Edward would watch from the safety of his fortress.

Two hours later, baseboard back in place and concealing the notched rectangle hidden by the washstand, one would never suspect that ten thousand dollars lay hidden inside.

He'd send word to O'Malley where to retrieve the money, and he'd send the latest shipment of opium to Curtis and Perkins. As he was an investor in Mrs. Winslow's Soothing Syrup, they would deposit his percentage into his bank account, further fattening his coffers. They'd repeat the process after his next raid.

Another stab of guilt.

Mothers across the country lived happier lives with calmer babies. Surely there was nothing wrong with a little peace and quiet. As it turned out, the syrup didn't only silence babies. It also worked to permanently silence women who wouldn't stop accusing their husbands of murder.

CHAPTER THIRTY

Andrea

Manhattan, Present Day

*T*he train to D.C. rocked Andrea's wounded heart like a baby in need of soothing. The scenery flashing past did nothing to distract her brain from replaying Beau's visit yesterday. He was the new owner of the Winderfield Apartments, and the Davidson-Quincy family demanded her silence.

Caylee snorted from the seat beside her. "Can you believe this guy?" She held up her phone so Andrea could view the screen. "Who's insane enough to try a stunt like that?"

A man with arms outstretched walked a tightrope over what looked to be the Grand Canyon. "That guy, apparently."

She went back to staring out the window.

Caylee elbowed her. "Don't be glum. We're having a girls' weekend in D.C.! There's no time for sadness."

When she'd asked Caylee to come with her, she'd alluded to wanting to celebrate Caylee's new leading role before the next year of performances took up all her time. They'd no longer see each other at Gant & Company, as Caylee had put in her resignation. Aside from treating her friend to a fun weekend in the country's most important city, Andrea wanted to take the counterfeit bills to her contact at the Smithsonian's National Museum of American History to see what information she could gain.

Holding to her promise, she'd told Beau of her intention. She'd also refused his father's suggestion of buying her silence. At first she'd believed that Franklin had honorably used Edward's identity as an alias for his missions. Now, with solid proof that Edward had institutionalized Franklin's wife for accusing him of murdering his twin brother and assuming Franklin's identity, and the link on the opium bottle being Beau's family crest, Andrea questioned her Pollyanna mentality. Margaret Davidson had either been a very ill woman, or she'd died sane and powerless under horrific conditions in an asylum.

Cause of death, unknown. How, when nurses patrolled and monitored patients around the clock? Brain trauma from ungodly experiments, or had she been murdered?

Beau had claimed that despite knowing about Margaret's insanity, his family was ignorant of any details regarding murder accusations, and they wanted Andrea to let the dead rest in peace. Nothing but harm could come from the story's exposure, and it would only harm those in the present, not provide justice to any past wrongs. For the first time since she'd met him, he'd been formal. Cold. Treating her as if she were a business acquaintance. Or a reporter.

Her chest ached with both longing for the man she was half in love with and from a warning not to put herself in the vulnerable position of becoming a modern-day Margaret. The Davidson-Quincys were powerful people, and Andrea had been trampled on before. No doubt they would desire to silence her. The question was, to what lengths would they go to accomplish it?

The D.C. sky had turned an angry gray, bringing with it the threat of rain. Andrea bunched her scarf for more coverage and savored the warmth of the coffee cup seeping through her glove. She'd met with the head curator at the Smithsonian's National Museum of American History while Caylee had gone to a local salon to refresh her cut and color. Her friend had already gone through all the hues of the rainbow, so Andrea was interested to see what style Caylee chose next.

Blessed heat warmed her face as she stepped into Hair Force One, a trendy salon with a vintage World War II atmosphere that was nestled in a corner building two blocks from the White House. Big band music played from the speakers, and the upholstery on the salon chairs was faux bomber jacket leather. The service counter and the furniture in the waiting area were chrome. There were even two little airplanes in the back where children could sit while they received a cut.

If Andrea wasn't so heartsick, she'd treat herself to some self-care while she was in town. But after an online conference call with a member of the Secret Service in the museum curator's office, pampering was the last thing on her mind.

Agent Winenger, who specialized in antique counterfeit equipment, money, paintings, and jewelry, had verified that the serial numbers and style of engraving on the bills matched records of ones supposedly seized by the Secret Service in 1874 but not turned over to the Department of the Treasury to be destroyed. The agency had long suspected there was a corrupt agent funneling the bills elsewhere, but they could never pinpoint who it was.

The agent said he couldn't declare anything for certain until the bills were analyzed and run through forensic testing, but it looked as if Andrea had helped solve one of the Secret Service's oldest cold cases. Or at least given the agency a good lead.

If Edward Davidson turned out to be the corrupt agent who built an empire in pharmaceuticals with the counterfeit money being exchanged for opium, Beau would be lost to her forever.

She stepped up to the abandoned counter, checking her email on her phone, when a woman came up beside her. She glanced up and said, "Go ahead. I'm just waiting for a friend."

"Andrea."

She pulled her gaze from her phone, focused on the woman, and blinked. "Caylee?"

Chestnut hair with a kiss of highlights framed her friend's face in an angled bob that had been curled to mimic beach waves. She'd never seen Caylee with a natural hair color and hadn't recognized her.

"You look amazing." Andrea tucked her phone in her pocket.

"I figured it was time for something different."

"It rocks."

Caylee laughed, paid the stylist for her services, and they walked back into the chilly air.

"How was your meeting?" Caylee stole Andrea's latte and took a sip.

"Time will tell. Why the change? Don't get me wrong, I love it. But why?"

She handed Andrea back her cup. "Mostly because my role in the Civil War era wouldn't be authentic if I had purple hair. I detest wearing wigs. Halo extensions I can do."

Caylee breathed a dreamy sigh. "And then there's Scott."

"The director's assistant?"

"He said my audition was brilliant. We've seen each other outside of practice a few times. I want Scott to like me for me. I figured I'd tried everything else since I've been in New York except being myself."

"My friend, you are a beautiful person either way."

For the next several hours, they shopped in nearby stores and took selfies at the Lincoln Memorial, the Capitol, and the Library of Congress. Though Andrea tried to be positive for Caylee's sake, being in this city again reminded her of Allen, which reminded her of Beau, which reminded her of the counterfeit bills even now being investigated by the Secret Service.

Which reminded her she stood on the edge of a precarious precipice.

CHAPTER THIRTY-ONE

EDWARD

Manhattan, Central Park, October 1879

A group of laughing children ran past Edward so closely he could feel the breeze. Despite being 843 acres of open land in central Manhattan, the park was congested. He blamed the permanent commission of the menagerie, goat rides, tennis on the lawn, and the new carousel. A park was meant for quiet recreation, and he preferred to spend a beautiful autumn afternoon with Cora in Gramercy Park over this crowd.

At thirteen years old, she craved excitement over quiet recreation.

"Would you like me to purchase you a ticket for the carousel?" he asked.

Her delicate fingers curled around his arm. "No, thank you."

She stared at the moving horses with longing in her eyes. When she started nibbling her bottom lip, he knew she was telling a falsehood. He could certainly teach her a few things about the ways of the world, but her innocence was what made his world less bleak.

"It's clear you want to ride. Let me treat you." He patted her hand gripping his bicep too hard for someone who had no interest in the carousel.

"Only if you'll ride it with me." Hope radiated from every pore on her face that no longer resembled a little girl but was quickly transforming into a woman.

He chuckled. "As appealing as it sounds to sit on a stiff wooden horse and spin in a circle, I'll leave it for the children."

Her shoulders fell. "That's why I can't ride it."

He raised a brow.

"It's for children." She sighed. "I'm no longer a child."

Was she not? When had she come to that conclusion?

Edward steered her toward the ticket booth. She was still very much a child, whether she realized it or not. He supposed this was one of those times a mother would know better what to say. "You sound disappointed."

"No." She looked away. "Yes."

"Which is it?" He kept a smile from his mouth.

"I want to be grown up and attend balls and dance and fall in love, but I also want to ride carousels and chase my friends at recess." She glanced around then leaned closer. "I'm not ready to give up my dolls yet. I don't play with them anymore, but putting them away seems like a betrayal. They've given me such comfort over the years."

He looked at the tree line to hide his amusement. How she'd loved each doll he'd brought her upon returning from a raid. She had to own close to thirty, all from different makers and cities. Those gifts would cease now that he'd retired from his duties with the Secret Service. Headquarters had moved back to D.C., and Edward was too settled in his life here to follow.

"You don't have to do anything until you're ready."

"All the other girls in my class have put away theirs."

She blinked away the moisture that had filled her eyes.

"So they say."

He supposed an all-girls school would still hold the same pressures as any other, one being to compete with peers. In this case, though, there'd be extra emotions and tears and a cruelty only young girls could execute. Maybe it wouldn't be bad to teach her a few things.

Edward looked at the carousel then the crowd around him, debating whether to enact this crazy idea. He was feeling better today, the fever and sores he'd suffered for several days gone for at least a week now. Maybe injecting a dose of childlike jolly into his life would finish setting him back to rights.

"We'll ride it together." He stepped into the line and paid for two tickets.

They raced each other to the carousel to see who could choose the finest steed first. The craftsmanship of the horses was to be envied, but the weather and rides from thousands of children were wearing on the detailed carvings. Once every saddle was filled, the ride jerked into motion. Edward gripped the pole stabilizing the horse and winked at his daughter.

Cora's laughter carried on the wind. In that moment, he didn't care that his life was a web of lies held together by glass threads or that he was the only adult on the carousel or what anyone thought of him riding it. He only cared about making his daughter happy, because at that moment he also knew he was at a crossroads. The little girl who trusted him, who thought him capable of doing anything, would soon slip away to marry a man she would trust and think capable of anything.

As life and time offered her experience after experience, she would learn the truth.

After several minutes, the ride stopped, and Edward dismounted with a sway. His stomach was woozy, his balance altered. He'd never understand how children found pleasure in spinning in circles. As a child, though, he'd have loved it.

Not that his childhood had held room for such entertainment.

Cora giggled and wrapped her fingers back around his arm. They strolled toward the Central Park Menagerie. "Thank you, Papa. You're so good to me."

The kiss on his cheek, and in public at that, surprised him.

"There's nothing I wouldn't give you, darling."

Except a mother.

Except your real father.

Except the truth.

The accusing voices held more frequent arguments in his head nowadays. He tried to silence them, but the more time that passed, and the closer Cora came to growing up and leaving him, the bolder they became.

"Why are you frowning, Papa?"

Edward shook his head. "I was just thinking how my father never would have allowed us so much fun."

"Us?" Her head tipped to the side.

"Me." He scolded himself for the mistake. The childish jolly had produced less clarity and more exhaustion.

They stepped around a dog that had stopped in front of them to dig. The mutt flung dirt on Edward's shoe. He swallowed a curse. Someone needed to keep this mutt under control.

"What was your papa like? You never talk about my grandparents. Or any of our family." Cora's top teeth nibbled her lip again.

He stifled a groan. "He wasn't a good man, and that's all I'm going to say. My mother, well, she was a veritable angel that only got to stay on earth until I was five. No woman has captivated my heart since. Except you."

He nudged her ribs with his elbow.

"And Mama, right?"

"Uh, yes, of course. And your mother."

The effects of his mysterious illness still lingered. He was always so careful not to reveal anything that would raise suspicion. Until today.

A grin lifted her cheeks high enough to squint her eyes. "You said my grandmother was an angel. That means you do believe."

"Not this again."

He'd like to strangle Mrs. Albany for guilting him into sending Cora to church. He didn't care if attending services was part of a proper upbringing for a girl in society. He was tired of being preached to.

"It's important." She stopped walking and faced him.

He gazed around then took a step toward her and whispered, "Stop trying to save my soul, Cora."

Her mouth opened in shock. Eyes watered. There was no need to be harsh with her, even if her evangelizing irritated him.

"But I love you, Papa."

"And I you. More than absolutely anything. That's going to have to be enough."

Her hand slipped off his arm in a listless movement. She crossed her arms over her middle and walked ahead. With that gesture, she looked exactly like Margaret. A glimpse of the woman to be.

The accusations jabbed at him again.

He forced himself to move and finally caught up to her, his foot throbbing. "I'm sorry for being harsh. Let's not let it ruin the day."

She shrugged.

A man selling roasted nuts walked by, and Edward stopped him to buy a bag. He offered them to Cora as they walked.

"I just don't understand." She popped a handful into her mouth and chewed. "How can you not believe? The evidence is everywhere."

Her arms spread wide.

Nature. People. Those didn't prove a heavenly power. Both

were cursed. "We're all different, Cora. What makes perfect sense to some is inane to others. Yes, there's good in the world. There's also evil."

Evil that ran in her father's veins. The man she believed to be her father, anyway.

"Believing is a choice," he continued. "You made yours, and I've made mine. Part of growing up is learning to accept things the way they are."

She swiped at her cheek. "Then I accept that until we're parted in death, there's still hope for your redemption."

He fingered a roasted nut before tossing it onto his tongue. Cora's sweetness made him want to change his wicked ways, but he was too far into sin to escape now. And he'd never understand why a God who claimed to be loving would give a boy with a clubfoot to a corrupt man to raise on his own. Surely a divine being could see that wasn't a wise idea.

He sighed. "See the monkeys with me?"

One corner of her mouth curled.

He put his arm around her shoulders, and they walked into the Central Park Menagerie.

They spent the rest of the day feeding exotic birds; watching the monkeys swing from trees; spotting camels, deer, and foxes; and staring in awe at the lions, tigers, and bears. Cora jumped when a lion released a ferocious growl from a cage next to her. Edward laughed, and she elbowed his side, scowling.

That made him laugh even harder.

Edward glanced at his timepiece. "It's nearing four, my dear. Mrs. Albany is preparing dinner."

Cora yawned. "I'm ready."

She giggled. "Can we walk to Bow Bridge before we leave? I'd love to see the changing leaves reflect on the water before we go."

His energy was waning fast, but he wouldn't deny her such a simple pleasure.

The walking paths weaved beneath trees bursting with green and gold and red. It felt as if they were strolling the countryside instead of on roads created by man in the middle of a city.

Cora yawned again, took his arm, and laid her head on his shoulder as they walked. He kissed the top of her head, fighting his own yawn.

"Mr. Davidson?"

He and Cora turned at the feminine voice.

"Franklin." A woman wearing a maroon dress with black trimmings and a matching hat clutched her reticule against her bodice.

Unease slithered through him. "Yes."

"I thought that was you." She rushed her approach, smiling. "Is this Cora?"

She reached for his daughter's hands. Cora looked to him for direction but allowed the woman to spread her arms and study her. "You've grown into a lovely young lady. Oh, you look just like your mother."

Edward's skin flushed hot.

Angelica Hackney.

Of all the people from his past to run into in the middle of Central Park.

He cleared his throat. "Cora, this is Mrs. Hackney. Her husband and I were partners with the Secret Service several years ago, before he tragically passed away."

"I'm sorry for your loss, Mrs. Hackney." Cora, always dutiful.

The mention of her dead husband elicited the reaction he was hoping for. Angelica blinked in surprise then looked down at her feet. "Let me offer my condolences on Margaret as well. She was a wonderful friend."

Cora perked at the mention of her mother. Something Edward made a point never to do. "You knew my mother?"

"We were good friends. Spent many an afternoon drinking tea, sewing, and filling the loneliness while our husbands were away. Are you still with the agency?"

"I am not," Edward said.

"What can you tell me about my mother?" Cora gripped the woman's elbows, attacking her with enthusiasm.

Angelica's eyes narrowed at him in confusion. Or was it an accusation for starving the girl of Margaret's memory?

Angelica licked her lips. "Well, she grew up in Illinois. She enlisted as a nurse when the war started. That's where she met your father."

The lines around her mouth and forehead wrinkled as she grinned at Edward. "She said as awful as that battle was, it was also the greatest day of her life."

Cora's gaze bounced between him and Angelica. "They met during the war?"

Edward's stomach cramped. He opened his mouth to speak, but

Angelica answered first. "He was injured, and your mother tended to him in the field hospital. That's where they fell in love. She prayed for him morning and evening and was so proud when your father received his Congressional Medal of Honor for his bravery."

"You received a medal?" Cora's voice rose with every word. "What did you do, Papa? Were you hurt in battle?"

"Have you never heard the story?" Angelica frowned, further deepening the lines on her aging skin. Her hair had grayed considerably since the last time he'd seen her.

"It's not a *story*." Edward stood tall. "It was an experience, and one I don't like to discuss."

Angelica took a step back at his snapping tone, causing Cora's arms to fall at her sides. "I apologize, Franklin. I didn't mean to offend."

Edward nodded. "I hope you are well, *Mrs. Hackney*, but we must be on our way."

He hoped she understood the formality in his tone. His brother may have once been close enough to her for the use of given names, but he was not.

The reticule had returned to her bodice. She swallowed. "It's Mrs. Holman now. I remarried three years ago."

"Congratulations." Edward placed a hand on Cora's shoulder, guiding her away.

Angelica watched them go.

Cora twisted and waved to the woman, who sorrowfully returned the gesture.

They'd almost made it to the bridge when Cora said, "Why have you never told me any of that, Papa?"

"I don't like to discuss it."

"You don't think it important for me to know that my papa is a war hero? And here I thought you couldn't grow any taller in my eyes. Will you at least tell me why you were awarded a medal? Tell me once, and I promise never to ask again."

Would there be any harm in telling her such things?

He couldn't chance it.

"I've a better idea. There's a confectionary on the corner of Forty-Second and Fifth Avenue that sells a revolutionary imported Swiss chocolate made by a man named Henry Nestlé. Milk chocolate, they call it. Produced in a solid bar. Let's spoil our dinner by sharing one."

Like always, Cora obediently accepted his authority. Someday, however, she would stop believing everything he said and would discover the answers for herself.

CHAPTER THIRTY-TWO

BEAU

Manhattan, Present Day

*T*he war room, as Beau's campaign committee liked to call it, was being transformed from a place to strategize to a celebration room. This was where Beau, his committee, his family, and his closest friends would follow the election and await the results. If he won, confetti would fall from the ceiling and they'd declare their victory long into the next morning.

Andi had promised to be back from Washington in time to join them. His dad's attempt to bribe her into silence had failed. Before she'd left, he'd gone to her apartment and explained his new role as landlord and his family's wishes for her to sign a contract of silence. Then he'd promised to respect her decision either way.

Her face, always so vibrant with color, with life, had paled to a sickly hue. *Devastated* was the only word to describe it. He'd felt like a cad. Worse. But he was on his way to becoming governor and, from there, maybe one day, president. No matter how much he loved her, he needed her reticence. If she loved him, she'd understand his position.

"Is this straight?" Wilson held one end of a patriotic banner he'd roll up that would be released upon the certified results. If Beau won. If not, it would remain coiled as if it were part of the decor.

"Up a few more inches." Beau squinted. "Perfect."

A young intern approached with hors d'oeuvre samples for him to choose from. Before he could reach for the tiny toast with avocado, his phone pealed from his pocket. Andi.

"I need to take this." He pointed to a table. "Set them there, and I'll decide as soon as I finish this call."

The intern nodded and left to be useful somewhere else.

Craving privacy, he opened a side door and climbed the steep wooden stairs two at a time as he answered the call. "You just saved me from eating food that was never meant for human consumption."

"Say what?"

He entered another door that opened to the second floor. This part of the building had yet to be restored and boasted an open floor plan with aged wood floors, walls, doors, and window casings. Beau looked out the window and down at the cars and moving pedestrians as he explained about the hors d'oeuvres.

"You'll be back by Tuesday, right?" He leaned against the wall. "I want—no, I need you here with me. No matter what the voters decide or how much tension there is over this counterfeit money."

"I'll be back tomorrow evening."

The hesitation in her voice put him on alert. "But?"

She sighed. "This is something I should relay in person, but you need to know now. Not on your big night."

There was nowhere to sit and brace for the news, so he leaned against the window frame.

"The Secret Service has seized the counterfeit bills permanently. Long story short, they went missing from a raid in 1874 at the hands of a dirty agent they could never catch. The style of engraving and the small details the engravers added to distinguish their bills from other counterfeits helped the Secret Service link them to drug lords who were convicted of exchanging large amounts of opium for counterfeit currency."

"And you think there's a link between this and my family...how?"

"Franklin Davidson was a Secret Service agent who built a fortune in pharmaceuticals. Specifically, opium used for medical purposes. I believe Margaret's accusation. I think it was really Edward, pretending to be Franklin. I think Edward murdered his brother. It's the only thing that makes sense, knowing Edward's criminal history. He had the means and the motive."

"Are you serious?" Curse the day she found those bills.

"When Cora and her husband inherited the family fortune, they transitioned from big pharma to real estate. Why pull out when the market was booming? Call it coincidence, or Cora wanting to forge her own path. I believe she discovered Edward's secret and wanted nothing to do with his investments."

Beau's hands shook. "Let me make sure I understand what you're implying. You're accusing my great-great-grandfather of not being who he said he was but instead a dirty agent and an opium addict?"

A threat simmered below the surface of his words, though he'd tried to stop it.

"I'm not implying anything negative about your great-great-grandfather. He was a good man. I am implying that your great-great-*uncle* wasn't. I think Edward saw a way to profit from other people's addictions and took advantage of it."

Beau paced the room, the groans of the old floor adding to his misery. "How could you think this?"

"I have proof. I possess an opium bottle bearing your family crest."

His pulse stilled. "And where did you find such a thing?"

His ears screamed for her to stop as she explained admiring the bottle in Grant's relic shop when she'd gone to get advice about the counterfeit bills. The very place Beau had suggested she go. Then, the day Beau had invited her into their study, she'd seen the family crest and remembered seeing it on the opium bottle in Grant's shop.

His gut roiled.

"I know this isn't easy to hear. Believe me, it's difficult to say." Her voice quieted. "I'm telling you because this news is going to be released, and I don't want you blindsided."

His phone dinged with a text. He wanted to throw it across the room and smash it to bits. "Is that all?"

She relayed the facts she'd gathered about the men being identical twins, the ear deformity, and Margaret's accusation and admission into the asylum. "I don't know how or when, but I think Edward murdered Franklin and took over his life. I think when Margaret discovered it, rather than go down for his crimes, he had her committed. After all, who would believe a woman already known for having a poor mental state over a Civil War hero who was an upstanding citizen and agent for the Secret Service?

"I also think he destroyed evidence of Edward's existence to cover his tracks but used his name when staying at the Winderfield so the name Franklin couldn't be tied to the crimes. I think he used the hotel as his headquarters when transporting the money he seized on his raids and later exchanged it for the opium."

She was accusing his family of building an empire founded on murder and lies. His brain was already conjuring up ways to discount the rumor. This would kill his credibility with the public, even if it came out after the election. His life was spinning out of control so fast it made him dizzy.

He pinched the bridge of his nose. "If the Secret Service releases this without solid evidence proving that it was Edward who pilfered these bills and committed these other crimes, I will sue them until the department bleeds."

More silence passed as Beau fought to control his emotions.

"The Secret Service isn't aware of my theory. I never gave them Franklin's or Edward's names. They won't be releasing any of the information. However, they've given *Smithsonian* magazine permission to release the information we've found."

It all clicked into place like the locking mechanism of a jail cell. "And I suppose the lead writer is Miss Andi Andrews herself."

Only the noise of traffic outside sounded in the following seconds.

His heart nearly cracked in two. He'd finally found what he'd thought was the perfect woman, only for her to blow his world to bits. Sucking in a deep breath to suppress his nausea, he said, "Congratulations on your new promotion. Exposing the Davidson-Quincy empire will no doubt be the biggest story of the decade and will gain you everything you've wanted."

"Oh, Beau. Don't misunderstand me. I called because I'm keeping my promise to tell you everything before it becomes public, not for a promotion." Her voice cracked, as if she had a soul. "Since you're such an advocate for the truth, I thought you'd want to know. I thought we could—"

"I am an advocate for the truth." The same fingers that used to hold her soft hand clenched into a ball. "You'd better be able to prove your theory with undeniable facts, or you'll be part of a defamation of character lawsuit for every single member of my family from Franklin to present day."

"You don't understand. I don't—"

"I understand perfectly. I also understand that when it came to you, I was an absolute fool."

He ended the call before she could defend herself further. There was no longer time to alternate worthless motives. His career was a house on fire, and the woman he loved had lit the match.

CHAPTER THIRTY-THREE

ANDREA

Manhattan, Election Night, Present Day

The beginning of November brought snow and an extra chill to her bones despite the infrared fireplace heater blowing at her legs. The cursor on her laptop screen blinked on a blank page. In twenty-four hours, she'd submit her article to be released as the top story in December's issue. Then the promotion would be hers. Her boss, Mark, was stoked about her discovery, and he was working on the logistics of her new position that very day, according to his latest email.

Andrea had finally achieved her professional goal, but victory didn't taste sweet. After Allen's betrayal, her life had split into two parts—the Andrea who'd lived in a world that was mostly good, who'd had a world of possibilities before her, and the Andrea whose eyes had been opened to the ways of the world, who could only rely on herself to make the good in life a reality. Her position at the magazine had saved her from drowning in the dark abyss of depression. It had given her purpose and drive and fulfillment.

Then came Beau....

She'd finally achieved what she'd been working hard for the last several years, and it felt all wrong. As palpable as the oncoming winter, she felt her life splitting into two parts again—life before Beau, where she kept her heart to herself, and life after Beau, where against her will, she'd given her heart away to a wonderful man she couldn't have.

Why had she found that money? Was she meant to discover the answers? She believed in a God who made no mistakes. But why her?

She drummed her fingers on the desk. The words she needed to make the article pop were bursting to be typed, but her fingers wouldn't do the action. No matter what she wrote, she'd lost Beau for good. She'd tried to explain her logic on the phone yesterday, but he wouldn't listen. He'd treated her as a rival, as someone he must defend himself against. Using the fortress of image and legalities and power, he'd let her go.

Her chest hadn't stopped aching since. Where she understood his position and need for discretion, his conjecture of her motive, his lack of faith in her, cut deep.

The postcard of Beatrice Everwood mocked her from its place on the bulletin board. Unrequited love. Andrea dragged her gaze to the wanted poster of Edward Davidson, a photograph of the counterfeit money, and other clues she'd discovered. There was still no birth or death record for Edward. Without solid forensic evidence, none of the clues could prove with absolute certainty that Franklin was really Edward, working for both the Secret Service and as an opium drug lord who committed his wife to an insane asylum to keep from being discovered and then raised his niece as his own daughter.

If this were a modern-day case being investigated through a court of law, her evidence would be probable cause for a criminal case. A jury who considered the facts and connected them as a whole picture would most likely agree with her conclusion. Beau was right. This could possibly become the biggest New York scandal of the decade.

Truth was, exposing the horrific choices Edward Davidson made during his lifetime wouldn't hurt the man. It would only hurt Beau. And his family. Since they'd had nothing to do with the choices of their ancestors and Beau had only used his platform to help others, it wouldn't be fair to drag them through this.

She didn't wish to.

Andrea closed her eyes and imagined Beau pacing his campaign headquarters, staying positive yet snatching every election update and report with anxious hands. Did he miss her at all? Did a part of him wish she were there with him, even though he was so angry with her?

Emotion tightened her throat. She wished she were there.

But casting her vote was all she could do to support his dreams, so she'd done that. Despite their brief history, there was no doubt he'd make an amazing governor. There was a good chance he'd be moving to Albany and the governor's mansion anyway. Even without this mystery between them, their whirlwind romance was doomed to end.

She blinked and swallowed her sorrow with a sip of pumpkin spice latte.

Her fingertips poised on the smooth keys of her laptop. Part of being an adult was working through the hard things. She had a job to do, and she was going to do it well.

❦

Edward
Manhattan, The Players Opening Night, December 31, 1888

"We do not mingle enough with minds that influence the world." A curl fell across Edwin Booth's forehead as he leaned toward the crowd. His commanding voice filled the room above the bodies crushed together to celebrate the opening of the prestigious establishment. "We should measure ourselves through personal contact with outsiders. I want my club to be a place where actors are away from the glamor of the theater.

"These words I said to my fellow actors, hence I stand here tonight, two years later, the vision a reality."

Booth went on to deed the building and its contents, the artwork, theatrical memorabilia, and his extensive personal library to the Players. His only stipulation was that by doing so, he could occupy the third-floor apartment that overlooked Gramercy Park to live out the remainder of his days. The man's fifteen colleagues who'd helped incorporate the Players had already previously agreed to the terms. The speech was merely a formality to the gathering of men from the theater, fine arts, journalism, and commerce who'd paid handsomely for membership.

Men like William Tecumseh Sherman and Mark Twain, who stood to Edward's left. There were dozens of others he didn't recognize but would know by name. Despite severe dishonor and embarrassment over his brother's assassination of President Lincoln, Booth had built a community in which members of the theater and other various arts could "convene to discuss their professions and have the freedom to be themselves as men."

Memberships to such places were all that Edward had now. His Cora had met Mr. Matthew Quincy while on holiday with Melanie

Appleton in the Capes. She was planning her wedding even now. Matthew was heir to a booming Michigan copper mine. Edward needn't worry about Cora's financial well-being.

He worried about his own welfare, however. His health was failing, and once Cora was married, there'd be no one to care for him. Oh, she'd gladly do it, but he wouldn't allow it. It was time she joined herself to a good man. Created a family of her own. Had all the unmaterialistic things Edward could never offer because they couldn't be purchased.

Like honesty.

Mr. Chelsea, an acquaintance he'd met several months back while dining at the Livingstons', offered him a cigar from a slim tin he kept in his pocket. Edward thanked him and fished one out. His shaky fingers refused to hold it in his grip, and the cigar fell to the floor. He bent to retrieve it while Mr. Chelsea watched in evident confusion. It took a few attempts, but Edward finally grabbed hold and righted himself.

The room swayed.

Mr. Chelsea kept him upright with his firm grip. "I dare ask, Franklin, have you already been imbibing this evening?"

Edward chuckled to mask his mortification. "I wish it were that. My health has been on the downturn of late."

Mr. Chelsea helped him to a chair and took the one across from him. "I'm sorry to hear that. What does the doctor say?"

That Edward had enjoyed the company of a prostitute one too many times, but he wouldn't reveal such knowledge. Especially here.

"Diagnosis is still yet to be determined." More lies. How truth cried to be set free, but he'd drag it with him to his grave.

Unfortunately, a permanent home in the ground was looking to be sooner rather than later.

It had all started with a few sores during his last raid with the Secret Service. He'd gotten treatment, and they'd healed quickly. Then, a few months later, right after Cora's thirteenth birthday, he'd come down with a fever and broken out in a terrible rash. He'd known ever since that the disease would slowly ravage his body.

He'd counted on it consuming him much sooner. It had been nine years, yet even if he had nine more, death would come too soon.

He and Edwin Booth had much in common. Both held a passion for transforming into other people. Both gave spectacular performances.

Both had a notorious brother. Only Edward held credit for playing both roles.

Like Mr. Booth, Edward would sit in his home overlooking Gramercy Park and await the sting of death.

CHAPTER THIRTY-FOUR

BEAU

MANHATTAN, PRESENT DAY

*B*eau wasn't sure which he felt more—elation for leading in the polls or bone-deep exhaustion. His crew was still going strong at two in the morning, and though he put on a good show, he wasn't feeling it. Andi should be here, the way he'd imagined it until two days ago. There should be no secrets from the past rising from the grave to strangle their relationship, their careers.

Maybe there was some truth to her theory. From an objective standpoint, the clues all pointed to Edward Davidson's guilt. If that was the case, his family's legacy was founded on lies and illegal gain. But that knowledge becoming public would end his family's stellar reputation. A legacy built on such evil made all the good things his family had done since insignificant.

Except that wasn't true, was it?

Just because one of his ancestors was possibly a villain didn't discount all the good things done by the man's descendants. King David of Israel had committed murder, after all—and Moses for that matter—but their descendants hadn't been held accountable. Sure, they'd been affected by the sin, but their future endeavors weren't sullied based on their ancestors' downfalls.

Cora Davidson-Quincy had spearheaded the move from pharmaceuticals to real estate and charity committees. Her children, grandchildren, and great-grandchildren had followed her path. No amount of rights cleared a wrong, but a wrong didn't make the rights any less credible. Though his committee had already come up with a plan to defuse the scandal once it became public, he would no longer fear truth's exposure.

His identity didn't lie in the world's image of him. He was more than his attempts to live up to the family name, to please his father. More than his career.

If only he'd realized this sooner.

Shouts exploded in the room. Confetti drenched him. Balloons popped. No, not balloons. Champagne corks. His father slapped him on the back before gripping him in a bear hug. Congratulations echoed throughout the room.

He'd won.

The next hour was a blur as he stood behind the podium to thank everyone who'd helped him along the way and discussed the first things he planned to tackle once he took office. Through it all, a hollow spot in his heart thrummed where Andi should be. But he knew better than to rely on another human to fill his voids. It was an unhealthy practice too many flirted with.

At three thirty, the celebration wound to a close. He instructed his crew to leave the mess for another day, go home, and get some sleep. He crawled into the car behind Jonas and beside his dad, letting out a mighty yawn.

The billboard lights of Times Square flashed colorful images over them as they drove south on Broadway. Beau leaned his head back and closed his eyes, thinking about his soft pillow and comfortable mattress. His phone pinged with a text. He groaned. Considered ignoring it. Since no one ever texted him at this hour, he opened his eyes and checked the screen.

Andi.

Congratulations, Governor. Well deserved.

He smiled. Call it fatigue or just plain crazy, but despite everything, he almost called her to meet him and celebrate. His finger hovered over the letters before reality slapped it away. Her gesture was appreciated, but making any rash moves in his current state of mind was unwise. Sleep first, react later.

Tucking his phone away, he returned to his napping stance. Maybe they could work this out and resolve the situation, and maybe they couldn't. Either way, there'd be plenty of time later to consider the ramifications.

For now, he was going to fall into his bed as a toast to a new era.

Edward
Manhattan, July 1890

It was all coming to an end.

Flames licked at Edward's feet, causing the sweat on his brow to intensify. Lesions covered his skin. Vision, dim. His legs refused to move, yet they twitched of their own volition. Cora sat vigilant by his bedside, though all he could see from this distance was her outline.

A shadow in the room moved, presumably the doctor. Edward had begged Dr. Duncan to be discreet when telling Cora he suffered from syphilis. Her knowing he allowed his fleshly desires to overcome him brought him shame. He'd failed her. The woman had finally come to understand that the father she worshiped as a child was not the man she'd thought him to be.

Worship. He despised the word. Nothing in this life deserved such reverence, least of all the things he'd chosen to worship with his life. Respect. Acclaim. Money. Power. As his aching body lay upon the bed, taking its last breaths, he could take none of it with him.

None.

But the good name he'd built and the fortune he'd amassed would help Cora as she went through life without him.

She'd hoped that after years of sharing her knowledge of the Bible and discussing the moral aspects of life, he would come to embrace the Christianity she clung to. It had been the very reason she'd turned down suitor after suitor after her coming out. She'd told him as much. Knew that if she left him, he might never find that peace.

But it had already been too late. His sevenfold vengeance had started the day his mother died.

Cora had eventually realized that by waiting on him to accept God, she might miss out on her own life. Her diligence didn't equal his redemption. She'd finally accepted Matthew Quincy's proposal.

Nothing could save Edward now.

The brass key was hot in his palm. He lifted his hand and rooted for Cora's. When her clammy fingers wrapped around his, he placed it in her hand.

"It's all yours, my sweet girl." Speech slurring, he barely recognized his own voice.

"The key to Gramercy Park." She huffed a laugh then sniffed. The wet sound told him she'd been crying. "I remember the first day you brought me here. It was like magic."

His mouth was as dry as the desert. The image of a cool mountain spring taunted him, making him crave water like he craved his next breath. Is this what hell would be like?

He licked his lips for all the good it did. "Choose to remember those times of magic…when I'm gone."

She stood and paced at the end of his bed, her hands shaking. "When I was helping Dr. Duncan yesterday, I noticed you possess both of your legs and feet. I know the story behind your Medal of Honor. Mrs. Albany told me when I was fifteen. I don't understand, Papa. So many things I thought to be firm are crumbling, and time is running out. Can you explain this?"

He'd known this day would come. The day when every lie he'd fed would turn and feast on him.

He coughed, hating the hope in her eyes that he'd offer a reasonable explanation. "Mr. Noble will provide you with accounts and stock information. All of my possessions are now yours."

His heart gave a twinge of pain, stealing his breath.

"As if any of it matters to me at this moment." The sound of metal pinged on the nightstand; then her hand wrapped around his.

He swallowed. "It will in the moments to come. Everything I've done, I've done for you. My sweet little girl."

He reached for her face. She pressed her wet cheek against his hand.

"It hasn't all been for me. You did it for you too." Cora swiped at her eyes. "What I don't understand is why Mother couldn't stay. Is it because she learned the truth? Are you not the man we all believed you to be?"

How much did she know?

"The only truth I can confess is that I love you. More than anyone on this earth."

A sob escaped, but she closed it off with a pinch of her lips. "It isn't too late. God will still forgive you, no matter what sins you've done. Even now in your final moments. He'll forgive it all if you truly believe. Just like He did for the thief pinned next to Him on the cross."

She'd come close to persuading him many times. But even if it was true, his wretched soul didn't deserve forgiveness. Not after all he'd done.

"Don't worry yourself over me, sweet girl. Matthew will take care of you, and that will comfort me in the next world."

The warmth of her face left his hand, and she started pacing again. "Why are you being so headstrong about this? My bank account—nor yours for that matter—will bring you one whit of comfort when your screams are filling the pit of hell!"

Didn't he know it.

"You should have been a minister's wife."

"Ugh," she cried. "Don't you see?"

She dropped onto the bed beside him, jostling his sore body. "You are the only father I've ever known. You may have a million secrets that'll rise and take their revenge on the rest of my life, but I love you. *Please*, Papa. Choose salvation this day."

His lungs felt like lead weights with every breath. He coughed again, but it came out as more of a gurgle. "You are my salvation."

Cora gave a groan of agony as the door opened. Footsteps approached. Cora turned and threw herself at the shadow. Matthew.

She'd chosen well.

Edward closed his eyes, assuaged that, with his parting, she had a good man to cling to.

The image of his brother floated in his memory as he slipped in and out of sleep. In the worst of times, they'd always had each other. They shared their entry into this world. Would they reunite in death?

Cora woke him a while later, wiping spittle from the corner of his mouth. She kissed his burning forehead. "I will fight Satan for your soul until the very end."

He winced in pain. They weren't all meant for the pearly gates. Otherwise, what would be the point of hell?

Edward closed his eyes for the last time.

The end came six hours later, at exactly midnight.

CHAPTER THIRTY-FIVE

ANDREA

Manhattan, Present Day

*T*his article is nothing like I expected." Andrea's boss rapped his fingers on his desk, frowning at the article she'd turned in two minutes before deadline. Typical office clutter littered his desk—paper, colored sticky notes, a paperweight, Newton's Cradle pendulum to entertain him when he got bored, and an oak nameplate with his name, MARK WITHERSPOON, etched to perfection.

His frown deepened by the second.

As if she were one of the stainless-steel balls in his desk pendulum, she waited for his disapproval to crash into her and knock her away from her promotion.

"This isn't the angle we discussed. There's no antithesis of brothers, no scamming, no insane asylum, no secrets from the grave to take down a modern family." Mark tossed the papers on his desk and leaned back in his chair. He cocked his head as if she were a science experiment.

He spoke the truth, though he exaggerated the modern-family part. She hadn't written what they had discussed. After agonizing in her apartment for hours, she'd pounded out the story that lay scorned before him. She'd slept for sixteen hours after sending the email, her body and soul depleted after the war of good and evil in her soul. Though the decision hadn't been easy, she'd decided that risking her promotion was worth a peaceful conscience.

Andrea tucked her hands under her thighs to keep from fidgeting. "I chose responsible journalism over salacious details that can't be accurately proven."

"Explain." Elbows on his armrests, Mark linked his fingers over his pillowy abs.

"The information I shared with you in confidence is what a judge would consider probable cause for a case, but with no birth or death record for Edward and no forensic evidence, the trail of clues would be hearsay and not damning enough for a conviction. That being said, the Davidson-Quincys threatened to sue the magazine for defamation of character, and no doubt would now that Beau is governor."

Mark lifted a brow. "This decision wouldn't have anything to do with that photograph of you two all cozy together at the Met Gala, would it?"

Her face heated. That magical night was long gone.

"Not at all." It had to do with much more than that. "While a tale of dueling brothers, unrequited love, opera singers, opium, and murder makes for sensational entertainment, our magazine is not a fiction novel. Or an *Entertainment Tonight* episode. We've built a reputation alongside the museum curators and are known for printing truthful history."

She took a steadying breath, untucked her hands, and straightened her spine. "I wrote the article objectively, using proven facts, quotations, and interviews with members of the Secret Service, who were finally able to close the case."

Mark's chair squeaked and groaned as he rocked, his mouth twisting in thought. "This is the article you're willing to stand behind, even if it affects your promotion?"

Good thing she was sitting, or his statement might've buckled her knees. She swallowed. "Yes, sir. I stand behind responsible journalism."

He nodded at the desk. Shook his head as if he thought she needed the asylum as well. "Okay. It's been great having you as an assistant editor and journalist, and I thank you for your service. However, I'll need you to clear out your office by the end of the day."

A rising tide of grief filled her chest and clouded her vision. Despite the pain, she'd never felt surer of her choice.

"Yes, sir." She stood and stepped toward his office door, wondering who she'd write for now that he'd fired her. Fired! Years of good work ethic down the toilet.

The doorknob twisted easily in her hand.

"Andi?"

She spun and found a smirk on Mark's face. "You can unpack your belongings in Pat's old office. I'll need you to sign this paperwork so I can give it to HR. Expect your raise on the December fifth payout."

Time stuttered. Her pulse swooshed in her ears. "You mean…" She couldn't finish uttering the words *I'm not fired.*

"I admit I'm disappointed we can't tell the story we'd discussed, but your decision shows you have this company's back over your own gain. Responsible journalism is what we do here, and you've done it well. Congratulations."

He hadn't fired her.

She wasn't fired!

Andrea smiled as she rushed to his desk, unsure if she wanted to laugh or cry. Oh wait—she was doing both. No decision needed. She blinked away the sheen of emotion blurring the page and took his pen to sign the papers.

Two hours later, she carried the last box of her belongings into her new office and closed the door. She looked up at the ceiling and whispered a grateful "Thank You" before putting the box on the edge of her desk.

A glaze of frost lined the corner window that looked out over buildings already decorated in reds and golds and greens. The meteorologist predicted a few inches of snow tonight, which would bring an even more romantic feel to the city.

At home, she'd already put up her skinny corner Christmas tree next to the fish tank. She'd spend Christmas with her aquatic friends, watching her favorite Christmas movies and eating her loneliness away with chocolate.

But first she had to survive Thanksgiving with her parents, her brother and his wife, and several aunts and uncles as she politely dodged the usual questions. *Why aren't you married yet? Are you ever gonna find a man? I know a great guy who's a friend of a friend. Can I set you up?*

Good thing she hadn't invited her parents to spend Halloween at Gramercy Park. They would've approved of Beau, making this whole thing even harder.

As she stared at the movement of cars and bodies below, she thought back on their time together. What was he doing right now? She imagined him moving his belongings into his new office ten times this size, with plush carpet and expensive leather chairs, a host of important people surrounding him as they greeted their new governor and discussed plan after strategic plan to make New York even greater.

She'd never know.

They'd both accomplished their career goals, which is what they'd been reaching for when they'd found each other. The only thing that would make this day greater was if they were on good enough terms to celebrate their victories together. That wish was nothing but a pipe dream. He'd never responded to her text on election night. Had probably blocked her number immediately the last time they'd talked.

Rubbing away the chill on her upper arms, Andrea went to the desk and started unpacking her boxes. She had her cake. It was too much to expect life to let her eat it too.

Beau
Manhattan, Present Day

The E line was down due to an unexplained fire. Brooklyn was facing a housing shortage crisis. Twelve homeless people had passed away in the freezing temperature last night. Drugs blanketed the city, and arrests and murders were on the rise. The checklist was already running a marathon in Beau's brain, and he hadn't even had coffee yet.

He descended the stairs, draping his suit coat over an arm. None of these issues were new, but they were his issues to solve now. He'd officially take office in twenty days and was already being briefed on the problems at hand.

At the base of the stairs, he rounded the corner into the dining room. As always, Marcy had lined the sideboard with delicious food, today's specialty being crepes with chocolate hazelnut sauce. If only he could bring Marcy with him to Albany. While there were many skilled cooks in the world, there was none like the woman who'd been like a grandmother to him.

Beau filled a plate and joined his dad at the table. He tucked a cloth napkin into the collar of his shirt.

"It's been many years since I've seen you wear a bib."

"Laugh now." Beau sipped his coffee. "In a few years, you'll be wearing one."

Rare laughter spilled from the man. "Careful now. You're my only heir. Get too cheeky, and I might leave your inheritance to the monkeys at the Bronx Zoo."

Beau winked and concentrated on his meal.

Dad had been in good spirits since the election. Smiling and laughing. Things Beau hadn't seen him do regularly in years. Had he finally earned the man's admiration? Respect?

The newspaper rattled every time his dad snuck a surreptitious glance his way. After the fifth time, Beau was getting irritated. "Something on your mind?"

"The December issue of *Smithsonian* magazine released yesterday." Dad waited for Beau to react.

"I know." Beau pushed his plate away, the few bites left spoiled.

"Have you read the featured article?"

"I'd rather not."

"You should." Dad carefully folded up his paper and laid it aside. He nodded to Malcolm, who'd entered the room carrying the magazine. "It's very interesting. Not only did the Secret Service finally get to close a one-hundred-and-fifty-year-old case, but your ownership of the Winderfield proved to be the perfect bargaining chip."

"I don't understand." Something akin to hope stirred inside Beau, but he stuffed it down.

Malcolm set the magazine in front of Beau. The cover sported a plunder of old bills and coins, an antique handgun, a few small bottles full of liquid, and a telegram. His father wouldn't be so jovial if the article had exposed their family's secrets. Still, Beau was afraid to look.

"I never used the Winderfield as a bargaining chip. I told her of our wishes, but I also informed her that her home was safe no matter what she decided."

Dad's brows lifted then knotted in confusion. "Sometimes the Davidson-Quincy name is intimidating enough. Or perhaps I misjudged her."

The magazine lay before Beau like a Pandora's box. Deciding to tackle the problem head-on, he opened the cover and skimmed the contents page. "Secrets in the Secret Service: How a Modern-Day Journalist Helped the Secret Service Solve One of Its Oldest Cases" was featured on page 14. He flipped through the glossy pages. The spread held the same photograph that was on the cover, spacing over the first two pages of the article with the title in white font. Beneath it the caption read, "Some secrets are so well kept, even the government can't decipher them."

Then his eyes landed on the name Andi Andrews, Writer-at-Large.

He smiled. She'd done it. No matter what hard information lay in the rest of this article, she'd accomplished her dreams, and he was proud of her.

Dad scooted away from the table and patted Beau's shoulder. "I'll leave you to it."

Beau ran a hand over his face and sipped the rest of his coffee. He curled the front cover behind the back and started reading. With vivid description and Andi's signature wittiness, she talked about her discovery in her apartment wall and how the counterfeit money had led her on a chase that led to the Secret Service. The article then gave a brief history of the department and how they identified the counterfeit bills. It went on to explain how the agents went undercover in those days and detailed how the raids were conducted. By the end of the sixth page, the article had circled back around to Andi, where she closed it with some of the most eloquent words he'd ever read.

"With the unfolding of history, we can learn about ourselves. History helps us steer our moral compass as we learn from the past and move forward as better people. This journey taught me many things. I learned that sometimes the answers we seek aren't the ones we thought we'd find, and that everyone is faced (at least once in their lives) with a difficult choice—to gain no matter the cost, or be willing to sacrifice for the good of humankind. Let us strive to never be counterfeit in our actions, our service, or our love."

Beau put down the magazine. Shame walloped him harder than the impact of slamming into a tree from his runaway skis when he was eleven. When it came to his gain—his career, pleasing his father, pleasing the world—his love had proven counterfeit. His image, his dignity, had meant more than trying to fulfill a relationship with the most wonderful woman he'd ever met. Andi was a woman of integrity, and he should've trusted her.

Instead, he'd hurt her.

She had all the qualities of a politician's wife and much more. Beyond that, he loved her. She was the only woman besides his mother who had seen past his money and his name and his image to see the man that lay beneath. At the end of the day, that was all he was. A man.

Could he fix the damage he'd done after weeks of silence? Could a meaningful relationship survive the challenge of her living in New York City and him in Albany? Was reconciliation worth the strain it would cost?

Yes. She was worth it all.

He would understand if she refused to talk to him. If she chose to cut him out of her life completely. But he had to try. In fact, if she'd let him, he'd spend the rest of his life trying.

CHAPTER THIRTY-SIX

Cora Davidson-Quincy

Manhattan, June 1905

*M*emories of her childhood danced with the breeze and toyed with her hair as Cora lifted her face to the sky. Fluffy clouds moved in an azure sky. Gramercy Park was in full bloom. African violets in the most vibrant pink she'd ever seen lined the pebbled paths. The gardener had molded the shrubs to perfection, some boxy, some rounded, some left to grow how they willed. The New York Times Building stood proudly in the foreground, surrounded by others made of steel and stone.

Being here was both comforting and disturbing. While her own children chased one another around the garden, images of herself at their age skipping through the flowers appeared as an apparition before her. Whenever her father hadn't been gone with the Secret Service, he'd given her his full attention.

How many afternoons had they spent in this garden talking, laughing, planning their future? He'd listened to her, considered her opinions, offered advice, and provided everything she needed. Many of the things she wanted. He'd been a good papa.

Except he wasn't her real papa.

She would prove it.

She would give her true father a voice to future generations.

Sitting on a stone bench beneath a shade tree, Cora spread a journal open on her lap. The brown leather binding was a stark contrast against the pale pink chiffon and lace of her gown. The warm breeze tickled her bare arms. She uncapped her fountain pen, cracked open her heart, and began to write.

> As I rest amongst the flowers and serenity of Gramercy Park, my heart grieves for two children lost. One, a creation of my womb. The second, the girl of my youth.
>
> How I wish my mother were here to sit beside me, to hold my hand, to tell me that the depth of everything I feel is all part of a woman's grieving. She would know. She would understand because she too lost a child.
>
> Only the child was not conceived with my father.
>
> The speaking of such things is not proper for a lady to discuss. Especially by an heiress, one of the wealthiest in Manhattan. But I cannot hold my silence any longer. I must confess or go mad the way my mother did when she was carted away to die in an asylum when I was four years old.
>
> The memories of her cries are vivid, as they've kept me awake many nights since. I was sick with fever, and her screaming pulled me from my bed. Her fear of the man I knew to be my father rattled the chandelier. "You are not my husband. You killed him." She screamed this repeatedly.
>
> That was the last time I saw my mother. Her history of melancholy and recent loss of a child made her hysterical accusations seem insane. Uniformed men took her away. I would not come to understand the words she screamed that night until the death of the man she accused of murder.
>
> The man I called my father doted on me. Somehow the Secret Service agent climbed his way up society to build our fortune in pharmaceuticals. Specifically, opium. Opium companies included in a syrup to calm fussy and teething babies. The same syrup a doctor recommended I administer to my child.
>
> That syrup killed my child. Evelyn Davidson-Quincy.
>
> In my darkest moments, questions and inconsistencies flooded my mind. Why did those night terrors haunt me from a young age? Why did our cook tell me stories of a

father that didn't match the details of the man I saw before
me? Why had my father gotten a Congressional Medal of
Honor for saving his comrades on the battlefield while his
own leg had been blown off by a cannonball, yet the man I
called father had two legs and two feet?

Needing answers to distract me from my grief, I
started by finding Captain Landon, former commander of
the Fifth New York Infantry. Aged but sharp in mind, he
confirmed my father's missing leg from the shin down. He
had wrapped the wound himself so they could carry him to
the field hospital.

Then I investigated the investments my father made to
a medical company in Bangor, Maine, that brought us such
wealth. Why opium?

How could my mother kiss my father with such passion
and then one day accuse him of murder? She would know
her husband better than anyone. No man could pretend to
be her husband without looking just like him.

For months I searched for answers before I found
someone who worked in the National Archives willing to
share a census record from my grandparents listing two
children. Boys. Franklin and Edward.

Twins. They had to be. It was the only explanation.

I was never able to find record of Edward, but what I
discovered sent me to my knees.

The man I called my father wasn't really my father.
He was my uncle, Edward Davidson. A man in possession
of both legs and feet. Though I may never know the true
identity of either man, I believe my mother died in Black-
well's Island Asylum a sane woman.

A female's heart is a well of emotion, deep and quench-
ing. Yet the expanse of such emotion during intense grief is
sometimes too much to bear. That did not make her insane.

Upon the completion of this page, I will close this book
and thus this chapter of my life, and I will move our family
fortune into endeavors that will assist families in this
city who are in need. And when this journal is unearthed

centuries from now, they will finally know the secrets
lurking inside Gramercy Park.

Cora took a cleansing breath and closed the journal with a thud. Though she'd forever be separated from the man she'd known as Papa, she had the hope of heaven and that, one day, she'd hold her sweet Evelyn again.

Her son Thaddeus ran at her, a butterfly poised on his little finger. She stood to greet him. The butterfly took flight and bumped her nose. They both laughed.

For the first time in a long time, her heart felt as light as those butterfly wings.

She gathered up her children and led them across the street toward home. After dinner, she would pass this journal to Mr. Mottleroy to add to the time capsule they would bury in Gramercy Park next week. Her other journals, she would burn.

Someday, when God's timing was right, that time capsule would be unearthed, and the truth of her family would finally be set free.

CHAPTER THIRTY-SEVEN

ANDREA

Manhattan, Present Day

*G*ant & Company had some of the most elegant Christmas decorations in the city, save for Rockefeller Center. Vintage and classy, they swept diners into an old-world charm of simplicity and happiness. Andrea would miss working the holiday rush, seating customers who brought flakes of snow inside on their coats and hats, seeing their faces light up as they broke bread with family and friends and chatted about the treasures they purchased. But like Christmas when it ended to usher in the freshness of the new year, so ended this page of her life to open a new chapter. Andi Andrews, writer-at-large.

If only the pain of a shattered heart didn't dull her joy.

Fifty days had passed since Beau had won the election. Fifty days of silence. Yes, she'd been counting. While she'd known a reconciliation was too good to be true, she'd held on to hope. But it was time to move on.

"Merry Christmas!" she said to the hostess staff as she exited onto the street shadowed by the sunset.

Warmth gave way to an icy blast whipping through the city. Pine garlands and red bows gracing the lampposts swayed with every gust. Snow piles collected along the curbs from Tuesday's nor'easter.

"Well, well, well. If it isn't the famous Andi Andrews."

She turned to find Caylee striding toward her, a bouquet of poinsettias tucked in her arm. Her cheeks and nose were red but still held mischievous undertones. Andrea smiled. "What are you doing on this side of town? Shouldn't you be at the *theater*?"

They laughed at Andrea's terrible aristocratic accent. Caylee pointed a gloved finger at her. "You need voice inflection lessons."

"How about I leave that to you? I'll stick to words on the printed page."

"Speaking of—congratulations! You deserve it."

"Thanks." If only she felt the smile she plastered on her face.

Caylee studied her for a moment. "Before we both freeze to blocks of ice, here. I brought you something."

Andrea took the envelope Caylee held and struggled to open it with gloves on. Inside was a glittery Christmas card and two tickets. "For your show?"

Caylee beamed. "Opens January twentieth. You'll come?"

"I wouldn't miss it for anything." She hugged Caylee then glanced down at the tickets. "Am I supposed to bring a date?"

"Oh yeah! I almost forgot. Here."

She thrust the bouquet of poinsettias at Andrea. "Thank you," Andrea said. "You certainly didn't have to do all this."

The mischievous glint returned. "The flowers aren't from me."

"Who are they from?"

Caylee rolled her eyes. "Open the card."

Andrea searched for one. Thankfully, the envelope wasn't sealed. *"Poinsettias symbolize cheer and success. Congratulations on your promotion."* She turned the card over, but there was no signature.

"If these aren't from you, then who are they from?"

"Well, you could follow the trail of poinsettias and see where they lead."

Andrea's face was too frozen to smirk, so she looked around until she spotted a sprig of poinsettias attached to a post box. She knew of only one person who would send her on a scavenger hunt, but she dared not let hope take root.

Yet.

She handed Caylee the bouquet and opened the next card. *"I can swap real estate and tackle New York's problems, yet I can't navigate my own heart. I'm an idiot. Please forgive me?"*

Andrea threw her head back and laughed, letting hope grow wings and fly. She searched the passing faces and then the landscape for another clue. A man wearing a long coat and a hat with fuzzy earflaps carried a pot of poinsettias across the street toward Gramercy Park. She faced

Caylee. "Do you think that's—"

"Go!" Caylee shoved her in the man's direction.

Andrea glanced both ways, waited for passing traffic, then darted across the street. "Sir."

The man turned.

"Jonas!"

He nodded, teeth chattering. "Miss Andrea."

"Are those for me?" She pointed to the pot.

"Well, I guess you'll have to read the card and see."

She reached for the envelope but paused. "Bless you, Jonas. For braving the cold for me."

He winked. "Love is always worth it."

Love? Did Beau love her?

Did she love him?

Yes. Yes, she did.

She tore open the envelope. *"Christmas is the season of miracles. I know it's too much to hope for, but I'm asking for one anyway."*

Her heart thudded, and her body shook. Jonas reached into his pocket and withdrew a key. "Go on in."

The key to Gramercy Park.

All this time, she'd suspected the gates held back the secrets inside. Just maybe, they were simply meant to protect the good things that lay within.

Her numb fingers struggled to fit the key inside the metal lock. After a few tries, the gate gave way and opened to a magical Christmas wonderland. She shut the gate behind her and followed the poinsettia petals deeper inside the garden.

Sparkling snow dusted the bare tree branches and everything beneath. Red bows, large gold ornaments, and twinkling lights adorned the gate perimeters and draped paths into the garden's middle. She followed the winding trail of petals, anticipation building with every step.

The sun descended, and the old-fashioned streetlamps blazed to life. Edwin Booth's statue was garnished in traditional garb as well. Faint singing floated through the air, perfectly harmonized notes blanketing the space in an ethereal mood. The sound couldn't be coming from the garden, because Beau had said entertainment was against the rules.

The poinsettia petals ended at a large fountain filled with oversized Christmas decorations and pots of poinsettias. She approached, scouring the basin for another card. After circling once, she tried again, bending to look in case the card had fallen on the ground. A pair of men's shoes stepped into her line of vision.

Beau.

She stood, a little dizzy from his sudden revelation and this amazing quest. Her mouth opened, but she couldn't speak. He was more handsome than she remembered, a confident yet vulnerable sense of gravity in his stance.

He hadn't been careful with her heart like he'd promised. A fact she'd let him grovel over for a while for both their sakes. People made mistakes. If those mistakes taught lessons that caused growth, how could she turn him away?

Grim lines bracketed his mouth and eyes. The singing grew louder then faded again. She waited for him to speak, but he only watched her, his brokenness clawing at her heart.

"Hi," she finally managed.

"Hi back."

"Thank you for the flowers."

"You're welcome. I meant it."

She took a step closer. "The part about Christmas miracles, or the part about you being an idiot?"

His mouth twitched in an almost smile. "Both."

She breathed a lungful of cold air. "In that case, what are our plans for Christmas? Your family's or mine?"

Beau closed the distance between them and warmed her lips with his. His kiss was possessive, apologetic, and even more delicious than the last one. One hand dove into her hair, the other pulling her tight against him. The frigidity of the night fell away.

She wrapped her arms around his neck and kissed him back as eagerly. When she finally broke away for air, he palmed the sides of her face, their breath clouds mingling. "Will you give me another chance? Forget the people of New York. I promise I'll work every day to be a man worthy of *you*."

She toyed with the ends of his hair. "How can a girl say no to that?"

He groaned. "Is that a yes?"

"It's a definitely." She kissed him again. "Can we continue this reunion somewhere warmer? I'm freezing."

"Patience, my dear. I know it's hard to keep your hands off me, but my evening of surprises isn't over yet."

"There's more?" She could get used to this groveling thing.

Beau smiled. He pulled his phone from his pocket and sent a text. A minute later, the singing grew louder as carolers dressed in Victorian-era costumes came down the sidewalk on the outer side of the gate. A man with an old-fashioned pushcart followed behind and offered them cups of hot chocolate.

She laughed. Rules *inside* the gates might be strict, but anything outside the gates belonged to the city. "You're a genius."

"Come on." Beau led her to a park bench he must have already brushed clear of snow. It was close enough to the carolers to enjoy their serenade but far enough away for privacy.

He sat beside her and tucked a giant wool blanket around them. "Your article was wonderful—and I'm not just saying that because you kept my name out of it. You're a talented writer. I'm proud of you, Miss Writer-at-Large."

Happiness swelled inside her. "I'm proud of you too, Mr. Governor."

Andrea nestled her head on Beau's shoulder and reveled in the beautiful voices singing "Silent Night" and "O Come All Ye Faithful," in awe of this gift. This man.

"What are you thinking?" Beau whispered against her hair.

"That this is the greatest Christmas gift I've ever gotten. I'm sorry I have nothing to give you."

He fiddled inside his coat pocket, jostling the blanket. "You could give me your heart."

A diamond ring appeared in front of her eyes. She sat up so quickly the blanket slipped from her shoulders. The generous diamond sparkled in the lamplight.

She swallowed. "You already have that."

"Then all that's left is to marry me."

"So soon? Are you sure?"

"When you know, you know."

Truer words were never spoken.

She kissed him. "Yes!"

The carolers stopped singing and clapped, offering their congratulations. Beau slipped the ring on her finger. A perfect fit. Just like the man.

CHAPTER THIRTY-EIGHT

BEAU

Manhattan, Seven Years Later

*B*eau stepped away from the podium and snatched Charlotte in his arms. His daughter giggled then howled as he tickled her ribs. "Now, go sit with Mommy and be a good girl. After this is over, we'll go for ice cream."

The warm June breeze rustled the four-year-old's curls. "And a pony?" Her little teeth gleamed.

Andi walked up and reached her arms out for her. "We've gone over this a hundred times. There's nowhere to board a pony in Albany."

Charles joined them, watching a tiny ant crawl on his finger. "But if Daddy wins the 'lection, we won't live in the city no more. We'll live in the big white mansion, and it has room for a pony."

Beau and Andrea exchanged glances. Charles was forever the problem solver. Just like his father.

Charlotte beamed. "That's right! Can we have a pony at the big house, Daddy? Please?"

Her small hands pressed together, accentuating the dimples on her knuckles. If only the entire nation had the confidence in him that his children had.

Beau kissed her cheek, which smelled of strawberry jelly. "It's called the White House, and we still have five months until the election. But I promise we'll discuss it later. *If* you're good during this ceremony."

She shrugged her shoulders as if the decision had already been made and she'd won. "Okay."

Just like her mother.

"Good luck." He handed her over to Andi, who gave him a quick peck on the lips before he stepped back up to the podium.

Gramercy Park was beautiful in the summer. He'd missed seeing it in bloom the last several years, though the garden at the governor's mansion was just as lovely. His father still lived across the street in the same house he'd pass to Beau upon his death. The doctor had given them two to three years if the cancer treatments worked as well as they hoped.

Andi settled herself and the kids next to his dad on the front row of folding chairs. "Aunt Caylee" and her new husband sat in the row behind. Beau had been afraid the construction from the water main break last winter would change the landscape of the park, but the crews had done a wonderful job of making it as close to the original as possible.

Beau tapped the mic. "We'll go ahead and get started. Thank you all for coming out. As you know, the park is a private garden open only to those who live on the square and possess keys. But today we open it to the public in celebration of the restored garden and to reveal the time capsule that was found by the water and sanitation department.

"For those of you who may not be aware, just after Christmas a water main burst, flooding the square and cutting off water to the surrounding homes and businesses. I tried to get Mayor Johnson to let us open the square for ice-skating, but he wouldn't agree."

Mayor Johnson chuckled along with the rest of the crowd.

"As the water and sanitation workers made their repairs, they discovered a time capsule that was buried in the center of the garden in 1905. Several items were found inside, including photographs, a newspaper, a few business cards, a pocket watch, a necklace, three pictures drawn by children who'd attended a local school, and a journal written by my great-grandmother, Cora Davidson-Quincy."

A bee circled Beau's head then flew away.

"The time capsule was taken to the New York City Public Library, where trained staff have been undergoing an extensive restoration process, as the items are nearly a hundred and twenty years old and, unfortunately, received some water damage. However, the items are here today for everyone to see and will be on public display at the library after today."

Cameras clicked from a cluster of reporters in the crowd.

Beau looked down at his family seated to his left, pride filling his chest. "I appreciate Mayor Johnson allowing me to present these items today in a garden my family has held access to since 1872. No one values this treasure more than I. Family is the foundation upon which we make our way in this world. If you're blessed to have it, value it. Honor it. Keep it. For our ancestors paved the way for this generation."

He recalled the day he'd met Andi and the whirlwind of their courtship—counterfeit money, clues, dark family secrets. He was grateful they'd worked past their challenges, and that the story of Edward and Franklin Davidson had remained classified. Such a discovery would certainly taint his chances of becoming president.

"I'll stop boring you with sentimentality, as that's not why you came today. Residents of New York, without further ado, I unveil the history of Gramercy Park."

AUTHOR'S NOTE

I hope you enjoyed the twisted tale of *The Keys to Gramercy Park*. While this story is purely fiction, I threw in some real-life events and characters just for fun.

Gramercy Park is an actual community in lower Manhattan. Only the residents of Gramercy Park have access to the keys. All the park's stipulations, plants, statue of Edwin Booth, and history mentioned in this book are accurate, except for the time capsule. I included that to twist the plot further.

The Irish Draft Riots mentioned in this story are accurate, according to my research. In Hart's Alley, residents threw pots of hot starch on the rioters to save their homes. Gramercy Park was unlocked during that time and open to the soldiers who were protecting the citizens of Gramercy.

Edwin Booth founded the Players and celebrated its opening on December 31, 1888. The club is still in operation today. Some of the most renowned actors of the nineteenth and twentieth centuries held memberships here. The historical tidbits mentioned in the scene where Beau takes Andrea to meet with the director are all true, according to the Players website, including Edwin's preserved bedroom on the third floor. See their website for more information.

Unfortunately, the Curtis & Perkins Proprietors of Bangor, Maine, really did produce Mrs. Winslow's Soothing Syrup in 1849. The concoction was a mixture of morphine and alcohol that caused thousands of deaths before finally being pulled off the market in 1930. One teaspoon of the syrup contained enough morphine to kill the average child. Many babies went to sleep after taking the medicine and never woke again. Throughout the years, the syrup was nicknamed "the baby killer." Parents had no idea what ingredients they were giving their children; they merely trusted their physicians. The Pure Food and Drug Act in 1906 forced companies to disclose ingredient lists on their labels. This eventually forced the company to remove morphine from their formulation and the word *soothing* from their brand's promise.

The Secret Service was created in 1865 as a specialized branch of the Department of the Treasury to combat the economic threat of counterfeit currency. After the Civil War, over half the money circulated in the U.S. was counterfeit. A few years later, the Secret Service broadened their responsibilities to include investigations into the Ku Klux Klan, illegal distilleries, smuggling, mail robbery, land fraud, and other infractions against the federal government.

The Secret Service headquarters relocated from Washington, D.C., to New York City in 1870 (as in this story) but returned to Washington four years later. The assassination of President McKinley prompted Congress to act, and in 1902 the Secret Service took over full-time responsibility of protecting U.S. presidents.

Asylum records from the Almshouse Ledgers, including Blackwell's Island Asylum, were as detailed with patient information as in this story. The record Andrea finds is modeled exactly on ones I found online in their public records. New York was awarded a grant several years ago to scan and preserve such medical records. Unfortunately, many patients during that time, especially women, were committed for ailments that didn't require asylum treatment. For more information, visit the Almshouse Ledgers online and read about Nellie Bly and her quest to expose such horrific treatment to the public.

ACKNOWLEDGMENTS

For an author, some books and characters come so easily, and others fight us the whole way. This dual-time novel—book #10! —was probably the hardest book of my career to date. Writing two different stories that intertwine while trying to keep all the details straight and then meshing them together at the end was the utmost challenge. But it was also a wonderful experience, and the plot was a blast to create. A big thanks goes to my agent, Linda S. Glaz, of the Linda S. Glaz Literary Agency, for encouraging me to write this story. Linda, you are my constant cheerleader and, most of all, my friend. I'm blessed to take this journey with you.

None of my books would be complete without thanking the "sisters of my heart"—the Quid Pro Quills—for critiquing my manuscripts before I sent them off. Robin Patchen, Pegg Thomas, Kara Hunt, Jericha Kingston, and Susan Crawford—your support, prayers, wisdom, and honesty push me to be a better writer. I couldn't survive my fictional worlds without you.

To the wonderful team at Barbour for the fantastic cover and to Ellen Tarver for her amazing editing skills. Working with you is always a pleasure.

Huge thanks to Nikki Jatindranath, Pegg Thomas, and Angela Raper for helping me proofread the galleys. You ladies were invaluable.

To my husband, Adam, who stumbled across Gramercy Park while reading a nonfiction book and asked me what it was. His googling skills led us to the answer, and we looked at one another and said, "That's a book idea." Thanks, babe, for always being willing to help me flesh out my plots and characters when I get stuck (even if I don't always use your suggestions ☺), for listening to me drone on for hours about books and writing, being patient with a messy house when I'm on a deadline, and always loving me no matter what.

To Levi, Silas, and Hudson—no matter how many books I write or what else I do in life, you are my greatest accomplishments. Our family dynamic sure is different now that you've grown into men, but it's a joy seeing God working in your lives. Thanks for supporting my dream all these years. Now go chase yours!

Above all, I thank my Lord and Savior, Jesus Christ. All honor and glory are His.

Thank you, dear reader, for taking the time out of your busy lives to spend it with my characters. Until next time...

Candice Sue Patterson studied at the Institute of Children's Literature and is an active member of American Christian Fiction Writers. She lives in Indiana with her husband and three sons in a restored farmhouse overtaken by books. When she's not tending to her chickens, splitting wood, or decorating cakes, she's working on a new story. Candice writes modern vintage romance—where the past and present collide with faith. Her debut novel, *How to Charm a Beekeeper's Heart*, was a 2012 ACFW First Impressions finalist and made INSPYs Longlist for 2016.

DOORS TO THE PAST

Visit historic American landmarks through the
Doors to the Past series. History and today collide
in stories full of mystery, intrigue, faith, and romance.

Passages of Hope
By Terri J. Hayes

Gracie Kingston begins renovations on the Philadelphia house inherited from her grandmother and finds a secret room. It is connected to a house nearby, the home of William Still, the man known as the father of the Underground Railroad. As she researches, she discovers a mystery in her house's ownership. In 1855 Olivia Kingston helps a sick mother and her young child by hiding them in a secret room in her home. As she helps, she learns that there may be an impostor conductor in their community. As Gracie's and Olivia's stories intertwine, they learn the meaning of sacrifice and love.

Paperback / 978-1-63609-406-9

In Spotlight and Shadow
By Rachel Scott McDaniel

Still dreaming of becoming a Hollywood actress, Sophie Walters moves home to Pittsburgh to accept an insignificant role among the shadows of Loew Penn's theater. But she becomes thrust to the spotlight when accused of being a jewel thief locals call the Mirage. Nearly a century later, Elsie Malvern is a disappointment to her family and herself as she works behind stage of Heinz Hall, too scared to audition as a violinist for the symphony. When she finds a mysterious paste necklace, Elsie enlists the help of a childhood friend turned country music star to research the piece, but will the story they uncover be the greater mystery?

Paperback / 978-1-63609-476-2